Moonstone Phoenix

By

Huckleberry Rahr

ISBN eBook: 978-1-959981-59-6
ISBN paperback: 978-1-959981-60-2

Editor: Weslee Imrisek
Developmental Editor: Angela Grimes
Cover Art: Getcovers.com
Formatting: Huckleberry Rahr

Books In the Ember Savita Series

1: Veiled Phoenix

2: Moonstone Phoenix

3: Battle Phoenix

Books by Huckleberry Rahr

- Jade Stone Chronicles
  - Wolf Healer
  - Epsilon
  - Alphas
  - Traitor
  - Pack
  - Battlefield
  - Pack Present
- Pebble Stone Chronicles
  - Xenagogue
  - Yugen
  - Zephyr
- Ember Savita Chronicles
  - Veiled Phoenix
  - Moonstone Phoenix
  - Battle Phoenix
- The Search – Short Story, eBook only

Acknowledgements

Every time I think I have the best writing community ever, more people sneak their way into my sphere. As always, my inspiration for writing comes from my immediate writing group, who includes my friends, critique partners, idea creators, and editors. I wouldn't be here without them. So as always, thank you Angela Grimes, Wes Imrisek, Lawrence Henry, and Nicole Maness.

This time around, I need to add a new person to the mix who had made this book, this series, what it is. At a book event in Kenosha, Wisconsin, I was lucky enough to meet Kassandra Novell, a narrator who has become so much more. She has not only brought my characters to life, she has helped ensure the book is clean and perfect. Reading is the best way to find those pesky mistakes!

I also want to thank my family. They are so supportive of all my work developing a story from the basic concept into a book that readers can consume. The help is everything from encouraging my stories to helping me brainstorm. My kids love D&D, and we always joke that the difference between them running campaigns and me is I have a bit more control over the characters. But not much.

In the end, I want to thank my readers. The lovely comments I get in reviews or directly in comments or messages is what makes all of this worth it.

Thank you!

To my readers

Ember Savita, the main character of this series, is nonbinary. They use they/them pronouns. There were a couple of nonbinary characters in the Jade Stone Chronicles, so I knew this path wouldn't be simple. As I wrote this book, I was excited to create this main character.

Writing a character with they/them pronouns is a challenge. I may have made some mistakes. If I did, I apologize. This book has been critiqued and edited by many people, but I'm sure some mistakes still found their way through.

Thank you for joining me on this journey. I appreciate all of you.

Chapter 1 - Meeting Of Minds

Ember

Whoever said, 'May you live in interesting times' had a nasty sense of humor.

Ember's family sat in a large hall with more people than they could imagine squeezing into the space. Next to them sat their boyfriend Felix and his family, who had invited them to this gathering. Everyone waited for the leader, Vi, to arrive and start the meeting. It warmed their heart to know that so many witches disagreed with Infinite Wisdom. The support for the end of this uprising between humans with and without magic was heartwarming.

Applause broke out. The door in the back of the FB Coalition meeting room opened, and a woman—probably the leader Vi—came out wearing a green business-appropriate dress. She had hair almost the same color as Ember's, pinned up on the sides. Her face could've been a mirror to Ember's Dad's. The woman took two steps into the room before Ember felt Dad move. They tore their eyes from the woman, so similar in looks to them that their heart thundered in their chest, to see Dad standing.

His voice echoed through the room. "Nuri? You're here?"

The woman, Nuri, the woman who had to be their aunt, turned to see who had interrupted her trek to the podium. Her brown eyes—the same color as Ember's and their dad's—widened and her mouth dropped open.

"Ash," she whispered, so soft that Ember thought only her phoenix-enhanced hearing allowed her to make out the word.

Next to them, Felix's head jerked back and forth, gaping at Ember's dad and his sister, who stood elegantly at the back of a room of over a hundred magic users, gathered in support of peace. His voice hissed out, "What am I missing?"

Ember shook their head. There had been so many changes over the last couple of weeks; they couldn't believe there were more surprises possible. An aunt they didn't even know about a month ago stood a few feet away. Their hands trembled as they gaped. Murmurs broke out throughout the room. Finally, they said softly to Felix, "She's my aunt."

Dad lifted a hand, palm up, as if asking for a dance. "I looked for you, but I didn't know how to find you." His eyes got misty. His mouth opened as if he wanted to say more.

Nuri lifted her hand, the mirror to him. "We'll talk after the meeting. I'm ... after." She gave a small shake of her head, and her face lost all its emotion. She straightened her shoulders and strode past them to the podium at the front of the room on the small, raised stage.

As she moved, Ember watched and listened to the crowd murmur. No one knew what to make of the two of them.

Before giving up the microphone, Monte, her assistant said, "And now Vi, our fearless leader. Again, thank you all for coming—both those of you who've been loyal for all these years, and the many of you new to our cause."

Nuri ... Vi looked in charge in her dark green dress. She looked powerful and put together. "As Monte said, I welcome you to our group." Her gaze swept the witches populating the seats in the overstuffed room. "As you know, Tad Shade and his cronies have started a campaign to drive a wedge between witches and non-magic humans in our world. They see competition where there is none, and feel a war is a way to purify our community."

Over the last few weeks, Tad Shade had used students to hold rallies at the school to build a following. The popular teens convinced the masses to follow them using propaganda and half-truths. When there were naysayers, some had been attacked and subsequently hospitalized.

A buzz went up amongst the people sitting around Ember. From what they heard, those around them were unhappy at the thought of the end of peace their world had had for so many years.

Someone sitting behind Ember stood. "How do you know they want war?" He didn't sound confrontational, just determined to know the truth.

Vi nodded. "That's a great question, and I want to say I'm excited to see so many new faces here. As pervasive as their message is, we are stronger and smarter, and I know we can get ahead of their wave if we work together. As for your question, did you go to the event yesterday or do you have any kids at the secondary school who attended either of the assemblies in the last two weeks?"

"No," the man said. "That farce yesterday would've been a waste of a beautiful day."

"You are absolutely correct, my friend." Vi smiled in agreement. "Many of us went to keep track of what Mr. Shade and his group are saying, what lies they are spreading. We also have some students who have attended the school gatherings. The message is clear. They are telling the magical community that the *humans* are discontent with the state of things, that *they* want to subjugate us. Their group is stating the only way to save our people is to bring the fight to them before they enslave us."

The man grunted. "Is this true? Has anyone here been to all of these meetings?"

Tansy shot up. "I went to all the meetings."

Ember hadn't seen their friend, though they hadn't paid attention when they arrived. They'd been overwhelmed with the number of people and immediately helped Felix with set up. This was their first meeting, if not Felix's, and Ember felt the pressure of being around so many strangers. When they arrived, not only did Felix realize they needed a distraction, he always helped out, and Ember decided it would be a good way to not have to talk to anyone they didn't know. They leaned over to whisper to Felix, "Did you know she was here?"

He shook his head. "She's new, like you."

Tansy continued to speak to the man who had asked the question. "Not only are they using students to get other teens spouting this, encouraging their friends and parents, they have goons who don't like it if you question their message. You just questioned the presenter." Tansy turned towards the podium. "I'm sorry, I missed your name."

Vi gave her a winning smile. "It's Vi, and you are?"

"Oh! Sorry, I'm Tansy."

"The hospital girl."

Tansy blushed. "You know about me?"

"Yes dear. Please continue your story."

Tansy shook herself and faced the man again. "I did what you did and questioned the presenters at the school. I ended up in the hospital with broken bones for being a 'human lover' instead of in the middle of a discourse, like we are now. Those people are serious about their message and goal. It isn't peace or equality they want. Another kid who questioned them when I did never got out of the hospital, so, even though I was there for four days, at least I survived." She sat before he could ask her anything else.

A lump formed in Ember's throat. They were proud of Tansy and the bravery she showed in standing up in such a large crowd and telling her story. After the full city presentation, Ember had been attacked, and like Harry, the second kid, they hadn't survived the brutes. Unlike Harry, Ember rose from the ashes of their death. The biggest advantage of being a phoenix.

Phoenixes were thought to be extinct. Because of this, Ember couldn't tell the group that they, too, had been hunted down as a human-lover. As of now, Tansy was the only one of them who could stand up and let the others know. And it was such a dangerous position to be in.

The man turned from Tansy to Vi. "They're beating up people who speak out against them?"

Vi nodded. "Yes, and any group who will do this to our children ... what further lengths will they go to?"

The man sat, face hard.

"Many of you are new to the FB Coalition. Our goal here is to continue the original mission of our founding leaders. We want to ensure the peace between witches and non-magic humans alike. For years that objective was simple because most people agreed. But in the last month, our job has become imperative. We need to keep track of what Infinite WISDOM is doing at each step, in the schools, within the cities, and when they branch out into a larger venue. As a group, we need to find ways to bring counter information ... accurate and reliable resources, to the public. We know their talking points are lies; we have easily found the facts. How do we disseminate them to oppose Tad Shade's messages? Is there a way to get ahead of them and support upholding the peace with the non-magic humans?"

She paused to let everyone think about the goals. "We will spend time this week creating committees. If any of you want to take a leadership role, please see Monte, who will now discuss with you each of the committees we would like to form."

Vi stepped down and Monte took her place. As she walked down the aisle, she stopped and spoke to Ember's parents. "Ash and ... you? Care to join me?" She pointed to Mom. Her eyes stopped on Ember. "And, I think, you."

Chapter 2 - Meeting Family

Ember

They headed through the door in the back of the hall into a large office. The center was taken up by a dark oak desk. A black leather chair sat behind it, and four chairs were lined up for visitors. On the left side of the room, there was a purple fabric couch, with a matching loveseat and a low, oval cherrywood coffee table. Behind the couch stood a double-wide bookcase filled with books and trinkets. Some looked old.

Nervous, and a bit overwhelmed, Ember let themself get distracted by the trinkets. *Maybe someday I can sit and investigate all the books and artifacts. I bet there are stories worth sharing.*

Once the door clicked shut, Vi turned and flung herself into Dad's arms. "Ash, oh my gods, I had no idea you were in the area. I should've guessed when kids started dying you'd be close. Never has there been a hotspot of disaster and phoenixes weren't nearby." She pushed back. "And you have a kid?" She shot a quick look Ember's way.

"Nuri Savita, I don't know that I thought I'd ever see you again." Mom laughed, a twinkle in her eye. "You look the same as the last time I saw you."

Vi's eyes widened. "Sadie! It really is you. As I live and breathe. I wasn't sure ... I mean, I hoped, but it's been so long and you're human, a witch, but still mortal. So, you actually mated with my brother. I thought you'd find someone better, but I guess you decided to slum it." They both laughed. "So, you did it?" She shook her head, but the smile on her face lit up the room. "The full kit and kaboodle? You got some of his immortality?" Vi ... Nuri chuckled. "*You* didn't think you'd see me, two hundred years later. I didn't think I'd see *you*! And, by the way, I go by Nuri Vita. I decided to separate myself from the family when the word went out that phoenixes were all dead."

Ember's mind whirled almost as fast as this twin sister of their father spoke. She was elegant and beautiful. *I hope to be like that someday. I can't believe someone so ... bold and ... gregarious is Dad's twin.*

Smiling wide, Nuri and Mom hugged. Mom pulled away. "This is Ember, our child. They are in their eleventh year of secondary school."

Nuri tilted her head and considered. "What are they? I mean ..."

Ember blushed, happiness bubbling inside them. They never thought they'd have more family then their mom and dad. "I'm everything." Then Ember winked, wanting to be bold. This was the only time they'd ever met someone new that they didn't have to hide who they were. Excitement surged through their body.

"Everything?" Nuri sounded dubious.

Holding out both their hands, Ember created a ball of fire hovering over one hand, and a small twister in the other. They winked. "If you want to go flying, I'd love to stretch my wings. Mom and Dad own some land up north." Ember had to keep from laughing. If they started, they weren't sure they'd be able to stop.

Her smile widened. "Oh, I like this child of yours. All Sadie's sass. That's good, if she—"

Both Mom and Dad said, "They," at the same time.

Nuri contemplated the word for a moment. "That would've made our childhood so much simpler ..., if they were too much like Ash, life would be boring."

Dad sighed. "Life with a half witch, all phoenix, is never boring, trust me on this. We can fill you in on that, but it's been years, Nuri. What have you been doing?"

"Isn't it obvious? I've been maintaining this organization you started. Someone had to do it. You made those laws in your Committee of Ten, then did nothing to ensure they stuck. You started this coalition then disappeared. You said *I* was hard to find? You're like the wind—you're not even a presence online. Completely invisible."

"*We* started." Dad grumbled. "I distinctly remember you being in from the start of Fire Bird."

"Fine, *we* started. Anyway, it was in place, and it had a mission of ensuring peace amongst magic users and humans. It seemed like a good thing to maintain. So I did. I met Monte maybe ten years after losing contact with you. She and I have been together ever since."

Ember sat up. "So ... so she knows you're a phoenix?"

Nuri smiled. "She had to, to become my mate and get part of my immortality, just like your mom."

"Do you have any kids?" Ember asked. "Do I have any cousins?"

"Not yet, dear, but now that I know it's possible, maybe one day." Nuri stared off into space for a second, a softness to her face.

Ember opened her mouth to ask another question, but the door opened. Monte walked in and shut the door quickly behind her. "Okay, Ash and …"

Nuri moved over to her and gave her a quick hug and kiss. "Monte, this is my twin brother Ash. Ash, Monte." They started to shake hands, but Dad pulled her in for a hug. "This is Ash's wife, Sadie. She was part of the ten who created the laws." Monte's eyes widened and she lost a bit of color.

Before she could move, Mom gave Monte a hug. "Lovely to meet you, Monte. I'm thrilled Nuri met her match in someone. I never thought that would happen."

A nervous laugh exploded from Monte. "It's a pleasure to meet you both. I mean, I know I'm almost as old, but the Committee of Ten has always been a bit of a … sorry, I'm geeking out."

Nuri shook her head. "Just don't. My brother is just that. Don't give him a big head. Maybe Sadie, she's always been the cooler of the two. Anyway, this is Ember, their child."

Monte whipped around to gape at Ember. "Child? A child between a phoenix and witch? That's possible?"

Ember shrugged. "Apparently."

"You are a miracle and give me hope." Monte wrapped her arms around Ember in a bear-hug then stepped back. "Oh, my gods. I just came in here to tell you we need to get out there so you can mingle, but gods above, this is so much."

Mom laughed at all Monte's exuberance. "I know. I just want to sit and talk too. It's been too long. Why don't you come for dinner some day this week?"

They both smiled and Nuri nodded. "Of course, any day. How about Tuesday?"

That decided, they opened the door and meshed with the horde of people waiting to mingle in the larger room.

Chapter 3 – Committees

Felix

Felix watched as Ember and their family went into Vi's office. He'd only been in there once. The room seemed so off limits, but something was going on, and it gave him chills. Ember said Vi was their aunt. Was that possible? Aunt on which side? What did that mean? Considering Vi ... *did she and Ash look similar? Her and Ember?*

Could there be three phoenixes alive, not just two? After the War of Peace, the story passed out to the public was that all the phoenixes were killed off. They'd sacrificed themselves to ensure the peace the war was fought for.

From the time Felix had first read about phoenixes, he'd wanted to learn everything there was to know about them. His dream had always been to see a real one. During a school field trip a few weeks ago, when he'd learned Ember—and then their dad—were phoenixes, he'd been thrilled. Now Vi could be one too?

Maybe there are more? Is it possible that some of the phoenixes survived the war?

He shook his head. Ember would fill him in later. *I don't even know if Vi is a phoenix. I need to focus on the meeting, not what's happening behind that door.*

The microphone squawked as Monte took a sip of water, fully bringing him back to the here and now. "Well, that was exciting. For those of you who know, these meetings aren't usually so ... well, thrilling, I guess. As Vi said, if we can count on a group this big each week, we would like to form some committees, and maybe get more things done."

Monte straightened her jacket, then gave a wide smile. "There are sign-up sheets along the back table. These are the committees we'd like to start building. First, we need to monitor the news from the other side and the message they are putting out. We need to know the lies as soon as they come up with them. Most of their messages are ridiculous, but we can't counter what we don't know."

The crowd shuffled and made noises of agreement. Nodding, Monte continued. "This brings us to the next committee. We need people who are good with research. This will entail both counter arguments to their false claims as well as finding our own messages to push out. What we, as a group, decide is public worthy, must be bulletproof. Nothing we share can be tainted with even the smallest falsehood."

A woman in the back stood. "Why? If they can lie, why do our truths have to be held to a higher standard? I mean, I get that we need to spread ideas that are true, but why under such tight control?"

Felix stood. He'd seen this type of thing every time he or Ember had been teased at school. "If there is any chance that a part of what we share can be shown as not true, our whole message will be belittled and smeared as false. They live for this type of, well, bullying. It's why everything needs to be above reproach, unfortunately." He sat with a small shrug towards Monte.

Monte smiled at him a bit sadly. "Okay, we also want to get a team that can find ways to strengthen our side, maybe bring new legislation to the table, or other acts that can enforce peace. It's a long shot, but we're looking for anything and everything. Along with these two groups, if we have anyone who knows about marketing, that would be a plus. We need to get our word out. Now, onto the less flashy teams. We need people to monitor the hospitals. If people, like Tansy and Harry, the boy who didn't survive, are ending up hurt, or worse, dead, then we need to know. I doubt the hospital will report it, so we need people, preferably on the inside, so we can track numbers. We'll need permission from the patients if we want to put information on our website. And that's my next hope, a one-stop-shop to show the public what's really happening."

She paused to get a drink of water.

A man near the front, Ronny Johns, stood. His light blue button down was tucked into his beige slacks. He'd been a member of FB Coalition longer than Felix and his family. "So much organization, Monte, a man doesn't know what to do with himself," he said with a laugh. "Are those all of the committees?"

"No, Ronny. We need volunteers to start organizing food and drink for these weekly meetings, not to mention the random Wednesday ones, which will probably pop up more often for committee work. Wanna volunteer to cook? Your chili and pecan pies are notorious."

"Ah, but are they notorious for being good or bad, my friend?" Ronny patted his belly as many of the people in the crowd laughed. "I do love the part where we get to eat and drink. Anything else?"

Monte threw her head back and laughed. "Nothing like a hint. We are considering one more, but we'll discuss it later. You are correct. Some of you have been here almost an hour. What will you do without your coffee and snacks? I'll go collect Vi so you all can meet her informally. Please, eat, drink, socialize, and sign up for committees."

Chapter 4 - Seeing Magic

Ember

Monday morning, Ember sat on the side of their bed gazing at the boxes edging their room. *Maybe I should get a second dresser for my two wardrobes.*

They snorted at their own thought. After years of homeschool, Ember and their parents decided they'd attend public magic school, both for educational and socialization reasons. They'd started secondary school just over two years ago in ninth year after they'd 'died.' As a phoenix, death was just a part of life.

One of the little known side effects of the death and rebirth of a phoenix was that when they reemerge from the ash, their sex changed. Ember had presented more female than male for just over two years.

A few weeks ago, when the eleventh years went on a field trip to collect night plants, pranks were as much a part of the experience as the assignment. When one of the jokes had gone too far, Ember ended up with a new masculine body. Thankfully, only Felix was aware of what had happened.

Historically, this would've triggered their family to move, relocate and start over. The only reason they stayed was some fast talking by Felix and his parents.

Then, in one of the quickest turnarounds ever, on the way home from the last citywide event of Infinite WISDOM, Tad Shade's group, Ember got tagged as a human-lover and attacked. As always, anything that can go wrong with phoenixes will, and an accidental knife ended up in their chest.

One death later, and they were back to the body they'd had for most of secondary school. The new clothes Ember and their mom had bought two weeks ago to hide their masculine body were repacked and put away. They debated keeping some of them out as a splash to their wardrobe, like the skirts everyone seemed to love. But most of the clothes would be saved for their next 'death.'

Ember contemplated the skirts. The nicer outfits they'd bought with their mom had been closer to how Felix always dressed. He loved to dress much more fashionably than Ember did. For that matter, so did Daisy. It was nice that neither of them cared that Ember always dressed comfortably. With a sigh, they pushed up from their bed and rummaged until they found a pair of jeans and an orange t-shirt that read, '*The sun may rise, but I won't shine.*'

Down in the kitchen, they poured a bowl of cereal and a mug of coffee. Dad sat swiping through screens on his phone, eating a bagel, and drinking coffee. His gaze flicked up and he smirked at Ember's shirt. "Morning, sunshine."

Ember flopped down with a grunt. "Yes ... yes it is."

"You definitely sound ready for the day."

"I was just contemplating the boxes of clothes in my room. Do you have two dressers?"

He laughed. "No, I just pack everything away that I don't want to wear in both forms. I generally leave everything out though. Our bodies aren't that much different. We never grow facial hair, our face is mostly the same, it's just a few small changes. If I were to go put on a dress, some make up, and style my hair, no one would be the wiser."

"That's true. I guess that's pretty much what I was doing the last two weeks, and hoping to continue to do if those goons hadn't attacked me."

"Think you'll still wear those skirts?" Dad said with a smirk.

Ember snorted. "Don't know."

Dad smiled. "Now, off to school with you, you'll be late. Don't you need to be super early to TA?"

Ember had started off hiding their magic in a feeble attempt to blend. In a cascading set of events over the last few weeks, it came out that their air magic was top of the class, maybe even better than some of the teachers. After Ember and their mom modeled playing catch while flying around on platforms, Ember had gone from a magical dud to one of the top students in the school. It had only been in one proficiency, but for many students, that was enough.

The administration and Mrs. Vintl, the Air Magic teacher, asked Ember's parents if they could help out in the Air Magic classes instead of wasting time in Earth Magic class, their weakest proficiency, not learning or accomplishing anything of note. Now Ember needed to arrive early to work with the teacher to figure out the lesson plan each day.

Ember got to school on time, before just about anyone else. They headed up to Air Magic, situated on the top floor of the school. The Air Magic classroom was huge, almost the size of a regular gym. It was at the top of the school because the roof could open up to allow more freedom for exercises.

There were dots along the floor, so students had a spot to create their air magic objects, and a goal to move to. Each student either chose or was assigned a color. In their class, Ember always used the green circle.

Mrs. Vintl had an office and there was a large private practice room.

When they got to the top floor of the school, they knocked on the Air Magic classroom door.

"If that's Ember, come in, if it's anyone else, I'll be available in twenty minutes."

Chuckling, Ember pushed through the door. "Hi, Mrs. Vintl. What are we working on today?"

Mondays and Wednesdays, Ember helped with the ninth-year students. On Tuesdays and Thursdays, it was their own class, a mixed class with tenth-and-eleventh-year students, since neither grade had enough Air Magic students to make a class alone.

"Well, this class is bigger than yours, as you know. I spent last week testing the students. I have them separated into groups by skill level. I want to do a bit of differentiation, where students can float depending on where they need the most help. I figured you could move amongst the groups, maybe continue to pull students out individually or in groups and help them."

Ember thought about her direction. "So, just do whatever I want?"

"Sort of? What you did with Betty—" She hugged her planner to her chest and looked off as if she could see the student doing the magic. "—I'd been working with her for over a month, and in a few minutes you figured out what was stopping her up. It was amazing. If you can do that with other students, I'm sure they'd be grateful. We may get to platform catch yet!" Mrs. Vintl's gaze sharpened, and she focused on Ember. "On that note, can you explain what you did with Betty?"

In her first class, the students partnered up to work. Ember saw one student working alone. Though the student resisted the intrusion, Ember asked to work with her. It didn't take Ember long to see how Betty could better manipulate the magic.

Later, talking with their parents, Ember learned it was probably a combination of their witch magic and phoenix sight that let them see what students needed to do to improve and strengthen their magical manipulations. Their parents determined that as long as it didn't move to fire it would be fine to continue what they were doing. That said, they weren't sure how to explain it to anyone else.

"I'm not sure." They gave Mrs. Vintl a small smile. "Maybe a feeling? I guess I can sense what they're doing. It's almost like seeing it, or something. I can't really explain it."

Mrs. Vintl tilted her head. "I don't follow, but I'm thrilled it's something you can do."

Ember's shoulders dropped. They hadn't realized how nervous they'd been that Mrs. Vintl would push to know more of their secrets. Thankfully, she accepted Ember's lack of understanding and just let it go. One less thing to worry about.

Once the mob of ninth-years were assembled and separated into groups, Ember circled the room, observing. Many of the students seemed to spend as much time watching Ember as focusing on their magic, and that didn't help.

One group worked on creating a twister, maintaining it, then adjusting its speed. The second, a step up from the first, created their twister and played with controlling the speed as it moved across the short end of the room, trying to follow a path. Some students even raced their twisters. The ones who raced followed a straight line and part of the goal was having the twisters not collide.

The last group was given an obstacle course. It involved movement as well as speed changes. It would be difficult for anyone, but even the top students would have to practice to master it.

After a quarter hour, Ember decided who they'd work with. Emerson, a tall, wiry kid with unruly blond hair and green eyes. He squinted at his twister as it continued to move off course, slamming into a wall and dissipating. He'd glare at the offending empty spot, scrunch up his face, and make a new twister on his yellow dot.

After Emerson's twister crashed into another student's magic spell, causing a few nasty words to pass between them, Ember approached him. "Hi, can I help you?"

One of his eyebrows rose slowly. "I've heard you have the healing touch. A few words from you, and anyone will do better, but I'm not going to hold my breath, Ember. I remember that just over a week ago everyone said you *had no magic*. So, instead, I'll hold off judgment, if you don't mind."

He didn't sound like a ninth-year. Hell, he sounded like an upper crust adult, but who was Ember to judge? They'd watched Emerson do the twister run twice. His magic flowed from his center to his hands and out, but the way he held his hands stopped up the power. Eventually, most magic users ceased using their hands as a focus, at least as a major one, but in the beginning, the hands were needed, or the magic wouldn't have direction.

Ember licked their lips. "You're holding your hands like this." Ember held both their hands out, palms facing each other. "And wiggling all but your pointer finger to create the twister. I'm guessing part of that is controlling the speed it spins on its axis."

"It's what the teacher taught us. Are you telling me now it's wrong?"

"No, you're creating the twister, and it spins just fine, right?"

"Yeah, that's always been easy enough."

Ember nodded. "You have a lot of power, and with the way you're holding your hands, it's all going into the twister, and you can't control it. It's like flying a kite in a blizzard."

He tilted his head. "Really?"

"Yeah. So, once the twister is created, only use your right hand to control the movement and the middle two fingers to control the speed, one for rotation, one for directional speed."

His face twisted into a mask of doubt. "This isn't going to work. I've always been bottom of the class."

"Kite. Blizzard. Too much power. Now, do as I've told you." Ember gave him a smile.

He rolled his eyes but followed the directions Ember gave him. His mouth dropped open as he finally developed finesse over something he'd never been able to control in the past.

Eyes wide, he stared at them. "Whoa! Ember, you must be, like, the most powerful witch in the school." *He finally doesn't sound snarky.*

Ember shook their head and had him practice again. At least they felt they were getting more accomplished doing this than struggling in Earth Magic class.

Chapter 5 - Mind Your Past

Ember

Ember walked into second period a bit late. Mrs. Vintl wanted to discuss Emerson after he gushed to the class about his new control and abilities. They ran down the stairs, but they still were one of the last to dart through the door.

"Ember, you're here," Cress said, sounding shocked.

Ember stopped in the front center of the room, halfway to their seat, and gaped at the popular kid. *Why does Cress care that I'm in class today?*

Ambrose made a small squawking sound. "Why do you care about *them?* They're always in class."

Cress looked back and forth between Ember and Ambrose like he were at a tennis match. "Um, yeah, that's it. I just forgot they weren't in my Earth Magic class anymore." Though it didn't sound convincing.

Ember raised an eyebrow at him, but then decided it wasn't worth pursuing. They turned and continued to their seat. Felix followed with his eyes until they sat then whispered, "What do you think that was about? Do you think he ... you know?" He waved a hand in a small circular motion.

"Maybe. I mean, who knows what people know. Why would he know and not Ambrose?"

Did the goons tell him they'd killed me after the last Infinite WISDOM event? That they destroyed the evidence with fire? Has he been waiting for the news of one less classmate? Do Ambrose and Cress know that the people they're representing hurt anyone for having an opinion counter to theirs? Does only Cress know? What's going on here?

They both spoke softly, but Ember was still cautious about being overheard. "We can talk more after class or in Math when there aren't others who may be listening. Or better yet, after school."

"Yeah, that makes sense. Maybe I can walk you home?" Felix looked worried.

"Sounds great." A small warmth blossomed in their belly.

Mr. Elias walked to the front of the class. "We've focused a lot on what led up to the war, why the war got out of hand, and who helped maintain the outcome so that the death numbers weren't so high. We're going to spend the next few weeks, until that mystical winter break you're all so focused on, trying to step into the minds of the non-magical humans."

"Oh, gods, can we not?" Cress drawled. "Isn't it enough we have to share land, work, and air with them? But now you want us to share brain space?"

"Mr. Walsh, if you can't control yourself, you can spend class in the office. We are in this class to learn about events that happened two hundred years ago during the War of Peace, not shoot our mouth off inappropriately."

Cress leaned forward heavily on his arms, eyes wild as he gazed at the teacher. "Mr. Elias, are you a human-lover?"

Mr. Elias's arm rose, and he pointed to the door. "Out. You can return once you remember how to behave appropriately in class. I'll talk with the principal later to make sure you made it and explain why you'll be spending classes there until you've written a paper on why your behavior today wasn't acceptable."

Cress sauntered to the door, bag thrown haphazardly over his shoulder. He stopped almost at the threshold and slowly turned. "You expect me to do what?" The impertinence dripped from his every pore.

"I'll email the exact assignment to you, the principal, and your parents, with an explanation as to why you were removed from class today. Don't worry, it'll be specific, so you won't be able to mess it up."

Nostrils flaring, Cress's mouth pursed together, forming a smaller and smaller scrunched stain on his face before he whipped around. "Fine. You'll get your paper, Mr. Elias. Human-lover teacher." He slammed the door on his way out.

It took Mr. Elias a few moments to turn away from the spectacle and face the class. "Does anyone else want to join Cress?"

The students all sat quiet and still, including Ambrose, and Josie, who was always boisterous and a big supporter of her friends.

Ember wanted to give Mr. Elias a standing ovation. It was about time one of the three biggest bullies got called out for their behavior. That said, they worried that Mr. Elias may have painted a target on their back.

Does the group target people who don't go to events?

"Okay, then back to the lesson. The war has ended, non-magical humans have learned that there is magic in the world. What do you think happened next? What was the human reaction to magic suddenly being real?"

Ember raised a hand. They knew they could get these answers from their parents but wanted to get a different perspective. "When the war first ended, did they know about both the magic users and the shapeshifters, or only one group? That part always gets skipped over. The war ends, the laws are made, but there was a year before the committee was created and, what, six months of the committee meeting before the laws were finalized and implemented, so, in that year and a half, did the non-magical humans know right away about everything, or was the information trickled out to them?"

Felix's hand went up, and Mr. Elias smiled wide, nodding at him to speak. "Well, the shapeshifters were instrumental in the war ending the way it did. Wouldn't that imply the humans knew about them from the start?"

In the back of the room on the other side, Lolli, a girl with spiky dark brown hair and brown eyes, raised her hand. "That's true, but only the magic users were fighting alongside the shapeshifters. The reason we as a group came out to the humans was they saw, felt, and experienced the magic. I don't know if I'm right, but my guess is they only knew about the witches at first. The shapeshifters had the good sense to stay away."

Olivia, Tansy's best friend, commented next. She didn't speak up much, being shy, and a bit of a mouse in most situations, but at times she would break out of her shell. Over the last few weeks, she was becoming more of a friend to Ember. "In the reading I've done, between the end of the war, and the forming of the Committee of Ten, thirteen months passed. We all say a year, because, well, that last month doesn't really matter. But, after eleven months, a group of shapeshifters, realizing that at least one of them would be sitting on the Committee of Ten, initiated their coming out to the humans. I'm trying to remember if the name of that shapeshifter had been listed in my reading or not."

"Does it matter?" Ambrose said, turning in her seat. "It isn't like that part is important. We don't need to know the names of any of the Committee of Ten, or which of them were witches or shapeshifters. It's not like any of them sought fame and fortune. It's history, not present. The question we were asked was what we thought the humans *thought* about magic suddenly being real, not the order in which things came out. Gods, this class is easily distracted."

"And, Ambrose, do you have a thought on my question?" Mr. Elias asked, coming to stand by her desk.

She huffed out a sound of disgust. "They were probably scared, hiding under their beds in fear. Then they tried to figure out ways to use us for their gain, as always." She crossed her legs and arms at the same time.

Tansy snorted. "Gods, you don't even agree with yourself in your answer. Which is it, Ambrose, were they scared or conniving to overthrow the magic users?"

"Whatever!" Then Ambrose narrowed her eyes. "No, you're wrong. It's pretty clear, right? When someone is scared they try to control or destroy whatever it is they don't understand."

A chill ran down Ember's spine. *Why is she so clever at times?*

Felix scoffed. "Not everyone thinks in such binary terms, Ambrose. Some people try to work towards understanding, peace, and harmony. You should give it a try."

Mr. Elias handed out a paper. "This is a copy of a diary of a teenage girl from that time. Take the rest of class today to read it. You'll be taking this week to write a report as if you were a teenage non-magical human at the time of the end of the war. Think of this as a creative writing project. Like what I'm handing out, you'll turn in a project with at least five journal entries." He passed the papers back then returned to the front of the room.

On the board, he listed the requirements. "The minimum will include one entry before the war started, establishing who the person you're writing about was. One as magic first becomes real. Does your person believe in it? A third should be several months later when magic has fully been established. Has your person met any witches? Are they friends? Are they scared? Hiding under the bed, as Ambrose predicted? Entry four is during the six months the Committee of Ten are creating the laws. Are they hopeful, skeptical, sassy? And the last mandatory entry is some time at least a year after the laws have been put in place. What is their work like, how does it look and feel? Try to make the reader understand how this change would affect someone your age from start to finish."

He moved to his desk and grabbed another stack of papers. "Please hand these back."

Ember checked over the assignment. It looked challenging, but interesting. They knew they could get more information from their parents, but they decided they'd do the journal entries first, then show Mom and talk with her about her memories. It would be nice to get stories from the past, now that they knew how old their parents were.

Ambrose took the page and rolled her eyes. "This is such a dumb assignment, a waste of time."

Before Mr. Elias could reply, Felix said, "It's a good thing you have people to do your homework for you."

Chapter 6 - It's A Dog-Eat-Dog World

Ambrose

Being popular meant Ambrose was obligated to sit in the center of the lunchroom surrounded by all her closest 'friends,' even on a day she didn't want to socialize. Cress sat next to her, laughing and joking with all his buddies, unaware of her feelings. He lived for the limelight.

She worried about his inclusion in this movement. Not that she cared about Mr. Shade, but she wanted power and Cress wasn't smart enough to know how to be subtle, something Father had drilled into Ambrose her whole life. The stunt Cress pulled in Magical History class was idiotic. He probably didn't even understand he'd made a tactical error.

Now all she wanted was to have a few minutes of downtime, but that wouldn't happen at school.

"Oh, my gods, above and below, can you believe that assignment? It'll be just awful!" Josie threw herself at the table, full of drama and flair. She wore a dark blue mini-skirt and a wine-colored Infinite WISDOM shirt. Her hair was back in a ponytail. She was a perfect supporter for the cause. As obnoxious as she was, unlike Cress, she knew when to shut her mouth.

Cress stopped talking and turned to Josie. "What assignment?"

"Right, you got kicked out of that awful human-lover teacher's class. Can you believe him? Just horrible. I bet he attaches the assignment in that email he's sending to you and your parents." She simpered at him. Ambrose should be upset, but her so-called friends always kissing up to her and Cress irked her, not to mention, she wasn't happy with Cress. Ever since they'd been on stage three times, his notoriety had skyrocketed, and he'd been impossible. Even when he was at her house, she could barely stand him and his newfound arrogance.

If the cause didn't need to see them together, if their popularity didn't revolve around them as a power couple, she'd walk away from it all. Father always said, power was more important than everything else. She had to remain where she was if she wanted to become the most powerful person in Feniks Secondary School's history.

Cress pulled out his phone and spent a minute searching, then he spewed some words that if the monitors could hear over the roar of voices in the lunchroom, he'd be back in the principal's office and in detention. "Ambrose, we should go to the hall and call your father. He and his *friends* should know what's going on at this school."

"It can wait until after classes, Cress. It isn't an emergency." His assumption that he could boss her around annoyed her. He needed to learn the pecking order in their relationship.

"You are as smart as you are beautiful, love, but if they're going to get anything done, the sooner they know, the better." He clenched his jaw, and she saw he was determined.

She massaged her temples. "What do you even think he'll do about a history teacher?"

He shrugged. "I don't know, that's the point. They're the brains of the operation, we're the image. If they want their movement to work, they have to keep us happy."

Ambrose wasn't sure he was as accurate as he thought. There were a lot of pretty, popular people in the world. What they were was convenient.

"Fine. Whatever." She didn't want to start a fight. Her day had been bad enough.

If I could go back and refuse doing this for Father and Mr. Shade, would I? Ambrose thought about it and decided no, she wouldn't. In the end she loved the attention too much.

They left their bags and food and headed out to the hall for a quick call. Her father answered on the fourth ring. "Ambrose, what are you doing calling during school?"

"Father. There was a bit of a situation in Magical History class and Cress suggested we call. I thought we could wait." She spoke calmly and business-like.

There was a pause. "Put the boy on."

"What?"

"Now, girl."

Gritting her teeth, she handed her pink embossed phone to Cress, but gave him a death stare. If he harmed her phone, she wouldn't forgive him any time soon.

He put the phone to his ear. "Yes sir." He winked at Ambrose, giving her a wide smile before turning his back to her.

He explained what he'd done in class and the assignment in succinct phrases. Once he'd finished, he'd added that Ember had been in class.

Ambrose followed everything until that last bit. "Why tell him that? Felix was in class, too. As well as most of the other students." *Why did I let Felix get away? He at least has brains.*

Cress waved his hand. "Alright, sir, I'll write that paper, hand it in tomorrow morning before school. I can tell Mr. Elias about next Saturday's event in Toresville, see if he's going. I'll do it before school. I'll let you know." Cress was quiet for a bit, listening. "Okay, I'll tell him Mr. Shade will be running it. I'll pay attention to his reactions."

When he got off the phone, he handed it back to Ambrose unharmed. She asked, "Does he want me to join you tomorrow morning when you confront Mr. Elias?"

Cress's brow furrowed. "He didn't mention you. No, I don't think that'll be necessary."

Ambrose realized she was being pushed out. Maybe she wasn't the top of the pecking order anymore.

Chapter 7 - Expanding The Network

Ember

Ember sat in the corner of the lunchroom with Felix. Felix searched the room full of loud students, distracted. "Where's Daisy?"

"I'm not sure, we headed out of class together, but she said she'd meet us here later. Something about asking a teacher a question. She ran off before I could get anything clear out of her."

He sighed. "Did you see the shirt she wore today?"

"Yeah." Ember slumped, taking a bite of pizza, hoping the cheesy goodness would help with their disappointment. "I saw her buying it at the event on Saturday. It gives me the willies, the number of students wearing the Infinite WISDOM paraphernalia. I want the people we attend this institute of education with to be smarter, but alas, the allure of the popular crowd outweighs their ability to think for themselves."

Felix scoffed. "I've wanted the intelligence of the masses for years, yet down that path only lies disappointment."

Ember nodded and took another bite. A student walked by with one of the evil group's shirts on.

The Infinite WISDOM symbol was an infinity sign with a cauldron in the left oval and a not equal sign in the right. Under the left swish was the word "Infinite" leaving WISDOM for the right. When the symbol was too small for all the bits and pieces, they just used the infinity sign.

"Do you really think it's all because Ambrose and Cress are leading the assemblies?" Ember tracked another student with a water bottle with the infinity symbol on it.

Felix grunted. "I want to believe some of them are following the words through ignorance and will *maybe* see the light and break away eventually. It's hard to believe they'd follow for any amount of time when all the facts are so easily found."

Ember snorted. "I don't think it would be this big if *I* brought this to the school. They took two of the most popular kids in the eleventh-year; because of that, they got the students in our grade and many of the students in the years below ours. They probably even picked up some from the twelfth-year."

Tansy and Olivia placed their trays at the table with them. Tansy smiled wide. "Hi! I know we usually don't sit with you two, but most of the people at our table had infinity signs on their shirts or necklaces, or bracelets, and well, I just can't. I know Daisy will join you two, but one to four is much better odds."

Ember liked these two and having them join their friend group made them happy. "You two are always welcome."

They spent a few minutes eating before Tansy gave Ember a mischievous smile. "So, Sunday afternoon. I've only been to those meetings twice, but how did Vi and your family know each other? That was ridiculous. And you all have the same red hair, which I've never seen outside of humans before meeting you, I might add."

Felix leaned in, a smile spreading across his face. "Yeah, Ember, tell us a story."

Shaking their head, Ember thought about what they'd discussed with their parents. They knew with the big display Dad had made, there was no getting out of answering the questions that would be asked. Dad had spent time on the phone with his twin forming a full backstory so everyone would get the *same* story.

"Vi is my Dad's sister. Their parents died before they graduated college. After college they each went their own way. It was a few years later that he realized he didn't know how to get a hold of her. Neither of them do the social media thing. So, it's been years."

Olivia's voice dropped, somber and respectful. "That's so sad. First they lost their parents, and then each other. Who's older?"

Ember couldn't help the twitch at the side of their mouth as they started to smile. "Dad, by about three minutes."

"Oh, my gods," Olivia squealed, totally invested in the story. "They're twins?"

Daisy dropped her tray on the table. "Who are twins? Hi, Tansy ... Olivia, nice seeing you here. Is this now going to be a thing?" Smiling, she sounded happy at the addition.

Tansy's eyes darted from Ember to Olivia to Daisy. "Yes, if you're okay with it. The table where we were sitting got ... I guess it's too much."

"Of course, you're welcome here." Daisy took a bite of her fries. "Ember." Daisy swung around. "You have to join me on Saturday. As I was coming in, I heard some people talking about another citywide event, but this time it's over in Toresville. It's being run by Mr. Shade himself. Will you come with me? You have to come with me."

Simon walked up. "Hi, Daisy, are you talking about the next rally? Are you going?" He sounded so pleasant when he spoke to Daisy, Ember almost mistook him for someone else.

It took everything in Ember not to roll their eyes. "Simon, what are you doing here? Aren't you scheduled to be in the library?"

His lip twitched. "It isn't a prison, Ember. Some people use that room to study. You should check it out. Books, reading, it's a thing."

They just gazed at him blankly. No reason to engage with someone who prejudged each person he met before any words were exchanged.

"Really, Simon? Ember has a higher grade than you in most classes. Are you just jealous?" Well, Ember may not say anything, but apparently that wasn't going to stop Daisy. "And yes, we're talking about going to Toresville to hear Mr. Shade speak."

Ember opened their mouth, then shut it. Then they shook their head. "You want to go to another one? You don't feel that you've heard it all by now?" They tried not to sound skeptical.

"There's always more facts, Ember," Simon spit out.

Daisy glared at him, then shot Ember a bright smile. "Come on! Of course not. There's always more to hear and learn. I've gotten something new every time I've attended. Witches supporting each other, lifting each other up to ensure no one goes unnoticed or forgotten. I love the idea of community and outreach. It's such a positive message. You know they have new information to deliver every time. So, can we go together?"

"I'll go with you," Simon cut in.

Ember saw Felix cover his mouth with his hand to keep from laughing and Olivia and Tansy exchange shocked glances. Simon never acted this ... smitten. Daisy was the only one who seemed oblivious, which made the whole situation funnier.

Daisy shook her head and gave Simon a weird look. "Ember?"

"Probably," Ember said slowly. "I need to talk with my parents. My Dad's sister just came into town, and I don't know if there's something planned."

Her eyes widened. "Your dad has a sister? Is that the twin you were talking about? Your dad's a twin?"

"Yep. So, let me get back to you after I talk to them."

"Okay, sounds great."

Daisy smiled wide, then dug into her food.

Simon grunted as he walked away, apparently done with the shenanigans of the people at the table.

Ember leaned against Felix. They knew Daisy was safe going to the farces since she seemed to believe in the message they gave, but deep down, Ember felt like they needed to protect their friend. Nothing good came from anything Mr. Shade or his group of cronies ran.

Chapter 8 - Pandemonium

Ember

Gym class was after lunch. Two weeks earlier, after all the eleventh-year students went on a field trip to the Bishop Bay Forest to collect night plants, a camel spider bit Ember. The spider, huge and scary, wasn't dangerous—unless the person bitten was a phoenix. In that case, the bite was deadly.

On their first day back to school, Ember forgot about gym, and hadn't prepared. They needed clothes that weren't revealing and a plan for putting on their gym clothes. The school had a single room toilet with a locking door. For the last two weeks, the gym locker room had been a minefield for Ember, full of challenges. Today, though they forgot their original clothes, they could finally stay at the locker without worrying.

First, they changed their top, replacing their forest green shirt with four cats piled on top of each other. The bottom was black saying, 'meow.' Flopped on that one, a purple cat had a bubble stating, 'them.' Next came a white cat proclaiming, 'their.' The last cat, at the top of the tower, a friendly yellow, had a speech bubble stating, 'they.'

Ember's gym shirt was the plain black one they'd gotten from their dad. They moved on to their jeans. They were just folding them into their small locker, when they heard a huff behind them. Spinning, they saw Ambrose glaring at them. In a flash, they remembered Ambrose walking in on them the previous week while they changed in the washroom and forgot to lock the door.

Everything about this was weird. The closed door should've been enough. Ambrose knew there were at least one or two students at the school who were trans, which was why the locker rooms had the private changing areas. In the end, they'd hoped Ambrose wouldn't be an issue.

Ember scrunched up their face at the other student. "What do you want, Ambrose?" They reached behind them and grabbed their shorts. They slipped them on. When they realized Ambrose was just standing there looking frustrated and confused, Ember slipped on their shoes, and headed out to the field.

At the field, the teacher had a board with basic stretches. It was a personal testing day. Ember gathered Daisy, and then began a five-minute run around the field to warm up.

As they ran, Daisy asked, "What was up with Ambrose in the locker room? I heard you call out her name."

"No idea. She's been acting weird since the school learned I had magic. I'm just waiting for all of the hullabaloo to go away."

"It won't, my friend. At least, not anytime soon."

"What? Why not?" Ember had a sudden fear Daisy was right.

"There's the novelty of you now having magic, but there's more. You're fixing people. No one can do that. Not the teachers, not the students themselves, no one. You've done more than shift who you are. You may be the top witch in the school. It's ... I dunno, it hurts my head if I think about all of it too much."

It saddened Ember when they thought about all the things they couldn't tell their best friend. And as Daisy believed more and more in the ways of Infinite

WISDOM, they wondered how long they could stay best friends. There was a fundamental difference in people who could suddenly hate all non-magical humans to the level that group preached. Ember knew to the depths of their soul Daisy didn't hate humans. They hoped that Daisy realized the truth about Infinite WISDOM before it was too late.

As Ember ran, they remembered their last few homes. When they were homeschooled, they spent time with the people in their neighborhood who were more often than not, non-magical. At the age of thirteen, Ember's family lived in this cul-de-sac and Alex, the next-door neighbor, was a year younger than them. The two of them were thick as thieves.

When Alex wasn't at school, they'd play games, go on walks, and talk about everything. Before Alex, Ember knew that non-magical humans were probably the same as them, but after, they knew the only difference was the ability to do some tricks.

Once Ember and Daisy finished their warmup run, they moved on to stretching. Daisy gazed into the perfectly blue sky with a few fluffy clouds. Ember wished they could be flying in that idyllic sky, wings spread wide, tail streaming out behind them, and the wind cooling their feathers.

"Is there anything in the message from the assemblies that you agree with?"

Ember pulled themself from imagining swooping through the clouds and focused on Daisy. "A message of segregation, lies, and hate? No, Daisy, I don't agree with it. It's easy to find scientific proof that what they're talking about isn't true. The counterpoints are easily proved. The non-magical humans are *not* saying anything that the group is crediting to them. It's propaganda and lies."

"So, you're not against it because of *who* is giving the message?" Daisy bit her lip, looking worried.

Ember's mouth dropped open. "You really thought my big argument was because Ambrose and Cress were their talking puppets?"

Daisy stared back, eyes wide. It suddenly occurred to them that she started to look worried halfway through her question. Daisy's mouth opened and shut like a fish. With a sinking feeling in their gut, Ember knew they weren't alone. Trying to keep their face blank, though they really wanted to roll their eyes, they turned and saw Ambrose standing behind them.

She stood in her perfect gym clothes, fists on her hips, glaring down at them. "What the hell are you, Ember?"

"I'm not really sure what you're asking, Ambrose. I'm a student, an air witch, and an eleventh-year? What answer do you want?"

The other students in the area stopped talking and stretching and turned to face them. One of Ambrose's eyebrows rose. "A student?"

Ember shrugged. "What's your problem, Ambrose?"

Ambrose rolled her eyes. "I saw you changing last week, and again today. What *are* you?"

Ember raised both hands to their sides. "I should ask *you* that. Why were you watching me?"

"Are you some sort of shape-changer? Is that a thing?"

"No. I think you're imagining things. Have you been under extra stress with all the assemblies you've been putting on?"

A flash of something crossed Ambrose's face. Ember wasn't sure what it was, but they thought they may have hit home with that last statement.

"Just what the hell is in your pants, Ember?" Ambrose wouldn't let this drop.

Face flat, Ember looked around, wondering if the teacher had heard any of this. They knew Ambrose could get into a lot of trouble for what she was doing. Unfortunately, they were without supervision. The terrible trio had a knack for getting away with everything. They huffed out a laugh. "Pandemonium."

The other kids chuckled as Ambrose slammed her arms straight. "You are so impossible. Whatever." She stormed off.

Ember had a feeling the topic wasn't dropped. They were exuberant they'd won the battle, but they knew the war was still real. Shaking their head, they got back to stretching.

Chapter 9 - A Lesson In Politics

Ambrose

Ambrose and Cress sat in the four season sunroom of her family's house. The living room was nicer, but the furniture wasn't comfortable. It was bought for looks, not to be used. These couches were sitting couches.

She was still fuming over Ember at Gym class. She usually just ignored Ember, but with everything going on, and Father taking Cress's phone call, she felt off. Part of her needed to establish some sort of pecking order, even if it wasn't something she normally cared about.

A human servant brought tea and mini cakes and placed them on the table.

Cress leaned back, his muscular body filling out his shirt. "Hey, you," he demanded of the server. "Bring us a plate of cookies."

The person, wearing the black suit and white tie that was the uniform of the house staff, bowed. "Yes, sir."

Ambrose watched him exit. "I don't recognize him."

"So?" Cress shrugged. "Does that matter?"

"I thought I knew all the people who worked for the family."

"Them? The *staff?*" He scoffed. "These human scum. I don't know why you even have them in your house."

Ambrose shook her head. "Who will write your stupid apology letter if there aren't humans? Or cook, or clean, answer the door? You know there are jobs that magic users don't want to do that humans are great at."

"Like what? Name one."

"Accounting? Baking? Fast food delivery? Vacuuming? I don't know. There are things that don't require magic." Ambrose was getting tired of assuming every job in the world was for magical humans only. She liked the idea of her people getting more power, but how far did they want to go with the movement?

"Fine, whatever." He grabbed a plate and filled it with small cakes and started eating them. "Can you believe that stupid assignment for history? Writing a journal as if we *were* human? Can we get your *staff* to do *that* assignment?"

"No, despite what Felix always claims in class, I do my own homework. The staff will help with auxiliary things, but homework itself I've always done myself."

In reality she could ask for anything to be done by the staff, but Ambrose liked learning. Cress's arrogance and his current obnoxious attitude was annoying her. She *wanted* him to do this assignment. The idea of him writing from a human point of view brought her a perverse sense of joy.

He grumbled under his breath. "Fine."

Father walked in and sat in his favorite chair. "How was your day, Ambrose? Cress?"

Ambrose gave him a tight smile. "It was ... okay. I've had better. What aren't you telling me, Father?"

His eyes narrowed. "What do you mean, daughter?"

"Don't patronize me. You and Cress have been keeping secrets. You know he's not very good at it." In reality he hadn't given much away, but there were a few tells. There may not be anything, but she was willing to bet there was something. "So tell me, Father. I don't like being kept in the dark."

He steepled his fingers and tapped his pointer fingers on his chin. "I don't know that you really want to know the seedier side of the movement. I knew Cress wouldn't mind learning all the aspects. He's a man and tough."

"That's very sexist of you, Father. I can be tough. Just tell me what I need to know." Her jaw tightened before she said more. She hated that she was losing ground in her father's and the movement's eyes.

He sipped his tea. "That's just it, I don't know that this *is* something you need to know." Her face tightened, but before she could say anything, he lifted his hands in defeat. "If you insist, I'll tell you. After the weekend event, someone caught that teen from your school. Ember, I think, the one with red hair."

"Yeah, that's Ember. No one else has red hair, only them. How is it possible for them to even have red hair? That's not a witch-born trait."

"I don't know. We'll set some people to do some research on that. I don't know that I've ever heard of magic users with red hair before you told me about them." He shook his head. "Well, one of our watchers caught this student talking back during the presentation, questioning our message." The last few words came out as a snarl.

When Mr. Shade started coming to the house, Father didn't really believe in the message, he just saw the power. His words and behavior felt like he was becoming a believer. Chills ran down her back. The idea terrified her.

Ambrose shrugged. "So? Several students questioned the message last week, too. We just rolled with it and moved on. No one paid attention to their idiotic questions anyway."

"This is why you're the face and body of the movement and not the brains, Ambrose. People will follow you because you're pretty, and popular, but you don't understand the dirty work behind running an organization like this."

Cress snickered and Ambrose glared at him. *Cress is the brains? How do they expect it to succeed?*

Father sighed as if he could read her mind. "We can't have discourse or challenges during our presentations. It will ruin the atmosphere we are creating and may diminish the number of new people joining our cause. Success is dependent on the number of believers we collect."

"So, what are you doing to these nay-sayers?" Ambrose finished a small vanilla cake with strawberry filling. "Aren't people allowed to think what they want to think?" Though she asked the question, apprehension filled her. Father had never been known for having a soft hand.

"What do you think?" His voice was hard.

She swallowed. "Those two kids who ended up in the hospital, the one who ended up dead, they were put there by your people."

Another sip of his tea. "No, Ambrose, they were put there by *our* people."

"And Cress knew? For how long?" She looked back and forth between the two of them, anger boiling in her. She wasn't sure what made her more upset, that Cress knew, and she didn't, or that the movement was harming kids.

Cress laughed. "From the start. I offered to be one of the men who rounded up the disbelievers, but I guess I'm needed for my pretty face. Not that I think any of them could've hurt me." He flexed his arm.

Bile rose in the back of Ambrose's throat and the cake felt heavy in her stomach. The idea of spreading this word had seemed like a game, but this game just took a turn for the worse. "But what about Ember. Why were you surprised? Did you think they had been hospitalized?"

"No, Ambrose," Father said, leaning forward. "I thought they were dead."

Chapter 10 - Take A Number

Ember

Tuesday morning, Ember sat in Math class with Felix. It was their third period of the day, and since they were in an Advanced Calculus class, everyone besides the two of them was a year ahead. It was usually a time to relax into relative anonymity.

Felix pulled his notebook out. "Tonight's the night, right?"

"Hmm?"

"Your aunt, Vi, she's coming for dinner tonight." He sounded as excited as Ember felt. They weren't sure how they'd ended up with such an amazing boyfriend.

Ember chuckled. "Haven't you known her for years?"

Felix gazed up in thought. "We joined the group and met Vi just over a year ago."

"So, I should be asking you about her, not the other way around. Both her and Monte." They poked him in the arm.

"I know Monte better than Vi, because she works with the volunteers, and I usually help out before the meetings. Vi usually mingles with the adults." He tapped his pencil on his desk.

"Well, start talking!" Ember laughed.

"Okay, okay, fine. Vi seems above it all. She always knows everything that's going on, kind of the master organizer. She knows everyone, but often only comes out at the last minute. Really busy. I don't know what it is about her, but she's amazing. She does socialize with us, but she's kind of intimidating." He tilted his head. "If she's your dad's twin, I guess I get it now ... maybe."

Ember nodded. "Okay, got it. I've never thought of Dad as intimidating, but maybe his sister is."

A wide smile spread on Felix's face. "Now, Monte, she's another matter. She's completely down to earth. Love her."

"Should I be jealous?"

"Yes, I'm smitten with a woman twice my age who's in a relationship with your aunt." His brow furrowed and he leaned forward. "Wait, *is* she twice my age?"

Ember shook their head. "You're so cute when you figure things out."

Before they could continue their conversation, a twelfth-year girl came up to their desks and stood over them, gazing down. Class was moments from starting, so Ember wasn't sure what was going on.

"Hi, can I help you, or do you want Felix?" They looked at Felix and back at the girl. Her light brown hair brushed her shoulders, and her mouth was pressed in a tight line.

After a few seconds, she huffed out a breath and her shoulders dropped. "You're Ember, right? That girl—or student, or person—that everyone's talking about. The one who did the air show a couple weeks ago?"

Ember sighed. Two weeks ago, Ember had been a freak that no one thought belonged at the school. A student with basically no magic. Then, they'd sat on a green platform with a bucket of balls, lifted up, and began playing catch with their mom.

When Ember and their mom agreed to do the demonstration, they'd failed to take into account that everyone in the school could watch the exercise through the windows. By the end of class, the end of the day, the end of the week, Ember had gone from magicless dud, to powerhouse air witch.

The school officials had shifted Ember's Air Magic class from student to teacher assistant, going as far as removing Ember from their Earth Magic lessons, a class they'd never been able to do much in, to assistant in the lower Air Magic classes as well. Who knew a training activity from when they were nine would change their life so drastically?

What started in Air Magic moved to other disciplines. It soon became apparent that they could help not only Air Magic students, but others as well. Ember wasn't sure if it was their witch magic, phoenix magic, or some combination of the two, but they could see how a person wove their powers. And now, random students kept approaching them for help.

"Yeah, that's me."

"A friend of mine ... well, my brother, told me to talk to you."

Behind her the teacher walked to his desk, signaling class was about to start.

"Okay, but class is about to start."

"Right. Could you meet me in the courtyard after school?" She darted a look over her shoulder, then looked back. "Please."

Ember shrugged, but sighed out a hesitant, "Sure." Just the thought of it made Ember tired. Watching the magic flow from students took more energy than one would expect. They debated telling this girl 'no'—what was her name?—but she dashed off to her seat too quickly and class started.

Math was a full bell to bell of notes. The teacher didn't stop talking and clacking his chalk on the board the whole time. *In this age of whiteboards and markers, where did he even find a chalkboard and chalk?*

When class ended and Ember and Felix finally put their math paraphernalia away, Felix asked, "Do you even know that girl's name?"

"No," Ember snickered. "I gave that a momentary thought between her walking away and class starting, but then ... well ... math."

Felix leaned over and kissed their forehead. "See you at lunch. Have fun in Magical Creations."

Ember waggled their brows. "That I will."

Magical Creations, like Math, had students from a variety of grade levels. It was an elective class that most students didn't take for some reason. The only student Ember really knew from their grade was Olivia. Ember realized they now recognized some of the students from the ninth-year Air Magic class, but they didn't want to socialize with them. Ember feared what they may request.

As always, Ember and Olivia sat next to each other, silently waiting for class to start. The room was full of lab tables that fit up to four students, but they got the table to themselves. The extra space was nice. There were times they'd talk, but both of them tended to be quiet and Ember enjoyed their silent time together.

Ms. Hewett stood from her chair behind her cluttered desk, her curly black hair a frame to her ebony face. She moved to the front of the room, and everyone immediately quieted down. "We've been discussing using different types of magic to create seamless vessels that can hold and carry elements. We've practiced taking glass and forming spheres with our magic. Today, with a partner, you'll create spheres around elements of air, water, and fire. Since not everyone in here has air, water, or fire magic, there are instruments on your table to help aid in your lab."

Ember turned to Olivia. "Do you want to go first or second?"

"You go first."

They nodded. "Sounds good. I'm going to encapsulate fire, since you can hold it out for me, if that's okay."

Her smile lit up her face. "Sounds perfect."

Ember chose fire because it was one of Olivia's proficiencies, and she was good; it was her strongest magic. Being a phoenix, Ember was born in fire—it was her second nature.

They took a few calming breaths. The magic in this class was based on generic magic. Since Ember was only half-witch, they struggled with doing most of these constructs, but Olivia was patient. They'd lucked out that she was in this class. Picking up a small sheet of glass, Ember imagined what they wanted: the glass to reform as a sphere.

They gave a quick nod and Olivia formed a small flame floating above the table about a foot away from both of them. One more focusing inhale, and they exhaled the mental spell with a push of energy. The glass lifted up, and Ember used an air current to shift it to the fire as it morphed into the shape of a sphere.

As the glass fell from the heart of Olivia's fire, Ember's hand shot out to catch the small glass ball. Olivia snatched Ember's hand back and caught the finished sphere, dissipating the fire outside the glass at the same time.

She glared at Ember, but her hands were shaking. "This is hot, and you don't have fire magic. This won't burn me, but it'll burn you. You need to be more careful." She placed the glass on a towel and took a slow breath. "You did a great job, but we should've thought through the landing. If you'd caught the ball, your hand would've been burnt ... like third degree burns type burnt." She shook her head. "I know you struggle with the magic ... or are you still pretending?" She paused, but when Ember didn't say anything she nodded. "You need to remember this is fire and fire is hot. I don't want to see you hurt, okay?"

Ember bit their bottom lip to stop their face from showing any reaction. They knew Olivia was just trying to be helpful. With a nod, they said, "You're right, sorry. Thanks for the catch, literally."

Finally, Olivia smiled. "Cute."

As they put the finished spell on the tray, they heard a few balls shatter around the room. Taking a quick look, Ember saw the other groups struggling with the assignment.

Ms. Hewett, who was walking around the room, stopped by the table. "Nice work. Who's fireball?"

Ember raised their hand. "Olivia provided the fire, and caught the thing after I formed it, so really it was a team effort."

She smiled wide. "It's great that you figured that out right away. This is a multi-part lesson. I usually have to give a hint that groups need to work together, but you two really are clever." She winked. "This type of magic always works best when done in pairs." Her head snapped to another table. "Oh, my, I have some healing to do. Back to work, you two."

It was Olivia's turn, and Ember helped them to create an airball. "What do you think we can do with this?"

Olivia's head tilted. "A small breeze on a hot day?"

"A *really* small breeze. I wonder if one of these could hold a more complicated spell, like a twister."

"That will be for another day, my friend." Olivia grinned. "It's almost time for lunch."

Class had flown by. They only had the two balls but, looking around the room, no other group had managed that many. *This process isn't easy.*

Chapter 11 - Welcome To The Inferno

Ember

"Wanna come to my house?" Daisy looked so hopeful as she asked, but Ember had promised to help the math girl in the courtyard.

Despite how much they'd rather join Daisy, they knew it wasn't in the cards for the afternoon. "I can't today, I'm busy. Maybe tomorrow?"

Daisy looked disappointed, and her eyes narrowed as Felix placed his hand on their back. "Yeah, tomorrow, that works."

Though guilt wracked Ember, they had made a promise, and knew that girl was waiting. Daisy had seen them help the student with water magic, but they didn't want Daisy to know how strong their abilities were. There were too many questions Ember couldn't answer ... not yet. And they knew Daisy, she would ask.

Tomorrow they'd have fun together ... as long as not too much of the conversation was on Infinite WISDOM. Ember froze in the act of lifting their hand to give Daisy a hug, the hurt in Daisy's face stabbed them to their soul. "I'm really sorry, Daisy. I just ... I'm sorry."

"Yeah, it's fine. But tomorrow, I'm going to hold you to that." Daisy's face was hard and determined.

Felix and Ember headed to the courtyard. Despite sharing a class, they didn't know exactly why the twelfth-year student wanted to meet them, though Ember assumed it was for magic help of some kind. Between being an assistant in Air Magic and creating glass balls, they'd used a lot of energy throughout the day and were tired, but they had a bit left. Ember figured they could help a student with something small.

When they arrived in the courtyard, the girl with the light brown hair stood with a boy with similar colored hair. Narrowing their eyes, Ember thought they recognized him. "Bear," they said, squinting. "Xander Bear. You're in the ninth-year Air Magic class, right? And this is your sister?"

He rolled his eyes. "Since we look alike, that isn't a very hard guess. I assumed you knew Zahra since you're in Math with her. Haven't you two been in the same class since the beginning of the year? You've only been in my class for a few sessions."

Zahra! That's her name. Ember shot a glance at Felix who looked like he was filing away the information of the girl's name as well.

Ember huffed a laugh and noticed Xander's sister, Zahra, smiling at his ire. Ember said, "That class isn't about socializing. You sit, take notes, and leave. If you aren't taking notes, it's a test day. To be honest, I barely talk to Felix, and we walk in and out of the class together."

Zahra covered a yawn with a hand, apparently as tired as Ember. "That's true. I didn't realize there *were* eleventh-years until Xander started talking about you, then it hit me, I knew who he was talking about."

Ember nodded but didn't want to chit chat. *I just want to get home, eat, and rest.* "So, what are we doing here?"

She bit her lip. "Look, I'm good with my proficiencies, but my fire magic is ... I keep getting messed up. There's a test coming up and I need to figure out what's going wrong. Can you watch what I'm doing and see if you can do what you're doing for other people?"

Ember froze. This was different. It was the one proficiency they wouldn't—shouldn't—coach. It was too dangerous. Fire magic was more than magic to them—it was *who* they were. But they couldn't explain that to these two. They weren't sure they could explain it to Felix. Their mouth was dry, and they weren't sure they could speak. After a moment, they forced their head to move up and down, agreeing despite that being the wrong answer. If they said no, they'd have to give a reason, and that would be worse.

Zahra smiled. "Thank you, thank you, thank you." She practically squealed the words. "Okay, here's the skill, It's two-fold. First, we create five fireballs." She created them floating in the center of the courtyard away from anything that could burn. Ember saw the power and the connection between the fire and Zahra. The tendrils were wispy, like lace strings. The fire witch didn't seem to have any issues with this part of the skill.

"We're supposed to have the balls dance, do an intricate pattern. Xander, can you show Ember the paper with the design?"

They heard a bag unzip and rifling but didn't take their eyes off the globes. Ember wasn't sure why they didn't look away, even if they had, they could've followed the fire. Felix put a hand on their shoulder. "Can you help her?"

They bit their bottom lip. *In for a pound and all that.* "I ... I think so."

"Here you go." Xander handed them the sheet.

The fire called to them. For a moment Ember just breathed. They hadn't spent time with other people's fire, outside their dad's. A part of them wanted to reach out and manipulate the flames, control the fire, make it part of them. *Gods, that would be a horrible idea.*

Forcing themself to turn from the fire, Ember looked down at the paper. Balls two and four needed to bounce up and down. The center ball needed to travel in a circular path perpendicular to the group. The end balls had to weave back and forth amongst the three moving balls in the middle, switching places and then moving back. It looked complicated but fun.

"Fun," Felix said with a sarcastic tone. "Are all your challenges this convoluted?" He rubbed his forehead.

Zahra snorted. "This one's particularly bad. The teacher decided some of the students were either cheating or sliding by. He figured this would weed out who knew their stuff and who didn't. I don't want to be lumped with the cheaters and sliders ... you know, separated out." She lifted her fingers to quote out the last two words. "I think he said he's creating two classes and I want to be in the upper class. I haven't been cheating."

Ember nodded. "Okay, show me what you can do."

Zahra's hands had been up like she'd been telling someone to slow down. Her right hand began to make a small clockwise circle and the center ball spun. She moved her left hand up and down and the two balls next to the center ball moved in time with her motion.

Sweat formed on her brow. "That's all I can do. I can't make the last two balls move. Well, I could, but not all five at once."

Ember studied Zahra and the gossamer threads. "Okay, this is going to be complicated, but we'll try. Stop moving your hands."

Zahra stopped and the fireballs resumed their spots in a line.

Ignoring the fire, and focusing only on the witch, Ember narrowed their eyes. "Let's start by pointing the palm of your right hand to the ground ... good, now, can you get the center ball to spin with just that right thumb? It's a bit of a different way to focus, but you're in your twelfth-year, you need to hone in your magic, use less hand motions."

Zahra's face tightened. "I don't think my year in school has anything to do with my abilities or control. I'm doing this because Xander suggested it. I don't need to be insulted."

Ember blew out a breath. "Sorry, I'm tired and would rather be home. We can stop."

"No, let me just..." They all waited while Zahra struggled, face scrunching up and she did what Ember suggested. Slowly, as her thumb rotated, the center ball began its path again. At first it wobbled, but as Zahra relaxed and got the feel of the motion, the ball's path smoothed out.

In a low voice Zahra said, "Okay, I think I got it. I can't believe it, but yeah, we're good."

"Oh no, not good yet, that was the easy part." Ember laughed. "The next two parts are tricky. I want you to move your right hand up and down, but only affect the second and fourth balls with that motion. With the thumb rotating the center ball, this will take concentration."

Zahra moved her assigned hand up and all five balls moved with the motion. She growled and tried again. This time only the center three moved. With a frustrated snarl, she shook her head, but kept her thumb rotating.

"I'm not going to lose my small victory. I *will* make this work." Zahra's voice was gruff with her concentration.

It took several minutes and attempts, but she finally managed to move just the two balls she wanted up and down while the center one rotated steadily.

Felix clapped softly while Xander whooped. "That's amazing. I've never seen that type of control."

"I've heard that once you get really good, you can do these things without the hand motions. Most adults do much less waving, if you think about it," Felix noted.

Ember saw the strain on Zahra's face. "Less chit chat, more finishing the task at hand. Speaking of hands, you now have your left hand free to work the hard part, moving the end balls back and forth. Start with that hand palm down. If you can, focus the movement with your thumb and pinky, the other fingers curled in. At the cross over, flip your hand over."

Zahra bit her lip, eyes wide, her shirt damp with sweat, and not because it was warm outside. The two end balls began moving towards each other. They dipped low below the balls going up, then needed to cross in the center of the ball circling.

As the end fireball's paths crossed, Zahra lost control and they collided, causing them to crash into the center ball, and fly out, collecting one of the bobbing balls. The large fireball flew right towards Xander.

His hand flew out in a traditional scoop and dissipate spell motion that all fire witches learn. It wouldn't be sufficient. The fire had grown big enough, and Zahra eyes widened and looked tired as she tried but couldn't extinguish her own fire. Her body trembled and she gasped out, "No!"

With a small flick of a finger hidden by their side, Ember absorbed a chunk of the heat, taking the fire from the out-of-control mass that flew towards Xander. They took enough that his scoop and dissipate spell should work. This was the danger with fire. They both should've just stepped out of the way. It was why they were in the fireproof courtyard.

When the flames went out, his eyes widened, and he leapt in the air. "Oh, my gods, Zahra, did you see that? Did you see what I did? I haven't been able to do that in class, and *when it mattered, did you see that*?!" He started dancing around.

Zahra gaped at her brother, looking from him to Ember. She shook her head. "I ... I don't know what happened. I don't know how I lost control or how Xander stopped it. That shouldn't have been possible. I'm really tired, and you've given me a lot to think about. The test is Friday. Maybe if you're up to it, we can try again tomorrow or Thursday?"

Ember shrugged. "Sure, I guess. I mean, you know the basics at this point."

"Yeah, but we wanted you to help with the scoop and dissipate, tell us what we're doing wrong since we can't seem to get the fire to fully go out when it grows past a certain point. I guess today isn't the best example, though, I'm really not sure what happened." The confusion in Zahra's voice echoed in the small courtyard. Brows furrowed, she looked back and forth between Xander and Ember as if trying to puzzle something out.

"I couldn't tell you. But I'm glad I could help you with part of your assignment." They forced a smile. "Dancing fire, who would've thought."

Ember left the courtyard with Felix. When they were halfway to their house, he stopped them. "That was you, wasn't it."

"What was?"

"The fire."

"I didn't start it, but I couldn't stand back and watch Xander get burned. It would've been bad, Felix, really bad."

He pulled them in for a kiss. "Just be careful, okay?"

His concern for them warmed them almost as much as the fire had.

Chapter 12 - Meanwhile ... A Bit Of Introspection

Daisy

"Wanna come to my house?" Daisy watched as Ember's face fell and knew the answer before they even responded. "I can't today. Maybe tomorrow?"

Felix's hand moved to rest on Ember's lower back. She liked Felix, she really did, but the longer the two of them dated, the more and more Ember pushed Daisy from their life. It wasn't that she was jealous, not really, she just missed her friend. "Yeah, tomorrow, that works."

Ember's hand lifted as if they wanted to give Daisy a hug. "I'm really sorry, Daisy. I just ... I'm sorry."

Daisy stepped back. It hurt to be left out of whatever they were doing, but as long as they still had friend time, she'd get over it. She just wanted to be upset right then. "Yeah, it's fine. But tomorrow, I'm going to hold you to that."

The two walked down the hall. Frustration bubbled in her as she grabbed her bag and walked the other way. Her walk home didn't take long. The weather over the last few weeks had turned cool, and she used the breeze to help calm down. *At least there isn't much time before winter break. One more week and we have a couple weeks off for good behavior. Ember and I have spent every winter break together since they came to Feniks Secondary School. I'm sure we'll do something together then.*

At home, she kicked off her shoes and headed for the stairs. In her room, she flopped on her bed, her arm falling over her eyes. *Just a few minutes, and then I'll start my homework.*

A knock came at her door before it cracked open. "Daisy, it's Mom. Can I come in?"

"Sure." She didn't move as she heard the swish of the door, a click, footsteps, and then felt a dip on the side of her bed.

Mom's warm hand rubbed her thigh. "You okay, dear?"

"Yeah, I'm just being dumb." She let her arm slide to the bed over her head. "I miss Ember. In the last few weeks, it feels like they're spending more time with Felix. I know they're dating, but ... I dunno, I miss our time being dorks together."

"Have you told them?"

"No, of course not. This is my own issue."

Mom sighed. "Is there anything else? Ember and Felix have been a couple for a long time. Your bristling over it seems new. Has school been getting harder?"

"Not really." Daisy rubbed her eyes. "It isn't classes. It may be ... well, there is something else. I asked Ember to go to another Infinite WISDOM event with me on Saturday. They haven't given me an answer yet. I know they aren't really into the message or the group, I just ... I think if they gave the organization a chance and ignored that the terrible trio ran it, I dunno, maybe?"

Mom's face tightened for a moment before relaxing. "How many of those have you gone to, dear?"

"Three so far. They're interesting. I've learned new things every time I go. Do you and Dad want to come along?" Hope ignited in her chest. Maybe she could finally get her parents to join something outside the house. Daisy loved spending time with her parents, and this would be fantastic.

"Tell me. You say you've learned a lot. Have you double checked the information they're sharing?"

Daisy pushed herself up to her elbows. She tried to ignore how annoyed the question made her. "You sound like some of the kids in the audience. The presenters hand out information cards with links to the evidence of what they're sharing." She sat up, crossed her legs, then pushed her hair back from her face. "Not to mention Simon, he's this kid from school, big smarty pants nerd. He agrees with the stuff being shared. I can't imagine him *not* double checking all the information."

"That's good, really good, dear. But what I'm curious about is, have you," she tapped Daisy's nose, "done any of this research? You rarely follow a crowd blindly. I've seen you spend hours doing research for school, studying, learning new things. You've never cared what other people thought if you were interested in a topic. Why not use that brain of yours now?"

With a grumble, Daisy rolled her eyes. "I've been busy, but a group wouldn't just lie, would they? They've spread their words to literally hundreds of people. If they hadn't told the truth in their messages, it would be known, right? Some other set of people or organization would call them out, wouldn't they?"

A single brow rose on Mom's face. "Okay. As long as you understand what you're supporting, dear. Dad and I have raised you to think on your own, and I just wanted to make sure you're fully aware of the message you want people to connect with the face and name of Daisy Autumn."

As Mom walked out, Daisy wondered if her parents had done any research. Though there were people who questioned Infinite WISDOM, no one presented counter-arguments with support. *You'd think Ember or Felix would have something if there was something to be found.*

Feeling guilty for her thoughts, Daisy realized her mom was right. *I really do need to do my own homework ... as soon as my real schoolwork is done.*

Chapter 13 - How Big Can One's Family Grow?

Ember

Ember helped in the kitchen, excited to learn more about their Aunt Nuri and her partner Monte. A pork roast had been slow cooking all day. When they got home, Dad asked that they chop veggies for a salad. Mom was preparing garlic mashed potatoes while Dad sat at the table and worked on lemon bars.

Ember took their veggies to the table and piled the lettuce, tomatoes, onions, peppers, mushrooms, and some cheese into a big bowl. They placed their masterpiece in the center of the table. "Do either of you need any help?"

"No, honey," Mom said. "Nuri and Monte should be here soon."

Ember dug in the refrigerator for a soda and joined their Dad at the table. "Do you think we should call her 'Nuri' or 'Vi'?"

"Unless there's a good reason, I'm calling my sister Nuri." Dad grumbled, "I'm too old to change my ways."

Mom moved to rub Dad's shoulders. "Ember, dear, you should ask your aunt what she prefers. Dad's a bit of a stick in the mud, but you're just meeting her. It would be respectful to let her decide. She'll understand your Dad's grumpiness."

"I'm not grumpy."

"Of course you're not, dear." Mom kissed the top of his head and Ember chuckled.

A few minutes later, the doorbell rang. Ember leapt up to answer the door. Their aunts stood waiting. As before, they both were immaculate-looking. Monte wore black slacks and a lavender blouse. Nuri wore a champagne dress with a black shawl. Her wavy red hair was pinned back on the sides.

Ember smiled. "Hi, Nuri, Monte, welcome to our home. Before I invite you in, I have to ask, can I call you both Aunt Nuri and Aunt Monte, or is it too soon? Or would you prefer Vi ... Aunt Vi? I just ... what should I call you?" They couldn't fight the smile taking over their face as they swept their arm from the door into the house in welcome.

As they all headed into the kitchen, Monte all but squealed. "I love that you want me to be your Aunt Monte. As for Vi—I mean Nuri, don't give her a choice."

Though Aunt Monte answered, Ember wanted Nuri ... or Vi, to chime in. "Which do you want me to call you, Nuri or Vi?" This suddenly seemed very important to them. This was the first family they had after their parents, and they never thought they'd have any. It was all so weird.

"Well, if you call me Aunty, it won't matter. That goes for here or at my job. But in front of people who only know me as Vi, that name's better, no reason to confuse the masses. If, as I assume is the case, my bull-headed brother calls me Nuri ... Well, twins always have weird names for each other."

Mom gazed at them over her shoulder. "Ember, why don't you show your aunts around the house while we get everything plated?"

"Sure, Mom." They led their aunts around, showing them the open-concept kitchen, dining room and living room. They pointed out the rest room, guest room, and den. "Do you want to see the bedrooms upstairs?"

Aunt Nuri chuckled. "No, I think we've seen enough, thanks."

"And the food smells great," Aunt Monte added. "Why don't we all get caught up on the last several hundred years of gossip." She laughed, the sound light and joyous.

The three of them sat, joining Ember's parents, and began dishing out salad.

Mom said, "So, Nuri, how long have you been in the area?"

"About five years," she answered, pouring some dressing on her salad. "We heard Tad Shade had settled around here and decided to move headquarters. We had a core of people working with us, but decided we needed to start recruiting." She turned to Dad. "What about you, Ash? What have you been up to after you made those laws then disappeared?"

He snorted. "I spent some time looking for you but couldn't find you. After the war there was all the politicking, which you know I hated. If it weren't for Sadie ... But then the committee was over, and it took a few years, but I finally escaped. I returned to the other phoenixes, until I heard the news of my exile. Then went out to search for you. Once I realized I couldn't find you,

Sadie and I found jobs, focused on education and survival."

Mom reached over and placed her hand on his arm.

It felt like a bucket of ice had been dumped over Ember's head. They had thought they and their Dad were the last two phoenixes for years. Then there was Aunt Nuri. Now Dad spoke of others. "What? There are more phoenixes than the three of us?"

Aunt Nuri smiled at Ember warmly. "Yes, Ember. All the ones in the war, except for your dad and I, sacrificed themselves for the good of peace, but not all the phoenixes fought. The ones that didn't fight thought the sacrifice of immortal beings wasn't worth it for mere humans or even magic users. They believed the mortals could fight and kill themselves off. Since Ash was the initial creator of the Fire Bird Coalition, the others have more or less exiled him."

"But not you?" Ember asked. "Even though you've continued his group?"

"They aren't too happy about that. Being immortal, a few hundred years isn't forever. They'll get over it eventually. In reality, it may be good for all of us to return to the phoenix compound and find our brethren. Me and Ash need to reconnect with our people, and Ember, you need to just connect. You have your dad, but there is so much more. You have to learn about who you are, where you came from, and what to expect, especially in the next few years."

Across from Ember, their parents looked pensive. Ember felt a warring of emotions. On the one hand, the idea of more phoenixes thrilled them. They could meet them, fly with them, learn from them. It almost overwhelmed Ember with the thought of it all. But the theory that their parents had neglected any part of their preparation offended them on their parents' behalf. Their education hadn't been lacking.

"I know you mean well, Aunt Nuri, but I've been given a great upbringing. I doubt you'll find holes in my knowledge. My parents have done a great job in my education so far."

Mom's eyes widened and her hand flew to her mouth. Suddenly, their confidence wasn't as ironclad. *What hasn't she told me? What has Dad held back?*

Dad's face softened. "Oh, love, we've done our best, but Nuri isn't wrong that there are holes in your knowledge."

Ember bit their lip. What didn't they know? Their heart started beating fast, and they made fists when they realized their hands were trembling.

Aunt Nuri watched them, then shook her head. "I'm sorry, I don't mean to create this tension. Can I ask a simpler question?"

Mom slumped. "Please."

"How long was Ember five years old? Did they make it the full year?"

Chapter 14 - Stopping Points

Ember

Ember gaped at Aunt Nuri, then at their Dad, and finally Mom. "What do you mean, 'Did I make a full year?' How could I *not* be five years old for a full year?"

Aunt Nuri's eyes widened, and her mouth opened, slack with shock. "Ember doesn't even know this? My gods, Ash, what have you taught your child about being a phoenix? Anything?"

Dad gave Aunt Nuri a long, flat look before shaking his head and turning away. He rubbed his lower face and gazed at Ember. "Phoenixes aren't human, dear, you know that. We're shifters. There are some developmental things that we need to do. Because of that, there are some ages that we stay at until we 'die' and are reborn. It's crucial for our development. These become stopping points. It is important to our kind and a point of pride for some."

"So, five years old is a stopping point? And how is it connected to pride?" they asked.

Mom slumped. "Yes, hon. You were five years old for about two years. It was a great age, and we were happy to have you that age for that long. Two years is spectacular by the way. Toddlers and young folk are so clumsy. We were very excited that we kept you safe despite being a young phoenix."

Dad mumbled, "Anything that can go wrong, will. The law of the phoenix."

"Two years!" Aunt Nuri exclaimed. "What did you do? Finally get fed up and throw the fledgling into traffic?"

Dad stiffened. "It wasn't like that. Ember really wanted to ride their bike. It was their obsession at the time. They'd never biked on their own before. One of the neighbors waved them across a small side street, but before they'd made it all the way past the damn car, the driver shot forward, knocking Ember into a car that careened into a truck that exploded."

"Gods above!" Aunt Monte said quietly. "Nuri was kidding." She shot her partner a look, and Aunt Nuri nodded. "But Ember really was thrown into traffic at the age of five?" At everyone's nods, she continued. "That's awful."

After a few seconds of silence, Ember realized Aunt Nuri was quietly laughing. They gaped at their aunt. "Sorry, Ember, it's just ... anything that can go wrong ... and what's a worse story than that? A nice adult waves you on, hits you with their car, you hit another car, and start an explosion. That's just ... so phoenix of you. You're only half phoenix, but that story tells me you're one hundred percent firebird. What about the other stopping points?"

Ember froze, their fork halfway to their mouth. "How many of these 'stopping points' are there? How old am I? With the two years at five instead of one, I'm already a year older ... so eighteen?"

Mom stared them in the eyes without blinking. "You know how old you are, honey. You're seventeen. Stop being silly."

"Me? I just learned I was five for two years. I think this is a logical question. Okay, how about this, how many years have I been alive?"

Gazing up at the ceiling, Mom started to count on her fingers. "You were five for two years, and you were at the next stopping point for four years. But the third you died almost immediately. It's why we allowed you to switch to public school. We knew once you passed the third stopping point we could stop with the homeschooling."

Aunt Monte leaned back. "That must be hard with jobs."

Mom shrugged. "Yes and no. Ash maintained his work at the think-tank, helping to gather evidence that peace was being maintained. He works from home. I took most of Ember's childhood off from academia. It has been nice to go back to work since they've returned to school."

Ember's head spun. "That last one, the one that didn't affect my age, it was that new bike you got me." They turned to their Aunts Nuri and Monte. "After two fatal bike accidents, I haven't gotten another new bike. Anyway, I'd gotten the bike for my birthday in August. I was riding along a path by a cliff. A small erosion just as I got to a bend sent me hurtling over the edge."

"Next thing we knew, we had a dirty and naked kid walking in the backdoor of the house. At the time, we lived remotely enough that Ember could make the walk home without being seen." The irony in Dad's voice wasn't lost on Ember.

They gave him a flat look. "You know, this last time I shifted and flew home. You made your opinion of me walking home naked, especially in female form, very clear."

Mom smiled, while Aunts Nuri and Monte laughed. Mom said, "It's true. You flew home invisible last time, which was exactly what we asked you to do."

Ember sat content for a few seconds before something occurred to them. "Wait, what age was I for four years?"

That got everyone laughing harder. Finally Dad said, "That would be when you'd turned ten. We lived in the southwest, a warmer climate. We'd moved there so that the weather wouldn't be an indicator for time passing."

Indignation hit them. "I *knew* ten felt like it lasted forever. I even said something to you a few times, and you said I was being silly, some ages just feel like they take more time." Ember thought about it for a second. "Is this why we never had a calendar?"

"No." Dad smiled. "I just think calendars are stressful. Too much pressure on the here and now."

Aunt Nuri scoffed. "Really? Still? You haven't gotten over that?"

He rolled his eyes at her. "And you were too young for a phone. You just played. I bet you could've stayed ten for a decade and just had fun. You loved it!"

"But what about the year?" Ember's brow furrowed. "Wait, we never discussed the year I was born until I started secondary school?" Their eyes widened. "Hold on, I remember my eleventh birthday, it happened right after that death when I'd gone rock-climbing, right? We'd gone to that nature preserve so many times and I'd climbed the rocks with and without you—gods! Now that I know it had been over four years, tons of times—but a giant spider popped out of the rocks, and I recoiled and fell."

"So that's what happened. We never did get the full story." Mom nodded. "We were setting up for lunch when the fire flared. We were both happy and sad. We knew you couldn't stay ten forever, and honestly, four years *was* a long time, but we'd been in such a wonderful groove. We gathered you up, headed home, and I went shopping for clothes while Dad packed. The next day we were on the road."

Ember had finished their meal. They began clearing everyone's plates as Dad got dessert plates for the lemon bars. Sitting back down, they narrowed their eyes at Mom. "So, once again, how many years have I been alive? How old am I? Do I age a year every time I die?"

Aunt Nuri reached over and clasped their hand. "Don't blame your parents. That's really not how it's done. For all intents and purposes, you're seventeen. You were five an extra year, ten an extra three years, so, in some ways you could claim twenty-one, but that's not correct. You're seventeen."

"Will there be another one of these stopping points I should know about?" Ember didn't want to pout, but this changed things. Their parents always filled out forms for them, and until they started secondary school, the date and birthdays weren't really a big deal, or anything at all.

Ember always assumed it was because Dad was older than dirt.

Dad said, "Not for a while. You have until you're twenty-four. And no, the only deaths that trigger you to age are the ones attached to stopping points."

It took Ember a second to remember their question.

Aunt Nuri leaned back in her seat. "Now, let's talk logistics. You said in the last few weeks you've had two events. That must've made school difficult."

"It wasn't too bad. Gym was probably the only problematic class." *And the weird run-in with Ambrose.* "I mean, if there was a way to keep this body, that would be great. I don't mind having male bits, it would just be easier for the next year and a half in school to have one body type." Ember leaned back, trying to think of the best way to explain themself. "The chance of having to explain the change is worrisome. I'll just have to figure out a way to not accidentally die, right?"

That got huffs and laughs around the table. Aunt Nuri spoke first. "That's always a good plan with phoenixes— just, you know, don't die. Easy peasy! But there *is* another way."

Chapter 15 - Everybody Wants To Get Stoned

Ember

Ember sat up taller and leaned towards Aunt Nuri. Excitement surged through their body. "Are you telling me there's a way I can avoid the accidental phoenix death?"

"No child, there is no way for a phoenix not to find every accidental event in an area and twist it in the worst way possible. It's our gift." Her face softened. "But," she said soberly, "there is a way to maintain the bits under your clothes. How much do you know about Everfire?"

"That's a myth, Nuri, and you know it as much as I do." Dad grumbled.

"Brother, let me finish my lesson. You don't know as much as you think." The two stared at each other and Ember could almost hear the silent conversation they had. They may not have seen each other in almost two hundred years, but they were acting like no time had passed and they'd spent every day of their lives together ... probably arguing.

With a small smile, Ember tried not to get distracted from the conversation. It was too important to their life. But it warmed their soul to see Dad with his sister.

He leaned back and crossed his arms over his chest. "Fine, but do not get my child's hopes up and then dash them away. It isn't fair."

Ember turned to Aunt Nuri, wanting to get the conversation back on track. "I know that when a phoenix dies a true and final death their fire, who and what they are, converts to Everfire, a fire that consumes everything in its path. It's called Everfire because it never dies out. If left unchecked, it would consume the world. One of the jobs the phoenixes have is protecting the unknowing from this fire since it destroys with a life of its own. They ... we, the phoenixes, have a cave where Everfire can be contained ... I'm not exactly sure where it is or how to transport it because I thought it was lost with the death of all the phoenixes. I didn't know anyone knew where the location was. Anyway, because phoenixes are fire, they can carry the Everfire to the cave and there it lives, safe from consuming the world."

"Excellent." Aunt Nuri turned to Dad. "Apparently, you haven't neglected all their education ... though they should be told the location of the cave." She faced Ember again. "Let me fill in a few other facts. The cave is lined with moonstone, the one substance that can contain Everfire. There is one other defense to Everfire, but it's less known."

Mom tilted her head. "There is? What is it? I've never heard of anything else."

A grumble escaped Dad. "I swear I've told you this before, Sadie."

"No, love, I don't think you have."

He sighed. "Someone with a powerful void proficiency can put a bubble around the Everfire flame and dampen the power that makes it unstoppable. Then any fire mage can put it out. If a mage has both proficiencies, it isn't good enough, it takes two magic users, or a witch and a phoenix. If the void mage is truly powerful enough, they can hold their spell over the Everfire until the flame dies out completely."

The mention of magical teamwork made Ember think of Magical Creations and working with Olivia. *Does my teacher know of other applications where more than one witch is needed?*

"That's amazing," Mom said. "Void is such a limited proficiency, it's really not a viable way to control Everfire. Except, there aren't many phoenixes either."

"There's more to the moonstone besides being able to contain the Everfire." Aunt Nuri said, sipping her wine.

"Nuri, you know that's all folk stories our grandparents and the elders babbled about. There was nothing real to them."

"Were they just stories? Are you sure? Every story they told us was based on a truth, Ash. We grew up in a community of phoenixes where no one cared if they changed—it just wasn't an issue. Within our world, it was all just part of who a phoenix was. The stories about moonstone locking your body to one sex didn't matter because no one cared. More than that, most didn't want that restriction. The tales were more precautionary than hope. Now that we're living here, among mortals with static bodies, the moral of the story changes. I agree with Ember, in general it doesn't matter to me, but while I'm 'Vi Vita' I don't want to appear any different. It would be too hard to explain."

Shock and excitement vied in Ember. "You have a stone, and you know it works, don't you?"

"Yes, I do." She pulled her necklace out from under the neckline of her dress. The pendant held a rough-cut, wild-looking, iridescent white stone with light blue veining. It was beautiful and called to Ember. A heat in their chest had them leaning towards the stone as if it would warm them.

"Is it different from any other moonstone?" Ember wanted to reach out and touch it.

Aunt Nuri smiled. "Yes. It's been burned with Everfire, changing its composition ever so slightly, giving it a magic of its own."

Ember sat transfixed for a few seconds. Their body quivered with hope and excitement. In Aunt Nuri's hand sat the answer to a challenge ... a big challenge every phoenix faced while hiding in plain sight out in the real world. They licked their lips and said quietly, "Is the lock permanent?"

A smile blossomed on Aunt Nuri's face. "No, Ember. I have to have this necklace on, otherwise I'd let you take this and use it to lock your body how it is now. If I weren't wearing this during my next accident, everything would change."

Aunt Monte winked. "I'm hoping when things calm down the necklace goes away, and we try for an Ember of our own. I always thought children were out of the question, but if I can be a mom ..." Her voice trailed off and Aunt Nuri wrapped an arm around her.

After a moment, Ember turned to their parents. "I want to go. Winter break is in a week. I want to travel to the cave and get a stone like that. Like I said, once I graduate next year it won't be such a big deal, but until then, it would make things so much easier."

Mom said, "I know you'd like to go, but neither Dad nor I can take the time off. You can't go alone."

Ember swung their gaze to Aunt Nuri, hoping after bringing up the topic, they'd have some support there. Unfortunately, she said, "I can't go either. FB Coalition just doubled and more in membership. My job just got a lot busier. I was going to ask you two to help, especially you Ash, since at one time, this was your baby."

Aunt Monte leaned forward. "I know FB Coalition is super busy, but there are other members who would happily do what I do. I know where the cave is, and I could take Ember."

Excitement surged through them. This was a dream they didn't even know they had prior to this dinner and now they wanted nothing more than to take this trek. They looked back and forth between their parents. *Oh, please, oh, please, say yes.*

Everyone got quiet. Finally Dad slowly shook his head. "It's still not safe. Ember has fire and air. I don't know your magic, but with just two of you, it isn't enough. Not in that forest."

"It's a pretty dangerous time," Aunt Monte agreed. "I have ice, water, and healing magic."

Mom's eyes widened. "Healing? I haven't heard about anyone with that proficiency in ages. They're down to one school and every magic user with that proficiency is sent there regardless of how weak their ability."

Aunt Nuri looked at Mom. "Better than spatial magic, which everyone thinks died out with your family."

"It did," Mom agreed. "It's just that my family isn't fully dead, yet. Actually, I think there are a few other families with a bit of spatial magic, we just had it in the strongest levels."

Monte gaped. "You can do spatial magic? Like, for real?"

"So can Ember. They have lots of secrets they've had to learn to keep."

"Okay, back to the subject at hand," Ember said. "What if I convinced Felix to come along? That would add earth, thaumaturgy, and his best, mind magic. We'd have a good cross-section of proficiencies to keep us safe and you know he's good in a pinch."

Mom's face tightened. "Is this really that important to you? Last week didn't seem that bad. You managed pretty well."

"I managed, but only just. It would be easier if I didn't have to worry about someone walking in on me while changing during gym, and that person wondering why some weeks I had male bits and other weeks female bits."

"Okay, honey. If Felix and his parents agree, then I'm okay with it."

With a growl in his voice, Dad grunted his agreement as well.

Shaking with excitement, Ember could barely focus on the rest of the discussion. It was probably good they shifted to stories of the last two hundred years.

Oh, my gods! I get to go on this trip and get this stone ... I may even meet a phoenix!

Chapter 16 - Take Off The Rose-Tinted Glasses

Daisy

Daisy debated: jeans or a skirt. Disappointment filled her as she realized that she wanted to wear her Infinite WISDOM shirt, but she'd already worn it that week and it was dirty. With a sigh, she chose jeans and a red shirt with a black cat holding a knife. It read, 'Bring me coffee and everyone will be safe.'

She'd just secured her dark hair in a ponytail when her phone vibrated in her pocket. Checking the display, she answered. "Hey, you're not canceling on me, are you?"

The silence made her nervous, and she started to pat her leg. Then Ember laughed. "Nope, not at all. I've missed our time, you know, just the two of us. But my parents are busy today. Felix said he could drive us." Daisy was about to complain, then Ember continued. "His grandparents live near the event. He'll drop us off and head over for a visit. We can text when we're done and all have lunch, if that's okay."

Daisy bit her lip, considering. She knew lunch wouldn't have been alone no matter what, if not eating with Felix, then Ember's parents. Felix meant an extra distraction for Ember. But three teens was always more fun than having adults around. "That sounds great. I'll see you two soon."

"Yay!" Ember sounded relieved. "I'm really excited to be spending the day with you. We'll have loads of fun."

Daisy could almost hear the unspoken words: *despite the event we're attending*. But shook it off. She wasn't going to let anything ruin her day because she wanted to get back to good times with her bestie.

It didn't take long for her friends to show up. As soon as they arrived, she slipped into the back of Felix's old model Toyota Camry. "Drive on, my man, to the event!"

Felix smiled at her through the rearview mirror. "You're in a good mood. A day standing in the cold? I'm going to go hang out with my relatives and be plied with cookies and hot chocolate. Are you sure you've made the right decision?"

Daisy waggled her brows. "I think so, though, if you could squirrel away some of the cookies, I wouldn't complain."

"I'll see what I can do." He merged into traffic and started the journey to the next town over.

It took just under an hour to get to the event. The three of them talked about the History of Magic assignment and what they'd done so far. Since Felix wasn't attending the event, once they arrived, he dropped them off really close to the stage. Daisy grabbed Ember's arm and dragged them to a vendor. They sold shirts, pins, pendants, and other odds and ends.

Daisy pushed to the front of the crowd to search for what she wanted. She'd gotten a shirt at the previous gathering, but she wanted something different this time. There was something she remembered from the last event. It had been available at one or two stands, and really wanted to buy it this time. She backed away after not finding it at the first table. After locating Ember, she led them to a second table and a third. It took four tables to find what she wanted: A small book about the history of the movement. *Infinite WISDOM - a History and*

Background. Everything you need to know about where the movement began.

Daisy slipped the book into her purse and thanked the man. She let her eyes rake over the table one last time before turning and joining Ember, who stood back, letting in those who wanted to purchase items. "Thanks for that, Ember."

"Did you find what you were looking for?" Daisy appreciated how hard Ember worked at being supportive even though she knew her friend really didn't want to be there.

"Yeah. At the last event I found a book. I was hoping to find it again. I want to read about Mr. Shade's background. You know, learn everything about this movement."

Ember wrapped their arm around Daisy's shoulders. "You really are excited about all this, aren't you?"

Her friend sounded a bit sad, though they were trying to hide it. "Just like you and Felix, I want to learn what I'm supporting, I don't want to go into this blind. Between this book and the internet, I'm going to become very informed."

The arm around her tightened and Ember's widening smile warmed Daisy's heart. "Good. I never doubted your integrity, my friend. Now, we still have about twenty minutes. Should we go get some coffee?"

"Yes!" Daisy agreed. "And a cookie."

"Always a cookie!" Ember agreed.

They found a good spot where they could see the stage. They weren't too close, but not very far away either. The warm coffee helped on the cool day. The weather never got too near freezing, just cool enough for a light coat or sweater.

Daisy stood arm to arm with Ember, trying to share warmth as the first speaker finished up. He hadn't said anything new, validating Ember's prediction that Daisy had already heard it all. Despite that, Daisy was convinced there'd be something worth their time.

As the first man left the stage—Daisy hadn't even bothered with a name—Mr. Shade walked out, and everyone cheered at a deafening level. While Daisy cheered, she saw Ember wince and cover their ears out of the corner of her eyes.

On the stage, Daisy saw Mr. Shade, in person, for the first time. He was tall and lanky with sandy brown hair and blue eyes that sparkled as he gazed over the mob of people thrilled to see him. His brow crinkled for a moment as his scanning of the audience snagged on something.

Daisy checked over her shoulder and saw at the back, a single protester, with a sign that read, 'You have no proof! You're a fraud!' She shrugged. One was such a small number for this type of event.

"Welcome to our humble gathering, my friends," Mr. Shade began.

Daisy's focus snapped back to him as his voice flowed over the people and silence descended, almost as deafening as the uproar when he'd taken the stage. "We are here to let you know that you, as magic users, are not alone." People applauded. "We know that you are worried about the current human uprising to subjugate us, take away our rights, and change the laws that have ensured peace and equality between our people for all these years. Are you as worried as I am?"

The crowd boomed, "Yes!"

He nodded solemnly. "I just want you to know, your fears have been heard."

So far he wasn't saying anything new, but this was just his opener and he sounded so welcoming. Tapping Ember's shoulder, Daisy pointed with a tilt of her head, to where the protester stood. When she looked, the man was gone. *Where did he go? Would he have left before the message was given? Huh ... weird.*

She searched the edges of the crowd, but she couldn't see him or his sign anywhere. Ember whispered into her ear. "What?"

Daisy shook her head and mouthed, 'later.'

"In the last week, new legislation has been proposed, behind closed doors of course, to start the process to undo the work of the Committee of Ten. The end goal is the unwinding of the groups, magic users and humans, so that one can be brought down, and the other can be elevated."

He's being really vague. Mom was right, I should probably check out what he's talking about. I meant to do it the other day, but my schoolwork took too long. Since school is winding down for winter break, I'll have lots of time to do my own research. I wonder which group he's talking about breaking the laws from the Committee Of Ten?

Her brow furrowed. He never said it was the humans who'd started this despicable action. He never directly stated whose end goal it was to separate, segregate, and elevate their own. These were the same words used in the last event she'd attended.

She'd always been a good student, and good with puzzles. Being in these large groups, it was so easy to get caught up in all the excitement. It was like being on a roller-coaster ride. Quick, exciting, and mind-numbingly fun, in a way. That said, she needed to start using her brain, take notes, and remember her skills as a top student to figure this out herself.

Daisy took off her proverbial rose-colored glasses and listened to the rest of the speech first Mr. Shade gave, and then the other presenters.

I'm still going to support them when talking with Felix and Ember. They are as against this as the people on the stage are for it. And the message has been pro-witch, which

I like. But after I do my research ... I don't know, we'll see.

When Felix dropped Daisy at home, she took the flier from this event and added it to her pile from the previous three she'd attended. She grabbed her laptop and opened an incognito browser. She wasn't sure what instinct told her to keep her search private, but for once she wanted to be careful.

She started at the beginning. The first flier only had the link to Infinite WISDOM's main page. The site wasn't anything to write home about. It gave information about the usual speakers and upcoming events. There weren't any links to evidence of what they claimed. They didn't explain the history of the group. Overall, they didn't have much. It really looked like a shell of a website. *Just like Harry claimed before he ended up getting sick.*

The second event had more. The same website as well as one site that they presented as proof of their claims. When Daisy typed the link in, it didn't lead anywhere. *Did I type it in wrong? It really should be available on their website. It's an obnoxious link.* She looked it over and retyped it in. Again, nothing. It was a fake website.

The third flier, the one given out at the city event, had four options, one being the one that she'd just attempted to type in twice. That was the last of the four. The first on the list linked to a news website that was well known for conspiracies. No one believed that site—at least she hoped no one did. The second one was a site asking questions, but it didn't have answers. The third led to a social media conversation on the topic; again, nothing with proof, just social support.

Frustrated, Daisy grabbed the flier from the event she'd just attended. There were only two websites listed, the same crappy homepage for the Infinite WISDOM website and a new page to prove their claims. *Does no one update their website? Can't they put the links here, so their supporters aren't forced to type all this stuff in? And why isn't there any information about the organization on the website? How hard would it be to update the page?*

Trying to bite back her anger, Daisy slowly typed in the last website. The page looked legitimate. It stated and supported the day's claims, almost too perfectly. It wasn't an academic page, nor did it have references, but the overall feel was solid. Despite that, there was something about the site that rubbed Daisy wrong. She searched but couldn't quite figure out what it was.

Daisy flopped back in her seat with a groan, glaring at the screen of her computer. "What is wrong with you? Why do you feel off?" She rubbed her temples hoping to figure this out.

In the end, the group had a website that supported them. It was only one, but that was better than none, right?

Chapter 17 - Bottling Up The End Of The Year

Ember

By the Wednesday before winter break, the students were mostly checked out. Three more days and then two weeks off from school.

Ember circled the ninth-year Air Magic class. Most of the students were doing well. They'd worked with the students who struggled the most, and now moved through the class helping in small ways, answering questions as they popped up. Because of their early success a few weeks ago, no one questioned their qualifications for being there.

Over the weeks, Ember acclimated to helping the class as a whole. At the start, they'd work with individual students, but now they watched all of them. Seeing that many people and their magic gave them a bit of a headache and took energy, but they ate a bigger breakfast and brought a bag of nuts in case they got hungry before lunch.

Class was half over, and Ember felt everyone knew what they were doing. No one seemed to need them. They headed over to Mrs. Vintl. "Would it be okay to sit and watch from the side? Everyone seems to be in their own groove. I think if anyone needs me, they'll come get me, or if I see anything, I'll jump in."

"That sounds fine. Everyone is squirrely this week anyway."

Ember walked towards the door, away from the noise of the class. Suddenly Xander stood next to them. "Could we spend a few minutes in a private session? I have, well, I could use your help."

So close! they thought with an internal sigh. "Sure, lead the way."

They got to the private room and shut the door. The private room was about half the size of a normal classroom. Like the main room, they could open the ceiling up to the sky if they wanted to do bigger spells.

Once they were alone, Ember asked, "What seems to be the issue? You've never had any problems in this class. You're one of the top air magic students."

"It's not that." Color rose in Xander's cheeks.

"Is it your sister Zahra? Did something happen with her fire magic test last week?" Ember thought they'd have heard about any big test failures. Rumors spread through the school like, well, wildfire.

"It isn't her. When you helped her, her fire went out of control. I extinguished the fire using a scoop and dissipate spell. It's weird, it's something I hadn't been able to master before then, but when it mattered, I did it. In the last week, I've tried to do it again, but I keep failing. I can put out my own fire, but a big fire, one that's bigger than a small, 'go away' flick, that you need a bigger spell to put out, I can't do at all. It's ... I've tried."

Ember gazed at him as his cheeks turned darker. "Xander, what did you do?"

He pulled up his sleeve and they saw it: burn marks. Ember lifted their arm, then let it drop. "Xander, are you okay?"

He nodded. "Yeah. I'm healing. I just ... can you help me figure this out? Why can't I stop a larger fire? I did it when you were helping Zahra."

No, Ember thought. *You didn't do it, I did. I let you think you did it, and now you're getting yourself hurt. I knew helping out with fire magic was a bad idea.*

They focused on the burn marks and came to a decision. "We can't do it here and now. It wouldn't be safe."

"How about after school? I don't want to wait until after winter break."

Ember wanted to say 'no.' It was so close to their phoenix power that they worried about being caught, but they worried more about what Xander would do if left to his own devices for two weeks. Playing with fire without supervision just wasn't safe. They wondered if Olivia would be able to help as well. "Will your sister be there?"

His only answer was a whoop.

Ember's muscles unwound as they sat at their table in Magical Creations class. Though the current lesson challenged them with their lower magical ability, it thrilled them with its potential. More than that, Olivia's presence was like a cool breeze on a stressful day.

They sat and began organizing the materials to create magic balls of elements while waiting for their partner in crime to arrive. It only took Olivia a few moments to drop into the seat next to them. "Hi, Ember. Ready to create magic?"

Ember snorted. "Mostly. I wanted to ask if you could join me after school today in the courtyard." They explained about Zahra and Xander.

Olivia's eyes widened. "Did he try to practice on his own? That's so dangerous. Yes, I'll come. I know you've been helping people, but he needs fire practitioners there, not just magic," she waved her hand. "Whatever you are. Even if Zahra is there, if she's creating the fire, you need someone else to be backup to put it out. Gods above, they are idiots."

They'd never heard Olivia say so many words, especially in a rant. Ember thought Xander was being dumb, but Olivia's anger confirmed it.

They opened their mouth to respond when Ms. Hewett said, "I know you all want to be on winter break, but I have a challenge for you today. This is an important lesson, so please check back in. You've all created small glass balls for each of the elements. Now I want you to create the balls again, but this time, transmorph the glass into a substance that, if thrown or dropped, won't shatter. I want the glass to dissipate. The second challenge is I want the spheres to be holdable. The heat, the cold, nothing should permeate the balls. What's the use of these balls if you can't hold them?"

Ms. Hewett held up a piece of glass, then pulled some water into a globe floating above her other hand. "Watch," she commanded. In a few seconds, she froze the water into ice, pulled out a small ball, wrapped it in the glass, then transformed the glass. She talked about what she had done at each step, after she had the ball of ice.

"Now that you see the ice ball, you'll notice each table has ice balls on your tray. I created those last week. I want each of you to pick up a ball."

Ember picked up a ball. It was warm to touch. It fit in the palm of their hand, about a half-inch wide. They could see that there was ice within; there was a crack in the ice.

"Okay, class, I want each of you to drop the ball on the floor."

The sound of cracking glass and rolling balls filled the room. Ember watched Olivia drop her ball. They both squatted down and watched as the ice rolled away, but the glass evaporated. Ember pocketed the other ball, intrigued by the process. They wanted to show their parents.

It took four attempts to create a fireball that they could touch. Olivia created the fire and Ember captured the element in glass balls. Once they had the balls on the table, they both worked on changing the glass to be touchable and so that it would break and dissipate on impact.

Once they did, they threw it to the floor and watched as the glass misted away. Afterwards they tried again. They both figured if they could do it with fire, they could do it with any of the elements.

Chapter 18 - Playing With Fire

Ember

Ember was exhausted by the end of the day. They weren't sure why their day had tuckered them out, but between helping students in the morning, and the magic outlay in making spheres, they felt completely drained. Morphing the glass into something newer, stronger, better ... it was fantastic, but so hard on their phoenix half. Ember needed to remember they didn't have the magical well the rest of the students had. They were only a half witch.

They leaned against the wall, waiting for the halls to empty. Daisy came by. "Are you busy again today?"

"Yeah, I'm helping a student with their fire magic. I tried to help their sister last week, and they thought they could up their game. They ended up burning themselves. Olivia's going to help. The more the merrier, right?"

"Do you want me to come?"

"To carry me home at the end?" Ember was only half kidding. Last week Ember hadn't told Daisy about the tutoring, but at this point, they were too tired to care. They needed the moral support more than they needed to try to keep things on the down low.

She snorted. "Something like that. Come on, magic guru, let's go."

Halfway to the courtyard, Felix caught up with them. When they got outside, they found Zahra, Xander, and Olivia waiting. Ember smiled. "It looks like a party out here!"

Xander's eyes narrowed. "I was hoping for fewer spectators. Why did you invite so many people?"

"Look, Xander, you are hurt because you're trying to learn how to play with fire." Ember wanted to stay calm, but they were tired. "Olivia is here because, like your sister, she knows how to handle fire. You need two fire witches to help you not get hurt. I may ... *may* ... be able to help you with your technique, but they know how to do the proficiency. Daisy and Felix are here for me. I'm already tired from the day and helping you will wipe me out. At the end of the day, it's not all about you."

He blanched. "Sorry, I guess I wasn't thinking. Thanks again for helping. Are you up to doing this now?"

Ember shut their eyes and took in a slow breath. They realized they may have been a bit harsh. "Yeah. If we don't do this now, you're just going to do it later, and you may end up getting hurt again. I'd rather help you before those burns get worse."

Shaking out their hands, Ember gazed around the courtyard. "Okay, Felix, Daisy, stand by the door. If things get out of hand, leave. Zahra, I want you to be on the far side of the courtyard—you'll be the fire starter. Xander, you take a spot just there." They pointed to a spot a dozen feet away where they could watch both brother and sister. "Olivia, stand a few feet behind him and help if it gets to the point that the fire is about to get out of control. We don't want anyone burned."

Everyone went to their assigned spots. Ember bit their lip. "Okay, Zahra, create the largest fireball you can put out." It took a moment, but the fireball appeared a few feet in front of Xander. "Perfect. Okay, move the fire a bit closer. Now stop. Xander, extinguish it."

Xander put out his arm, hand out in a stop sign. He twisted his hand in a quick fist until it faced the sky, like he was picking up a bucket by its handle or scooping the fire. Ember watched the magic flow from him. It didn't pass his arm or reach the fire. It wasn't doing what it should. His focus, the one that worked for so many magic users, wasn't working.

"Stop," Ember said, gazing at everything, a pounding starting in their head. "Olivia, do the same motion, but only once."

They watched as the magic flowed and the fireball shrank to half its size. The magic flowed easily from Olivia, the motion almost a hinderance for her. "Zahra, enlarge the fireball, half again as big as it was. Olivia, do what you just did, but just flick your fingers, don't do the full motion."

This time almost the full fireball dissipated. Olivia gasped.

Xander grumbled, "You aren't here for her."

"I know, but I had to see a working spell," Ember said, annoyed. "Zahra, again. Xander, when you scoop your hand, leave the fingers flat and make your motion slower. At the end, lift your hand higher. With your left hand, swat beneath, as if shooing the air to the right."

He took a moment to think about the directions. "That isn't like anything I've heard before." He didn't sound like he was arguing, just noting a difference. He did as directed and the fireball shrank. Not as much as when Olivia did her bit, but Olivia was a strong fire witch.

Xander did the motion again and again. Finally he did the motion one last time and the fire went out completely.

His body shook with tremors when he finished. "I can't believe I did that. It took so much of my energy, but, gods above, I actually did it. I don't know how you do what you do, Ember, but that was … thank you!"

Ember felt dizzy from watching the magic. The sight took so much of their effort. They nodded, trying to stand motionless, lest the world tilt. "You're welcome. You'll need to practice. Hopefully you'll get to the point that you won't need to do as much to snuff out fire, but for now, getting your power to work for you takes more focus."

Olivia came up beside them and spoke softly. "I didn't expect you to do anything for me. Thank you. That was … just, thank you."

Felix slid an arm under theirs and provided a bit of support. "Time to head home, teach?"

With a snort, Ember nodded. "Yes, please. Maybe you, me, and Daisy could go watch a movie and be brainless for a bit. Olivia, you could join us if you wanted."

Daisy came over and slid her arm around Ember's waist, chuckling. "I'm in. I hear Firestarter is a relaxing movie."

Chapter 19 - Fire In The Sky

Felix

Winter break was about sleeping in, avoiding studies, and eating sugars. Well, one out of three wasn't bad, right? Felix packed the last of the items he wanted to bring along on his trip and headed down to the kitchen for breakfast. He wasn't sure when his next big meal would be during his travels, so it thrilled him to see pancakes, eggs, and bacon waiting for him, with coffee on the side.

"Thanks, Mom. This looks great."

She sat down to join him with her own plate of food. "I can't believe you decided to travel north and into a wild jungle during your short time off, but I figured this was the least I could do."

He ate a few bites of the delicious food, then sipped the coffee. "I was invited to travel to find a cave with the infamous Everfire of the phoenixes. Do you really think I would turn that down?"

She laughed. "My son? Turn down anything to do with his lifelong obsession? No, I don't. Part of me thinks you manifested Ember and their family with all your hopes and dreams."

He laughed, not trying to deny that he'd been intrigued with shifters and particularly phoenixes his whole life. It was a topic he'd talked about for as long as he could remember, and his parents had received the brunt of hearing about what he'd learned. He may try to downplay his love of phoenixes to Daisy ... and anyone else who teased him, but it wouldn't fly with his parents.

Thinking about Daisy, a stab of guilt pierced him. He wished he hadn't had to cover up the fact that Ember was a phoenix. He sometimes wondered if he'd made the right decision. The two had always been so close; maybe Daisy could've been trusted. Then again, Ember and their family were so secretive. He just didn't know.

As he finished up his breakfast, his phone vibrated, and he checked the display—a text from Ember that they were on their way with Monte. He grabbed a travel mug and filled it with coffee, slipped on his coat, grabbed his bag, and headed out to wait on the stoop.

They arrived in Monte's Subaru Impreza. The trunk opened and he placed his bag in the back before climbing into the back seat. Ember sat in the back next to him. He realized Ember's mom was driving with Monte in the passenger seat. "How long do we have to drive before we get to the cave? Mrs. Savita, did you decide to join us?"

Monte laughed. "Oh, that's cute. You kids are just hilarious. We're driving up to Ember's parents' woods. Vi and Ash are driving in a car ahead of us. Sadie needs to introduce us to the wards. From there, it will take about six hours."

The drive up to the woods was a completely different experience this time. As they approached the property, Felix watched the trees fly by. It intrigued him to see the wards effect Monte as she looked away, unable or unwilling to see the woods. As they pulled into the gate entrance, a shiver ran down her body, and she finally covered her face with her hands.

Once through the gate, Mrs. Savita leapt out and headed to the fence. A light glowed down the length of the tall wrought iron boundary in both directions.

Monte shook her head and shivered. "Gods above, that sucked. Whoever set those wards was powerful." She rubbed her temples.

Back in the car, they continued to the glade where he had seen phoenixes for the first, and only, time in his life. Excitement surging through him, he turned to Ember. "Are you flying as a phoenix? Do I get to see you in bird form again?"

He knew he sounded like a fanboy, but he didn't care. The idea of seeing a phoenix again was just too exciting.

From the front of the car, Mrs. Savita said, "That wasn't in the plans, though, letting the three phoenixes stretch their wings may not be a bad idea. It's been awhile since the twins have flown together. Ember, do you need to stretch your wings?"

"Always."

Felix trembled with excitement. "Really?"

"We'll see," Mrs. Savita said. "I'll need to talk with the others. I know that you three need to get to the edge of the forest today and be given some time to find a campsite. Despite that, an hour to fly may be a good bonding experience. Let Ash and Nuri reconnect. I don't understand everything about phoenixes, but I do know that in their flights something links between them that can't join in human form."

Ember nodded, a wide smile on their face.

Once they arrived at the clearing, they parked, and Ember's parents spoke with Nuri. The smile on Mr. Savita's face let Felix know that his hope was coming to fruition.

Mrs. Savita set up three chairs as Ember, Vi, and Mr. Savita slipped behind the cars. It didn't take long for two huge white phoenixes to explode out, streaming towards the sky. Both had shimmering blue bellies and red and orange wings. Their tail feathers, streaming down below them as they rose, as if rising from the ashes, shimmered the color of fire. They looked like twin birds emerging from the ground.

Felix turned to Mrs. Savita and Monte. "Can you tell them apart?"

Mrs. Savita's eyes twinkled. "Gods above, it's been too long since the two of them have flown together. They are majestic, aren't they? Nuri is a pinch bigger and her belly is a bit more purple than blue, if you can focus. Beyond that, the twin phoenixes are almost impossible to tell apart."

Before Mrs. Savita could say more, a fireball of red burst from behind the second car, the tail feathers streaming down red, orange, and purple. Felix waited, heart pounding, for the moment Ember reached the height of the other two. When they did, they snapped out their wings, a perfect transition from red to orange to purple, gorgeous and breathtaking. The three swept the field before darting off towards the ocean.

Smiling as she faced the sky, Mrs. Savita sighed. "They'll be gone for a bit. This really was a good idea for all of them. There are some sodas in the car. Felix, why don't you grab them? We'll just relax while they burn off some energy."

Felix wanted to laugh with his own giddy excitement. Would he one day be this blasé about seeing phoenixes fly? He hoped not.

Chapter 20 - A Sky Dance

Ember

Ember followed the pair of white flames as they flew towards the ocean. With a push of power, they turned invisible just as Dad and Aunt Nuri did the same in front of them. As they crossed the beach, Ember looked down and saw it was empty.

Yes! We get to play over the ocean.

Mom must've called and complained that tourists had invaded their beach. It had really frustrated them last time that Ember and their dad had been restricted from flying over the ocean. Ember really wanted to fly and feel the wind and spray of the water as they soared. If people saw the extra movement of the water it could end in discovery. The family hadn't been careful for hundreds of years only to be careless for a single flight.

But today ... today they could play.

The three shot out over the ocean. When they were far enough out, they dropped their invisibility, though as phoenixes, they could still sense each other in any state.

Ember flew low, letting their tail feathers drag in the cool waves. With a spin, they flew up in between the other two phoenixes, who twisted and darted after them.

An obstacle-course of fire rings appeared. Words flashed in fire. "Can you do it?"

Ember formed words, replacing the question with: "Challenge accepted."

Ember entered the rings. They twisted and dove, dipping down towards the ocean before they shot back up towards the sun. As Ember zoomed, spinning and diving, dodging and rising, they thought they heard an echo.

'They're really very good. Better than you at that age, Brother.'

'Better than either of us. They love to fly, we just don't have much opportunity to drive out here. With their

magic ... they're an amazing kid. You really should get to know them.'

'That's the plan.'

Ember shot out the end and hovered in front of their dad, baffled. They'd never spoken to their dad mind to mind in phoenix form, they didn't think it was a thing. Were they imagining it?

What the hell am I hearing? Mentally they tried to yell. *'Are you two talking about me?!'*

Both birds gaped, if birds could gape. They both turned to look at each other, then at Ember. Ember waited for something but when nothing happened, they went back to flying. They went invisible and headed back to the woods, flying over the trees and in and out around the trunks. After a close call, they heard an echo of their dad's voice. *'Careful child!'*

With a huff, they tried shouting back. *'I am being careful!'*

Realizing it had been close to their hour, they popped above the tree line and found Dad and Aunt Nuri still in flight over the ocean. Digging into their fire, they flashed the words, 'It's time.' Then they turned and headed back to the clearing.

Hovering for a moment, they descended behind a car and started their shift. It took a few minutes to let their body envelop the fire back in and let the person back out. Once they had legs and arms, they dressed in underclothes, jeans, a long-sleeved shirt that stated "Love is Love," a zippy sweatshirt, and socks and shoes.

Coming around the car, Ember noticed Dad and Aunt Nuri dressing.

Mom called from a camp chair, "Come, get some food and drink. You need to leave soon but eat first."

Ember found a camp chair in the back of their parents' car, set it up, then accepted a sandwich and soda. They relaxed with the food. "So, Felix, have fun?"

"Well, I mean, I didn't get to fly, but we're not all lucky in our air travel."

Mom and Aunt Monte laughed more than Felix's comment deserved. Ember narrowed their eyes at them, wondering what they were missing.

Dad came from behind a car, grabbed a chair, a sandwich, a soda, and flopped down. "We have an interesting situation." He sounded like he was about to launch into a story.

Taking a similar path, Aunt Nuri planted herself down next to Aunt Monte. "It was rather interesting, wasn't it?"

"Oh?" A single eyebrow rose on Mom's face. "Do tell."

Dad's gaze shifted from Mom to Felix and back with a sigh and a small shrug. Then he turned to Aunt Nuri. "Does Monte know?"

Aunt Nuri shook her head. "There wasn't a reason to tell her. You may as well start at the beginning. Even if Sadie knows, she's always willing to hear stories again."

Dad faced Ember and Felix. "Nuri and I are twins. In the world of phoenixes, twins are not very common. To some, twin phoenixes are considered a good omen. To us, it meant our unique plumage wasn't as unique as everyone else growing up. It also meant that Nuri and I can speak mind to mind."

Just the idea of that gave Ember the chills. *They can talk telepathically? Even in people form?*

"Yes," Dad said, as if he could hear their question. "It's easier in phoenix form, but yes, in both forms. We're us no matter how we look, Ember. You need to remember that."

Ember narrowed their eyes at him. "I didn't ask that out loud."

"You didn't?"

Mom's eyes widened and Felix's jaw hit his chest. Aunt Monte sat perfectly still, waiting to hear the rest. *I wonder how used to hearing crazy information she is?*

Mom shook her head. "No, Ash, Ember didn't speak. What do you think she said?"

Aunt Nuri snorted. "I heard them ask if we could talk telepathically even in people form."

There was a chorus of gasps as everyone started to speak.

Dad put up his hands. "Hold on, everyone quiet down. Let me get this all out. Nuri and I can talk in bird form easily, just like we're talking now. If we concentrate we can talk mind to mind in human form, just not at as great a distance. This was the reason we were the leaders of the armies in the last war. We could communicate over great distances and use our fire magic to give commands."

Felix sat forward. This was one of his favorite topics. "Did you have other qualifications?"

Dad quirked a half smile. "Yes, but we're not going to get into them now."

"One of us did, at least," Aunt Nuri said with a shake of her head. "But Ash had Sadie to help him out, so it was fine."

Mom snorted, covering her mouth to stop the sound. "Children, children, please, you're both adorable. Do you need a participation ribbon? I can get two that say, 'I'm Number One'."

Sighing, Dad stared at his sister. "Can I go on now?" It sounded like this was an old joke. At Aunt Nuri's nod, he said, "During our flight, Ember caught some, but not all, of what we said. They seemed to be able to project some words at us. I don't know if we heard everything they said, but we did hear some of it."

Aunt Monte leaned towards Ember. "Can you 'think' something at them right now? See if they can hear you?

This is really fascinating. I had no idea about any of this, but my geeking out meter just keeps going off."

'I hope you can hear this because I feel like a fool thinking to myself!' Ember bellowed in their mind.

Both their dad and aunt flinched. Dad said, "Maybe try thinking in a bit less volume. I mean, it's nice that you can throw words at us, but yelling—" he shook his head as if he'd been hit, "—may be a bit extreme."

Ember smiled and ducked their chin in their chest. It was cool, if not a bit embarrassing to think other people could read their minds. *'What if I don't want you to hear what I'm thinking?'* they thought more conversationally.

As if being controlled by the same marionette puppeteer, Dad and Aunt Nuri leaned towards them. They both tilted their heads to the side. Then Aunt Nuri said, "I think you asked about privacy. Not wanting us to hear you. The trick is, don't project out. I'm not sure that you can hear us as well as we can hear you. I've tried sending you a few messages, but I don't think you've picked any up. So, it's hit and miss. The child of a twin phoenix and a witch. You're kind of fun."

Ember snorted, wondering if they wanted to be 'fun.'

Mom slapped her thighs. "Yes, Ember is, but these three need to be off. It's late and they have a long trip ahead of them."

"That's right." Dad said, standing. "Why don't you get the ride arranged, and I'll start cleaning up. Nuri, Monte, you get the rest of the food packed. Six hours is a long trip. You'll get there in time for sleep. I'd suggest getting a room tonight and starting out into the woods tomorrow."

Ember helped fold up chairs, listening in on the plan. Aunt Monte nodded. "That sounds good."

Felix turned to Mom. "Which car are we taking? I'll get everything situated."

Mom patted his cheek. "You are a doll. Where you're going, a car just won't cut it. We've arranged faster transport."

At the tail end of her words, three griffins appeared from out of the shadows of the trees.

Chapter 21 - Life In A Sphere

Ember

The three griffins stepped out. Their red lion's fur shone in the sun. All three beasts had tucked their white wings in, and their eagle's heads bobbed a hello.

Ember squealed in delight. They darted forward and wrapped their arms around the neck of the smallest beast.

"Zorn, my friend, it's wonderful to see you on this fine day." They gave the creature a scratch under his chin.

Moving to the next griffin, Ember gave him a slower, more sedate hug. "Tort, ever vigilant. Are our lands as safe as you can make them?" Once Ember moved back, Tort stomped a foot and dipped his large head down in a bow.

When Ember got to the third griffin, they performed a curtsy. "Roan. Again, I thank you for the service you and yours does for my family."

Hands landed on Ember's shoulders. Looking back, they saw Mom. "Roan, we would like to request that you and one of your brothers transport Monte, Felix, and Ember to the Phoenix Forest. If, at any point, you get tired, Ember can fly with you. However, I don't think they can fly the full six hours. I know your job is to keep our land secure, but we feel the safety of our child is a priority, and for the next few days, a single sentry should be sufficient."

Roan lowered down in a bow. Straightening, he flicked his tail at Tort, who trotted off.

Mom bowed her head. "I thank you. I've brought a saddle to hook the bags onto Zorn's back. He can take the bags and Monte, and you, as strong as you are, can carry Ember and Felix. From my family to yours, again, we thank you for your honor and grace."

Ember shot a glance back at Aunt Monte who stood stock still, eyes wide, and jaw hanging open. Ember wasn't sure she breathed. Aunt Nuri stood next to her, rubbing her back and whispering in her ear.

Next to Ember, Felix gasped. "We get to ... ride ... fly? Am I dreaming? Did I ... oh, my gods."

"Are you going to faint? Are you okay?" Ember gazed into his eyes, worried for their boyfriend.

"Um, yeah?" He shook his head. "Yes, yeah. I'm great. Gods above, the life you live. I just ... this is incredible."

Walking up to stand next to Felix, Aunt Monte nodded and pointed her thumb at him. "What he said."

As a group, they quickly gathered and packed their luggage onto Zorn. Felix had a look of excitement and fear as he helped some, but mostly watched.

Ember intertwined their fingers with his and walked him first over to Zorn and then Roan and reintroduced him. "Roan, remember, this is Felix. If you are up to and willing, he and I will be riding on your back."

He made a squawking sound and bowed at them. Ember leaned in to scratch his neck. They showed Felix where Roan liked the affection.

Felix trembled, but his arm was steady as he reached out to scratch the magnificent beast. Roan made a low purring sound and Felix huffed out a soft chuckle.

Once they got everything secured, Aunt Nuri helped Aunt Monte up onto Zorn's back and Dad helped Felix and Ember onto Roan's with Felix in front. Ember had more experience riding the griffins, and if they fell, they would survive.

Ember felt Roan bunch his muscles. They tightened their arms around Felix and legs around the back of the beast right before they launched into the air. It felt so much different in human form, the air rushing over their face, hair streaming back. In front of them they heard a small yelp from Felix as his body shook.

It took mere moments for the two griffins to reach a height near the clouds, the cold wind lashing at them, when a bubble encapsulated them. Air still streamed through, but it was diminished.

Voice shaky, Felix asked, "What just happened?"

"It's their magic. It keeps the harshness of the cold from us, allows us to talk, even to Aunt Monte, and blocks anyone from the ground from seeing us. How else would the general populace not know about them?"

From a few feet away on Zorn, Aunt Monte's face was lit with wonder. She smiled wide as she looked down. "This is amazing. The trees, they look so small. And the cars, they look like toys. I've been in a plane before, but we're closer to the ground, I can see better detail now. This is ... I just can't believe it."

"Are we really going to travel all six hours before we land?" Felix said, leaning over Roan's neck. Ember held his hips, worried he may slip off.

"No. I think we'll go for a few hours, take a break, and get dinner." Aunt Monte didn't look any safer in how she gaped at the world below. "Then we'll take off again and rest at a hotel near the woods. Ember, your dad said he'd make a reservation for us."

The first leg of their journey took a few hours. The sky was a deep blue, speckled with white clouds.

For the first part, Ember just reveled in the difference of being in the sky under someone else's power. They'd flown as a phoenix for their whole life but being in the clouds in their human skin was so different. Flying on Roan was exciting.

Felix leaned his head back. He was a bit taller than Ember so his head could land on their shoulder. "Is this what it's like when you're flying as a phoenix?"

"No." They had to speak loudly. The sphere made it a bit warmer, but there was still noise from the wind. "I get to stretch out more when I'm a bird, and I feel lighter and hotter ... you know, being fire."

He laughed. "Well, I don't care, this is amazing." He sat up. "I'm flying! I'm actually flying!"

Aunt Monte laughed. "We sure are. You don't know how long I've dreamed of this. It's so ... I've lived through so many things, and I can't believe I'm riding on a griffin." She patted Zorn's neck. "You, Sir Zorn, are majestic."

Ember snorted at both of them. They loved the big beasts and enjoyed Aunt Monte's and Felix's reactions.

"Well, I'm glad you're enjoying it. We'll be up here a long time. I've flown for almost two hours in my bird form, so this is going to be a new record for air-time for me."

There was a few moments of silence, then Felix asked, "I've been wondering. How is it you help everyone with their magic? Is it a phoenix thing? Can you tell me?"

Resting their head on Felix's back, Ember shrugged. "That's the thing, I don't really know how to explain it. Neither Mom nor Dad can do it. I didn't even realize it wasn't something everyone could do until after I tried to explain it to them. I just ... see the connection and flow of magic from the person to what they're trying to create. As for how they should manipulate their motions? It just ... the patterns make sense to me. Like with Olivia, I didn't mean to help her, I just needed to fix her flow to get a better feel for what she was doing."

He shifted and Ember pushed back from him. "Why did you need to see her do the magic in the first place? Don't you know that skill?"

"Yes and no." Ember thought for a moment, trying to find the right words. "I don't do a lot with gestures. The fire is strong in me. I also think my approach is a lot different than a witch's. Fire is a part of me. If I want to do something with fire, I just do it. With air and the other proficiencies, the gestures make more sense. If I'm going to guide someone in fire, I need to know the limits, I don't want to go farther afield than I'm already going. Knowing what they're taught is a good starting point."

He huffed out a laugh. "That makes sense. You had to dumb down your understanding to help build up Xander's."

"Something like that."

Flocks of birds passed them, veering away as they got near.

"Does the shielding the griffins use have a similar effect on birds that your magic has on humans? A sort of repelling force?" Felix asked, the third time a V-shaped group of geese shifted course to avoid them.

"It appears so. I don't know that anyone knows much about their magic. It's hard to talk to griffins. I mean, I talk to them all the time, but they don't really speak back. It's more just gestures. I wonder if the griffin shifters up north have similar magic. They're very private. I'll have to ask Dad when we get back."

Felix sighed, leaning back into them. "Griffin shifters. I thought I knew so much but knowing your family ... it's just amazing."

Chapter 22 - A Bit Of Truth, A Lot Of Reality

Daisy

Daisy sat at the dining room table reading *Wyldling Snare* by A.R. Grimes. She'd read the book to the point that it looked well loved. Two of the main characters met for the first time as teens, but immediately felt like brother and sister to each other. Daisy loved that. As soon as she met Ember, she felt like she'd met a sibling. Even though it felt like Ember was pulling away from her, Daisy knew if she ever needed her best friend, they'd be there for her.

She sipped her coffee and ate some fruit. Daisy's dad joined her, reading something on his phone. After a few minutes, and a refill of coffee, he grunted and put down his device. "Are you and Ember doing anything over vacation?"

"I don't know." She placed the matching bookmark with the main character, Enoch, on it in the book, and put it aside for later. "They said they'd be busy for at least the first week of vacation, a trip. But they'd let me know when they got back."

"So, what will you do to use up your time?" He gave her a challenging stare over his glasses.

She leaned back and sipped her coffee. "Read, do some research. I don't know. I'll figure stuff out."

His head tilted. "What type of research?"

"I've checked out the sites that were on the fliers for the Infinite WISDOM events, but I'm curious if I can find anything else to support their claims. What they provided was kind of awful. I dunno. What they say about supporting each other and creating a community sounds great, but I just want to get a bit more information."

Dad gave her a smile, though it didn't reach his eyes. *I wish he'd give this group a chance. Maybe if I find something in my research.* "Good for you. I'm glad you aren't blindly following the masses. You should always figure things out for yourself."

She smiled at the familiar words. "You sound like Mom."

He just smiled back and went back to reading on his phone.

Thinking for oneself, not following the crowd, being independent and clever, these were all hallmarks her parents had instilled in her. It was time to remember and apply that to this new group.

Once Daisy had finished eating, she headed back up to her room and logged into her laptop. She decided to start with seeing if humans were really trying to pass legislation to eliminate witches from government. That shouldn't be too hard ... right?

She searched for new legislation. The number of sites that popped up overwhelmed her. Starting with the first site, she read over the current issues being debated on the floor. There were several big issues; the biggest were international affairs and equal rights ... for all genders, not humans versus witches. There was nothing like what Infinite WISDOM had brought up at their events.

Not wanting to be discouraged or disorganized, she started a document where she listed the link and summarized what information it gave her. The next link gave a few of the future laws that were being pushed from the conservatives, liberals, magic users, and humans. The four-pronged table delineated each focus for a six-month and twelve-month window. There were links for the major goals.

Daisy lost herself in each of the links, reading and recording what she found. There were a lot of issues out there, from equal pay to vacation time. What she couldn't find, no matter how deep she searched, was anything about the humans trying to close the magic users out of politics or anything else. There was nothing about subjugation.

The lack of proof began to frustrate her. Could an organization just lie, especially about the most important part of its platform?

What is another fact that I saw or heard that I thought wasn't true, but may be true? Daisy pinched her nose between her finger and thumb and thought. *Didn't Tansy say it was Infinite WISDOM that had put her in the hospital? I couldn't believe it, it was ridiculous. Could that have been true?*

Starting a new search, Daisy found a website titled FB Coalition. She didn't know anything about them, but they had a bunch of resources and links that refuted what Infinite WISDOM had been spouting. It looked like a new group that had been formed to counter Mr. Shade's claims.

One of the pages on their site, much better put together and organized than Infinite WISDOM's one page, led Daisy to medical stories. There was an asterisk linked to the bottom with confirmation that all the patients had agreed to have the information put on the internet and a link to a form if someone wanted to be added.

Scrolling back to the top, Daisy went through the names slowly. She found several people, some with pictures, some just names. She clicked on Tansy's picture, and it led her to a page with her story and a news article about what had happened to her.

Backing out, Daisy saw a story about Harry Lows, the boy who died. *Did the school say his parents told them he'd died of a sickness? Why is he on this page?* A lump formed in Daisy's throat as she read about how he got attacked after the second meeting. He'd questioned the presenters and got tagged as a human-supporter. The article went on to describe that at his funeral a group of protesters came and disrupted the services, harassing everyone in attendance. The father requested those in attendance not react during the service and ruin the remembrance of his son.

Daisy's hand shook as she scanned the names of the people currently in the hospital. The page was organized as a table. A list of people who'd been and were released to go home, like Tansy. Those who were expected to leave soon. Some people in critical condition but expected to recover. The last column was people who may not survive.

As Daisy read the stories, the words on the screen blurred. She didn't know them, but there were a dozen or more people who had been hurt for doing nothing more than disagreeing with a movement. That wasn't what she thought the group supported.

A name on the page jumped out at her. She gasped in shock and tried to swallow in a suddenly dry mouth. Tomas Elias. She hadn't realized that was her History of Magic teacher at first because she was used to seeing his name as 'Mr. Elias.'

She clicked on him. He'd been in the hospital since Saturday. He'd been shopping, heading back to his car. He was supposed to meet a friend that night. When he didn't show up, his friend called the police. His body was found beaten and bruised in an ally downtown. From the state in which he was found, the police believed he'd been left for dead. He had several broken ribs and wasn't conscious.

He'd woken up late Sunday and given his tale. They hoped he'd be able to leave the hospital on Monday or Tuesday after his second visit from the healer. With the number of injured people, healers were having a hard time keeping up.

After finishing her notes, Daisy closed her eyes to think. None of this looked good, but at the same time, was there really any hard evidence? Did anything really point back to Tad Shade and his organization? There were people saying they worked for Mr. Shade, but anyone could say they worked for Infinite WISDOM and start beating up people they didn't like.

On the other hand, not everything the group said had merit. She'd done that part of the research herself. She wanted to believe in a movement that supported magic users. She didn't like the idea that they were lying to get there. Maybe Simon knew more. He was smart and supported the cause. These people couldn't be pulling the wool over his eyes, could they?

Chapter 23 - The Dryer Isn't The Only Place To Lose A Sock

Ember

Morning coffee at the hotel wasn't awful, but the rest of the continental breakfast was.

Ember's legs were sore from being on the griffin for so long the day before. That said, they'd do it again in an instant—they didn't regret a minute of the experience. Once the group had landed, the three had thanked Zorn and Roan before they took back off to the family property. Then they checked in and collapsed.

The hotel was a few blocks from the edge of the Phoenix Forrest. Their walk over wasn't bad, but once they started cutting their way into the thick foliage, Ember realized their hike wouldn't be easy. "I take it there isn't a path? How do we know we're going the right way?"

Aunt Monte looked at them, brows furrowed. "Well, that's the question, isn't it? I came here with Vi ... Nuri, about five or six years ago. We entered the woods just about the same place we just did. We walked for a bit and then, I don't know, I can't explain it, she just knew. I was hoping we'd get to a certain point and," she gave a small smile and shrugged, "I dunno, you'd just know where we needed to go."

Ember's jaw dropped open. "You thought *I'd* lead us? Like some phoenix thing would snap on and I'd just point, *that way!*"

Aunt Monte laughed. "Maybe ... sort of. I know it's in these woods and the general direction, just not exactly where it is. Look, your dad and aunt have confidence in us."

There was a dense patch of trees and bushes, and they stopped talking to focus on making their way through. As they worked on cutting a trail, Ember thought about their aunts and wondered how they'd met. They knew now wasn't the time to ask, but maybe once they were walking on the trail.

Once they passed some brambles, the air felt lighter, and Ember heard the singing of birds in the trees. They closed their eyes and let themself sink into the intoxicating song. It felt like their body grew, their feet merged with the soil below them, and they stretched their arms out to the side.

Lifting their head towards the sun, its warmth radiating from behind the clouds, reaching through the canopy above to stroke Ember's face, they suddenly felt a heat in their chest. Ember jerked their head in the direction of the tension and saw ... nothing, just more trees. They rubbed their chest, but the pressure remained. When they rotated, the tightness moved in their core to their side and back, always in the same spot.

They suddenly noticed Aunt Monte and Felix watching them. "I um, think I know the direction we need to go. I can't really explain it, but I believe we need to go that way." They pointed in the direction the heat pulled at them in their body.

A smile blossomed on Aunt Monte's face. "That's exactly what happened with Nuri. Excellent. Let's go."

Felix followed slowly. "I assume, like any other forest full of magical creatures, we shouldn't move too fast." His statement sounded like a half question.

They slowed their pace. Aunt Monte nodded. "Fair point. We need to be watchful for all the creatures that live and lurk in these lands."

The three walked for a bit in silence. Ember enjoyed looking at the different trees and plants. "Aunt Monte, do you know the names of everything I'm looking at?"

"No, dear, but we can probably get a book or ask your dad or Nuri. I'm sure they know."

Felix let his fingers drag over the bark of a white tree that looked covered in paper. Some of the trees stretched so high that the tops were hidden in the clouds. Part of Ember wanted to fly up and find the tips of the majestic vegetation.

A spark flashed in the leaves before winking out. Ember squinted but didn't see anything again. *Maybe I saw a bird flying to its nest.*

A rustling ahead of them and to the left had them all stopping. Two men walked out. They were tall, well over six feet in height, thick with muscle, wearing jeans and jackets. They had dark hair. The one on the left had facial hair and appeared to be older, in his forties or fifties. The one on the right was younger, maybe between twenty and thirty, and had longer hair. Neither looked happy to see them.

The older man stepped forward. "You don't belong here. This is the forest of the shapeshifters, not a vacation spot for magic users."

Ember took the lead, signaling the other two to hold back. They pushed out their magic in the same way they felt when they watched and helped witches use their magic. It took a moment, but they got the flavor of the two men who faced them. Their eyes widened for a moment, but they tightened their jaw, trying to hide their reaction. "You're griffins. What are you doing this far south? And what makes you think we don't belong?"

The older man's eyes narrowed, then he lifted his nose a bit and sniffed in Ember's direction. "From a distance all I could smell was magic on you girl, but now that you're closer I sense fire. You're a phoenix? No ... you don't quite smell right to be a phoenix, but their stronghold is near ... I don't recognize you."

Unclenching their fists before their nails cut into their palms, Ember tried to relax. They needed to portray calm command. "Not everything is as it seems in the world anymore. There are magic users trying to undo the War of Peace. And a phoenix coming on a pilgrimage to the Phoenix Forest."

The same griffin-shifter said, "If you know your history, then you'll know that the griffins didn't get involved last time, and we're not getting involved this time. I don't know why you're here, but I'd suggest leaving. There's something off in the woods lately. Your safest move is to go home."

"I appreciate your wise words, my friend, but we're going to finish our quest." Ember bowed their head. "If you bury your head for too long, you may lose all your allies, and then what?" Ember raised an eyebrow in question at them. "Safe travels."

The man grunted, spun on his heel, and walked off. The younger man watched them for a few minutes as they headed away. There wasn't malice in his gaze, just consideration.

As a group, they tried to ignore him. Though, once they'd walked for about five minutes, Felix leaned in close to Ember's ear. "Did you say they were griffins? Like for real? Gods, my mind will just be blown to pieces a few times every day. No worries, I'll adjust."

For the next few hours, their trek was peaceful. The day was warm and once they'd passed the first half mile or so from the border, it didn't feel like the forest was trying to actively keep them out anymore.

Ember's head started to hurt. They wondered if they needed water. They didn't normally get this much exercise in a day. A thought flitted through their head: how important was this moonstone? They were doing a lot of work for something they didn't really understand. Not to mention, the two weeks they had to cover up the shift in their body hadn't really been that bad. What was the point in all this? They could be home. Hanging out with Daisy. Going shopping, to the movies, baking. There were so many better things to do than walk for hours in an unforgiving forest.

With a shiver, Ember turned around and bunched their muscles to run. They suddenly knew they had to get away. They saw Aunt Monte's eyes, wild, darting looks in every direction, ready to do the same.

Felix reached out and grabbed one of Ember's arms and one of Aunt Monte's. A cool chill ran over Ember's mind, like a glass of water washing away dust and debris. After a few moments, he slumped. "Gods above, with two of you, that really sucked."

Ember began to tremble. "Why did I want to run? What was I thinking?" They shook their head. "What in Hades was that?"

"I don't know," said Felix. "I just saw you turn, and felt the wave over my mind, but I always have shields up. You two have shields for the next couple of days. If we're here longer, I'll have to reset them."

"Mind magic? Who is attacking our mind?" Ember glared around them, staring down random tree trunks.

Aunt Monte sighed. "We may never know. The forest seems to be filled with beings trying to get us to leave. Thank you, Felix." She massaged her temples.

"It's one of the purposes of the eleventh-year night-time field trip. They let us do the pranks because they know in the real world we may face these challenges."

She sighed again. "If I remember from my last trip, The cave is about an hour away, maybe two. My vote is that we should camp here and finish our journey tomorrow. Nuri and I took two days, and I think we should, too. Though for us, there were less challenges."

As they got themselves ready to sleep under the stars, Ember set up a fire and moved a few logs around for them to sit on. Felix began cooking a meal.

After the food was served, Aunt Monte asked, "Is there anything interesting you're learning in school?"

After thinking about all their classes, Ember told them about the magical spheres in Magical Creations class. "It's not the easiest magic to do. Olivia, another student in class, doesn't seem to struggle much, but it's weird. Changing the property of the glass to make it more, then less. It's crazy."

"Could you do something like that with other objects?" Aunt Monte asked.

"Why? What would be the purpose?"

"You know," Aunt Monte said, narrowing her eyes. "Every time Nuri has an accident, even with the moonstone, her body burns up. The moonstone, I think, makes the fire a regular fire, not some sort of phoenix-death-changing fire. I'm not sure, though. I wonder if you could change the property of your clothes to make the fire not burn them up. Then when you die, you wouldn't be naked every time."

Ember froze with the hot dog halfway to their mouth. They gaped at Aunt Monte. Their mind whirled with possibilities.

They pointed to the bag and waved. "Hand me a pair of socks." When the two just stared at them, Ember used a bit of a push and a sock ball appeared in their hand.

Aunt Monte's jaw dropped, and Felix laughed. Aunt Monte got out, "Did you just use spatial magic?"

Feeling wild with their thoughts, Ember focused on the woman. "I forgot you hadn't seen it in ... have you ever seen it?"

"Not in over a hundred years."

Ember gave a curt nod. "I want to test this out." Their mind wouldn't stop. They pulled apart the blue-and-white striped socks and focused on one of them. They thought about everything Ms. Hewett had taught them, centering on the theory, not the glass.

Closing their eyes, they composed the spell they wanted and pushed it out. A shiver ran through their body as they used a part of themselves that was harder to tap into. Once done, they held the sock out and called on phoenix fire. The sock burned to ash.

"Gods above and below!" they said in frustration. They explained the theory to the other two while eating their hot dog.

They each tried to effect a sock after they'd finished dinner. Ember thought they knew what to do differently, but their magic wasn't ever going to be as strong as a full witch.

All three socks were lined up on the ground. With a single flare of fire, Ember set out to destroy them all. Two socks burned to ash, one remained pristine, light blue with unicorns and rainbow tails. Felix was a powerful witch. "Too bad I only have one of those now," they said with a wry smile.

Felix winked. "Should I go about fireproofing the rest of your clothes?"

"That would be nice."

As he worked, Ember realized now was the perfect time for tales and asked, "Aunt Monte, can you tell us how you and Aunt Nuri met?"

Chapter 24 - Monte And Nuri's Story

Ember

Aunt Monte smiled at them. "Do you really want to hear a story about something that happened so long ago? It's ancient history."

Excitement bubbled up in Ember and they smiled. "Yes, of course we do ... well, *I* do."

"Oh, I do as well," Felix said, working through Ember's clothes, making them fireproof. "I can't imagine. I met Ember at school; we're the same age."

"Mostly." Ember sighed.

"Wait, what?" Felix jerked his head to her, brows drawn together.

Ember waved a hand. "There hasn't been time to tell you. Aunt Monte's story first. My craziness can wait for another time." They turned to their aunt. "I want to hear this story, something with a happily-ever-after ending."

Felix's eyes narrowed. "Are you saying ours won't have that ending?" As hard as he tried, the sides of his mouth twitched for a few seconds, a smile spread across his face.

Ember rolled their eyes. "Just stop playing. We're too young for that." They moved so Felix could wrap an arm around them, and they could slip theirs around his waist. "Now, Aunt Monte, story time." He gave a squeeze, then got back to working on Ember's clothes.

She smiled. "I was working in a women's boutique. The shop specialized in upper-end clothing. I could sew a wardrobe like you wouldn't believe. I probably still could, but over the years a person gets tired of one occupation and needs to move on. I haven't sewn in years. Come to think of it, I may pick it up. Fashion these days is getting exciting again."

Ember snorted. "Well, you have fun with fashion. I enjoy my jeans and t-shirts. The snarkier the message, the better."

"I don't know," Felix said, bumping shoulders with them. "Looking put together isn't always bad."

They looked over at Felix and realized he usually looked dapper, in fairly nice clothing. With a mischievous smile, Ember said, "Maybe the two of you could start a business together in the future. You both seem to care about nice clothing more than I do."

Felix leaned over and kissed their cheek. "I like the way you dress. I dress the way I do because it's what I like. That's the point. Now, let Monte speak."

"Okay, where was I? I had just finished up a commission, and was debating making a few items for quick sale, when this woman walked in. With her brown eyes and auburn hair, I was a goner. She wore trousers and a bib shirt. It isn't something that's around today, but the outfit wasn't what ladies wore back then. She explained that her house had caught fire and she'd grabbed her brother's clothes. She needed a whole new set of clothing quick as could be. I felt horrible for her and offered her a dress that would do until I could make what she needed. She agreed and, once she changed clothes, she left the shop."

Ember laughed. "How long until you realized the boy's clothes were hers and she'd just shifted because of a death?"

"Hush! You're ruining my story. Now, to continue, over the next few weeks, she came in for measurements and fittings. When she said she wanted a full wardrobe, she hadn't been kidding. We discussed fabrics and items for warm and cold weather. I found myself pining for the days she came to the shop."

Aunt Monte stopped, her cheeks red with a blush. She stood and headed to the bags to grab a drink. She gave each of them a pointed look, but Ember shook their head; they still had some water. When Aunt Monte didn't grab anything else, they assumed Felix didn't need anything either.

When she returned she gave Ember and Felix a small smile. "I don't know why I'm being so open about this. Maybe it's because I've never been able to really tell anyone about it. It's been hiding within me, struggling to get out and be shared."

Ember got up and grabbed a blanket for themself. Felix could share when he was done with the magic. "So far, I love the story. Tell us more!"

"Okay," she laughed. "After maybe a month or so of us only talking business, my business, her clothing, she asked me to lunch. I was beyond giddy. I couldn't believe we could continue our interaction outside the boutique.

While we ate I finally got up the nerve to ask about what she did. She said she worked for the government. That surprised me since that wasn't something I thought a woman could do. She went on to explain it was a project, a job, her brother had started, but she'd lost contact with him, and felt the business was worth continuing. If not him running the office, then her. I grew in awe of this spectacular woman who was willing to fight to keep her brother's work alive."

Aunt Monte leaned back, staring up at the sky that darkened as the sun went down. Stars began to stain the blackness. "It's funny. I remember telling Nuri how impressed I was, and she laughed at me, telling me about how she scoffed at him and his dreams. But after a few years she saw the reason behind his madness. She began to feel in her soul, her bones, why he'd begun his group. When he disappeared, she decided his dream was worth adopting and continuing."

Ember was lost in this story from the past. They could imagine Aunt Nuri and Aunt Monte sitting at a cafe having their discussion. If Aunt Nuri was anything like Dad, she could spin a great story. Ember could picture Aunt Monte falling in love with the vision and their aunt.

"I knew by the end of that first lunch that I was falling for Nuri." Aunt Monte's words followed Ember's thoughts so closely, it felt oddly like she read them. "Knowing I could lose her and the commission of a lifetime, on the way back to the store, I took a chance and pulled Nuri in for a kiss. That was it, that kiss did me in. I was completely lost for your fiery aunt. After that, my soul seared by her, she tried to push me away, but I'd have none of it. It took another month, but she finally gave in to my pursuit."

Felix leaned into Ember, sharing heat. "How long did it take before you knew what she was?"

"That took a bit longer. Dating, love, commitment. She had a friend who, like you, was good with mind magic. I agreed that if I couldn't handle some news I would allow her to erase what I had learned. It was the last step of our bonding. Once I knew, I never wanted to not know. I promised to keep the secret. We went through the mating ceremony a couple years after that first kiss, and a few dozen years ... well, centuries later, here we are."

"What's the mating ceremony like? How do you get a piece of a phoenix's immortality?" Felix's voice had gone soft, as if he were asking for something he'd been wanting for years.

"I could tell you," Aunt Monte said, a single eyebrow raised. "But then I'd have to kill you."

Felix froze, even his breathing stopped, until Aunt Monte laughed. "I'm just teasing you. But the ceremony is private. I'm going to let Sadie and Ash explain it to you. Though it's something I went through, I don't feel right divulging the secrets."

Slumping a bit, Felix nodded. "I get it. Thanks for sharing your story. It was ..." He looked up towards the tops of the trees, even more lost in the night's sky. "Just, thank you."

Ember got up and gave their aunt a hug. "I'm so glad you're part of my family."

They cleaned up their dinner and Ember packed their clothes away. After that, the three decided to get to sleep. They still had a long trek to get to the cave the next day, and then they'd have to re-do all their walking to make it back home.

Chapter 25 - Becoming Unhinged

Daisy

The weather was cool, and Daisy planned to meet Simon at an outdoor café. She decided on a coat over her sweater. When she arrived, Simon wasn't there. Instead of coffee, she ordered hot chocolate and a snickerdoodle cookie.

As she waited for her items, Daisy thought about the incident in ninth year when she and Ember had been mistaken for shoplifters. They'd been walking by the store when the owners ran out and chased them, yelling that they'd stolen something. After that, they'd never gotten good service, or so they believed.

Today the line was long. Daisy observed and realized no one really got good service here. It was the only shop with decent coffee and pastries, so everyone in town ended up at this café. The baristas were gruff, slapping orders on the bar as quickly as they could, snapping at everyone.

When Daisy came with Ember, they were always in their own world until they got to the counter to order. *I guess I never realized it wasn't us, but the business that was at issue.*

"Are you going to gape or take your order?"

The snap of the voice got Daisy's attention. "Oh, thank you."

She took her items and found a table outside. Almost every table inside was full, and even the ones outside were gathering patrons. She knew what she wanted to talk to Simon about and hoped he'd be willing. Their conversation would be controversial, from everything she'd seen and read online ... they needed privacy. She chose a location away from the others and pulled out her notebook.

It didn't take long for Simon to show up. She watched as he entered the café and came out a few minutes later with a coffee and a muffin. He sat in a seat across from her and smiled. "Hi, Daisy. I'm glad you called to meet me. It's nice seeing you over winter break."

She couldn't believe how normal he sounded. There wasn't a sneer or sound of condescension coming from him.

Daisy smiled. "Simon. Thank you for meeting me. I wasn't sure if you'd be around, or how busy you were."

"Of course. I always have time for you." His eyes widened like he was surprised he'd said the words. He picked up his overly large mug of coffee and hid behind it as he took a sip.

She was a bit confused by his statement. *Why would he always have time for me? That's so weird. Could Felix be right—that he likes me? I wish Ember was here so I could get their take on this.* She mentally shook herself. *Focus, Daisy, you're here for a reason. Pick Simon's brain for information.*

Straightening, she sat up taller. "I was hoping we could talk a bit about Infinite WISDOM, if that's okay."

Simon's face dropped, and his mouth tightened for a second, but then he smiled wide. Daisy wondered if she imagined the look of disappointment that flitted across his face for a moment. "Sure, that sounds great. I'm so happy you've seen the *wisdom* in that group." He chuckled, leaning back. "Saw beyond the faces they are using. I get they want to attract people to their cause, and Ambrose and Cress are popular, but couldn't they have found someone with brains and beauty ... someone like you?" He blushed, then rushed on. "What I mean is, I'm really glad you've heard their message."

Daisy held a smile on her face. She wasn't sure what to make of the compliment, so she decided to ignore it.

Of course she would listen. did he think she was an idiot? *Well, Simon thinks everyone is below him, so, yeah, probably.* "I did go to the events to get the message—not focus on the messenger. I've been to four of their assemblies and collected their fliers. I went through all the websites they provided, and for the most part, they didn't support what they promised they'd support. Not even their own website gives much evidence. That's what I wanted to talk to you about, why I asked you here. Have you gone through everything?"

"I did," he smiled smugly. "But didn't you find on the fourth flier, the sky-blue one from Toresville, a website that met your needs?" He leaned back and sipped his coffee.

"Hmm." Daisy narrowed her eyes. "I guess. It *looked* good, but something about the site still felt off. I've studied a lot of academic sites, and it was close, but not really what I'm used to seeing. Why?"

His mouth scrunched up. "At the start, I searched their 'resources' and came to the same conclusion you did. I talked to the computer club, who got me in contact with the people who asked *them* to create the website. Anyway, I created that last website for them."

"Oh!" Daisy tried to keep her voice neutral. "You provided that last site, for the event in Toresville?" Her mind spun. This huge organization, and they used the school's IT to create the website and Simon for their only legitimate website? Was anything about the organization real? They were using students to create their proof and gather their supporters. Everything was fake. An illusion ... it was all just smoke and mirrors.

His eyes sparkled, as if excited, and he leaned on the table. "Part of winter break I'm working on their main website. I agree with you, it's awful. There needs to be so much more. But what didn't you like about the one site I provided?"

"Ah, well, it's nice, it just ... it wasn't very academic, you know. It didn't have references and resources that I usually see when I look for evidence. That's all. I mean, at least it wasn't social media like their other sites they provided as proof."

He nodded, scrunching his mouth together. "I guess that's a good critique. But you have to understand, Daisy, this group, what they're saying about humans, it's real. Last summer I worked at the University library. I worked in the reference area. Anyway, they fired me so they could hire a *human*."

"Are you sure that was the reason?" She furrowed her brow and tilted her head. "It's not that I don't believe you, just, what's the full story?"

"I went back and saw who they replaced me with, this mouse of a girl, sweet and prissy, and completely human!"

She clenched her jaw, trying not to react. A reference job at a library, like so many other jobs were just that, jobs. Magic wasn't a requirement. "When you were hired, did they know you were a witch?" Daisy tried to stay neutral. People on the hiring committee often didn't care if the person they found could perform magic. "What did they tell you when they let you go?"

"*Let me go.* Isn't that always the way they put it? As if they're being nice. Yeah, that's what they said. They told me I was rude to the students coming in asking questions. I made the poor college students feel inferior." He started to wave his hands with anger. "Can I help it that these students, years older than me, who should be my intellectual superiors, were such imbeciles?" He leaned forward and glared, lowering his voice. "I wasn't even in the eleventh year of secondary school yet, and they couldn't find their way from under a rock! I mean, really, Daisy, can you blame me?" He slapped his hands to his chest. "You figured out my website wasn't good enough, and you're just in secondary school. These University kids, ugh! They were numbskulls!"

She rubbed her hands on her thighs and tried to stay calm, hoping it would affect him. "So, they said you were fired because you weren't being respectful, not because of magic?"

He scoffed. "That's what they said, but you know it was because of the magic. Why else hire a *human* to take over? Some idiot *girl?*"

Because she wasn't being an arrogant jerk? But that wouldn't help. "Wow, Simon, I'm sorry this happened. That sounds awful."

"Oh, you can't even begin to understand how awful. They were imbeciles." He crossed his arms and slouched with a sneer on his face. At least he looked more himself.

Daisy bit her lip and one of her eyebrows shot up. "You don't think some of that attitude showed up in your work? Maybe *that's* why you were fired?"

"No, Daisy. You're cute, and book smart, but not job smart. That's not how the world works. Everyone at that library was intimidated because I was a witch." He placed his coffee down hard enough that some sloshed out.

Clenching her jaw, Daisy forced a smile. "Right, got it." She wanted to be supportive, but he made it so hard. He was obviously still seething about the injustice he saw, so she'd forgive him for the patronizing remark. "At work, did you tell them you were a magic user?"

His face scrunched up into a scowl. "No, but with my superior intellect, isn't it obvious?"

After a pause, Daisy gave him a wide smile. *It's a good thing he doesn't seem to recognize social cues. Ember or Felix would know this wasn't a real smile a mile away.* "Of course. So, you're all the evidence that the group has right now? Your story and a site you've created? Nothing else? I did some searching but couldn't find much."

"What?" he snapped out. "My story isn't good enough?"

Daisy flinched at his outburst, nervous that he'd make a scene. She couldn't agree with him, but worried if she disagreed he may get worse. Taking a sip of her hot chocolate, Daisy leaned back, trying to think of a way to dissipate his rising anger. "No, I think it's pretty amazing you put it all together, honestly. I'm impressed you did it while keeping up with all our school responsibilities." She let her eyes widen suddenly and pulled her phone out of her pocket. "Oh, no! My mom just sent a text, she needs me at home. I'm so sorry to end this early, I'm having such a great time. I really need to run. Again, I'm super sorry. Can we maybe reschedule?"

The scowl that started when Simon thought Daisy hadn't approved of his website, deepened. "Sure," he snapped out. Then he took a slow breath and his face contorted. *Is that a smile?* "Maybe we can go to the next event that's happening. It's coming up soon."

She plastered on her fake smile once again. "That would be great. Text me the date and I'll make sure I'm free." She gathered her stuff to return to the store before heading back home. She wasn't sure why she felt she had to leave, but she knew the conversation was about to take a turn for the worse. She couldn't keep up the fake façade while Simon bragged that the only evidence the group had was fabricated by him.

Isn't he smarter or better than creating fake evidence? ... Because his making an 'academic site' is fake, I know it. Does he believe his story is enough? Don't we need three to five pieces of evidence for every paper we write? Shouldn't an organization like this need even more proof? Is he hurting that much?

He still sat at the table as she headed down the sidewalk towards home. She knew he would text her about the next event. She just hoped Ember would be back by then. Either she could use Ember as an excuse, or they could go as a group. The last thing Daisy wanted was more time alone with Simon. *Gods above, I hadn't realized how unhinged he was before today.*

Shaking her head, she contemplated the websites and their lack of proof as she walked home. The walk was nice, and once she was a couple of blocks from the town's center, she was alone and could relax with her contemplations. She needed to work things out and walking helped her mind work.

She thought about the people in the hospital she found on the website that actually *did* have references. As much as she loved the idea of witches supporting each other, nothing she'd found out on her own about Infinite WISDOM supported that claim. Moreover, she feared the opposite. She mumbled softly to herself, "How could I have been so foolish? They're brainwashing everyone and have no proof."

"You know, Daisy." Her head snapped up and she saw Cress step out from a doorway. "When you question a group that's growing in popularity, you shouldn't do it where you can be overheard." He tapped his head. "You know I hear everything."

"Cress!" She stepped back a few steps. "What are you doing here? What do you want?"

Fear sliced through her. *Has he been reading my thoughts? That's illegal!*

"You've been such a great supporter of ours. I just wanted to hear that you still believe in our cause, Daisy. We hoped you'd bring Ember over, maybe even Felix."

"I don't know what you're talking about. Everyone has to follow their own beliefs. If they want to follow your group, they can."

Cress stepped into Daisy's personal space. She tried to step back but ran into someone standing behind her. A big beefy man. She shot a quick glance at the large man, but Cress continued talking. "What about *your* beliefs? You've always seemed like one of ours. You even wore a shirt to school. But hearing your talk with Simon ... what's your next move?"

Chills of dread and fear coursed through her. *I wish I could fly like Ember did on that platform that day. Just shoot straight up and be away.* "I'm just going to go home. I need to help my mom. She's expecting me."

A man to Daisy's left with a low gruff voice laughed. "She may have to wait awhile. If you're not with us, you're with the humans, and we can't have people like you running around."

"I ... I never said I wasn't with you ... please, I need to go." She thought about screaming but wanted to try to talk her way out. She was safe, right? People didn't really go around hurting others ... did they?

A sharp pain in her lower back was the only warning she received that they didn't believe her words.

Chapter 26 - Right To Move Freely

Ember

Ember woke to the smell of coffee. They groaned as the scent practically lifted them from their sleeping bag and led them to the fire they'd set the night before. Aunt Monte sat stirring a pot with what smelled like oatmeal. She handed Ember a mug of liquid awake.

Halfway through drinking their first coffee, Felix stumbled to the log and took his own wake up magic. Aunt

Monte smiled at both of them. "Teens are so fun. Wake of the walking dead, but after some coffee and food, I may have civility yet."

Ember grunted, and wondered if their aunt's hopes were too high. But maybe coffee and food *would* transform them into a working member of their group.

They took about an hour to first break their fast and then break up camp. They wanted to make sure they left the woods as close to how they found them as they could. Once the fire was out and the logs transported back to roughly where they'd been, packs repacked, they found their direction and started hiking.

Ember's feet were a bit tender. They sighed.

"What's the problem, Ember? Not looking forward to a day on your feet?" Aunt Monte sounded concerned and amused in equal measure.

"It isn't that. I'm just sore. I'm not used to this."

Felix huffed out an agreement. "You and me both. Just when I thought I was in good shape."

"Kids, I tell you. Just when you think you know them," Aunt Monte grumbled. "You do know I'm a healer, right? I can easily make you feel better for today's schlepping."

Ember slapped their forehead and Felix chuckled. They stopped and let Aunt Monte do her magic, literally. Their trek became a lot faster after that. Ember continued to feel the warm pressure in their chest. It seemed to heat up as they got closer to the cave ... at least that's how they translated it. They really didn't know what was happening.

Once the soreness was gone, a nervous excitement grew. *Is this really happening? Am I going to actually visit the heart of where my people come from?* A giddiness bubbled within them.

The group had been walking for over an hour, and Ember thought they were close. A sound like something large sweeping through the trees had them stopping. Felix and Aunt Monte stopped behind them, following their lead. From above, a flash of fire dropped, landing behind some trees.

A tension grew in Ember, and they put out their arms, pushing the others behind them. As with the griffin-shifters, they pushed out a bit of energy and felt ... fire.

As they waited, Ember whispered, "I think this is a phoenix. Either way, remember, let me do the talking. The denizens of these woods are obviously prejudiced against witches."

Both Felix and Aunt Monte mumbled their agreement, though Ember could feel Aunt Monte's tension.

I have the fire and am the phoenix; she'll just have to trust me.

A few moments later, a man walked out, young looking, wearing only a pair of pants. He didn't seem to mind walking barefoot in the woods.

Ember stepped forward. They didn't know who this was, but the number of phoenixes in their life kept on growing. "Hi, I'm Ember."

"Ember," he scoffed. "Wishful thinking? You should leave before you get hurt. You are invading our territory. Your kind is not accepted here. You need to leave. Now."

Anger swelled in Ember, like an erupting explosion. Ember tired of this. "My 'kind,' you say. And what kind is that exactly?"

"Non shifters. Those that do not know the beauty of the sky."

"Test me," Ember shot back. "You and those on patrol need to get better at figuring out who is walking in these woods. Whoever is training your ability to sense and judge is awful. We're here on a mission, and all this gatekeeping is getting old and tiresome. The griffins tried to stop us, and then let us through. Now you're here. How many more people will tell me I don't belong? Should I travel as a phoenix? Maybe blaze my path in fire?" Their eyes narrowed and they stepped forward. "Should I burn my way to the heart of your compound—then would you leave me alone?"

His eyes grew as their tirade continued. "You're a phoenix? But I know all the phoenixes in the area."

One of Ember's brows rose in challenge. "Obviously not. And has no one trained you to use your sense?"

Eyes narrowed, he flicked his hand at Ember, as if shooing a pest, but in the wake of his hand, a small ball of fire shot out towards them.

Behind Ember, they heard Felix's intake of breath. Aunt Monte softly whispered to him. They needed to focus and would deal with their companions later.

They debated and decided to catch the ball above their hand, let it hover, harmlessly. "You know, that's rude. Do all the phoenixes you know have such a hard time controlling their tempers? Throwing fire at strangers in a forest is not only childish, it's dangerous." Ember juggled the ball back and forth between their hands. They let the fire land in their hand and squeezed until the flame went out. "I know I threatened to burn my way through these woods, but apparently you really would." It took everything they had not to roll their eyes. "So, now that we've had our fun, will you tell me ... us ... who you are and then let us proceed?"

His face hardened. "I'm Declan. How did you capture my fireball?"

"I *am* fire; it's easy to control what you are." Ember sighed. "You should know that. Are you saying if I threw a ball of fire at you, you wouldn't have been able to catch it? And if not, why throw one at me?"

"Stop it, but not play with it." His face tightened. "Who *are* you?"

"I told you, I'm Ember. Ember Savita."

Eyes widening, his jaw dropped. "You're a Savita? How is that possible?"

His reaction interested Ember, but they saw no reason not to go on. They knew their Dad was exiled, but they were on a mission. Aunt Nuri wasn't exiled, and Ember wasn't either. "I'm the daughter of Ash and Sadie Savita. My aunt is Nuri Vita. They are powerful people, apparently. If you can't do what I did, they must be very powerful. Now, will you let us pass or not? We're on a quest. This is Monte, mate of Nuri, and Felix, my ... friend. I am only seventeen, but I desire a small piece of moonstone. I don't live in a phoenix community, so my lifestyle and needs are different from the average phoenix."

Ember shook their head. *Why am I telling this jerk so much?* They tried to blank their face and stare at the other phoenix.

Declan took a deep breath before releasing it quickly. "You may pass, but do not linger. The cave of Everfire ... it isn't safe, especially now. Be quick. If you have need of me or mine, just call my name. I won't be far. This area is always patrolled. If I am not on active duty, someone will find me, or come to speak with you. Again, I highly suggest reconsidering this foolish quest and just leaving." He melted back into the shadows of the trees.

Ember took a moment to watch the spot Declan disappeared into. He was the first phoenix they'd ever met besides family. Felix came up and wrapped an arm around their waist, giving them a moment to acclimate to all the feelings surging through them. Happy that there were others, sad that the first meeting wasn't more pleasant, and frustrated that it was short and sour.

Felix released a breath. "You're doing great."

"You are," Aunt Monte agreed. "I wish, as the adult on this trip, I could help more, but I'm just a witch. To them, I'm nothing."

Ember huffed out a laugh. "I know. This is the Phoenix Forest. It has to be me if we're going to get through it."

Before they moved on, a red and orange fireball shot up into the sky, as Declan flew back into the clouds. Ember's head dropped back, again marveling at the height of the trees and wondering how many phoenixes may be hidden in the clouds above.

Chapter 27 - The Cave of Everfire

Ember

"Okay," Ember said to the others. "I think we should finish this quest. We must be close. If we weren't, Declan wouldn't have tried to stop us."

"Agreed." Aunt Monte came up beside them and rubbed Ember's shoulder.

With a nod, Ember felt the heat in their chest, and continued walking towards the cave. The heat wasn't painful, but the small point that they'd felt at the edge of the woods had grown to the size of a large nut. Their goal had to be close.

While circumnavigating a copse of trees, an acorn hit Ember on the forehead. Their fingers came up to rub the spot as a second projectile hit their stomach. Behind them, they heard Felix and Aunt Monte grunt.

"What the hey," Aunt Monte mumbled. "Acorns? Who is attacking us with small tree seeds?"

Ember threw up an air shield as they all searched the trees but couldn't see where the nuts came from. Three more acorns hit Ember's shield, hard, before she stepped out and yelled, "I will burn down these trees, take the woods down to ash, if you do not stop. I have been questioned and now attacked. I came here in peace and have not been given peace back. If you want to fight, I *will* fight back." They formed two large fireballs hovering above each of their palms. "One more blow, and I start burning things down."

Ember burned with rage. Every step of the way had been a struggle. Getting into the forest had been brambles. Then the griffins, the mind attack, sore feet, then Declan, and now this? They knew this was a private sanctuary, but they hadn't done anything to deserve what they were being put through now.

The air cleared of flying missiles, but Ember's anger kept them ready to return fire.

Aunt Monte's hand landed on Ember's shoulder. "I think you can put out your fires. They've stopped. Let's get to the cave."

Releasing the flames, Ember searched for their attackers. If anything came at them, they wouldn't hesitate to reignite and attack. "When you came with Aunt Nuri, did you face all these discouragements?"

The hands on Ember's shoulders gave a squeeze of support before slipping away. "No, it was much easier. Something must have happened. They've upped their protections."

Ember finally relaxed and dropped the air shield. Behind them, Felix huffed out a sigh. "Okay, good. Can we continue?"

Ember just nodded.

The path cleared up and the beacon of heat within them intensified.

Soon, they saw a large hill that the trees had hidden. They'd seen it while in flight, but it hadn't occurred to Ember that that was their final destination.

Felix whistled. "The trees really hide a lot, don't they? I had no idea we were so close to something so large."

"Finally!" Aunt Monte said with a sigh. "I was beginning to wonder if we'd make it with all the obstacles."

The way from the edge of the woods to the cave didn't take long. Outside the small mountain, there was rocky terrain. A dark opening, large enough to fit two griffins side by side, awaited them. A yearning to enter filled Ember, a desire to know what lay within.

"Do you think it's safe?" Felix's voice quivered. "I'm wondering if ... I don't know. I just ... what do you two think?"

Aunt Monte put a hand on his shoulder. "Breathe. Clear your mind. You have your mind shields up, but the cave really doesn't like non-phoenixes to enter. Ember, maybe you should invite him. I think that's what Nuri did with me. Maybe that's why I'm not being repulsed right now."

Ember looked from the cave to Aunt Monte to Felix, then gave a curt nod. "Right, an invitation." They had no idea what they were supposed to do. "Um, okay." They went up to Felix and placed a hand on his shoulder. "Felix, I invite you to enter the cave with us ... with me, a phoenix of the land."

Ember tilted their head and made a hopeful smile. "Did it help? Are you okay with going in?"

Felix squinted and took a shaky gulp of air. "It's ... do you need me in there?"

Shoulders dropping, Ember thought hard. It appeared a bit more formality was in order. They took Felix's hands and tried to push a bit of energy out with their words. "I,

Ember Savita, invite you, Felix Porter, to enter the cave of Everfire with me. Enter in peace and leave everything as you found it. If your intentions are not to harm the phoenixes then your presence in the cave is welcome."

This time, Ember felt a bit of their magic, not the witch magic but something deeper, shift within them.

Felix shook his head. "Um, I come in peace and harmony. My intentions are to observe and not to harm. I honor the phoenixes and wish no ill will on any of them." Ember could hear the passion and belief behind his words. This was something he'd felt his whole life.

It felt like the cave sighed. A smile grew on Felix's face. "Oh, my gods, I no longer feel like fleeing. That was ... I don't know. Every day with you." He leaned over and gave Ember a quick kiss.

The three slowly walked through the wide entrance. The first part of the cave looked like any cave a person would imagine, but further in, the temperature rose, and the walls began to take on a white, iridescent shimmer. A tension overtook Ember as they walked to the part of the cave where the walls and floor were covered with the moonstone.

Oh, my gods! This is real, this is happening. I can't believe how much in my life has changed in such a short time. And this rock that surrounds me ... it will simplify so much.

Ember stood in the heart of the cave of their ancestors. The fire of all the phoenixes that had come before. One day, their fire would burn here. It wasn't a sad place, but rather a depository of remembrance and joy. From the stories Dad had told them, the fires here came from phoenixes who'd lived long lives and chose to move on. Their fire lived here in celebration of their life.

Dragging their fingers down the wall, Ember moved farther into the cave. The heat on their skin was an indicator that the others probably stayed behind.

"I think you two should hang back; it's getting warm."

Felix laughed. "It's getting more than warm, Ember. We've already stopped. Go, we'll hang out and wait."

They smiled and continued on alone. Ember didn't go as far as where the fire was, but the stories in the fire seemed to resonate within their bones. They thought that if they sat and let it, the fire would tell them stories of its life. Each phoenix that came before them and their life was burned into the walls of the cave, the heat in the air, and the soul of the mountain. If Ember continued, they'd be filled with the history of their people as the fire licked around them. The thought drew them forward towards the pit where the fire danced, but they knew now wasn't the time.

I wish I were here with Dad. He would understand.

After a few minutes, the weight of the history became too much. Ember almost felt queasy. They knew they needed to leave. This wasn't a place to sit and commune with the elders, it was a place to drop off the fire and leave. They reached down and found a small chunk of moonstone that fit in their palm. The stone buzzed in their hand, a shiver overtaking them as they lifted it.

They made their way back to the others and held their hand out to their aunt. "Aunt Monte, until I'm acclimated to this, why don't we put this in your bag. It's ... it's really weird. I can't explain it."

Felix gazed at them. "It's pretty. To me, it's just a stone. That's really interesting. I wonder where the Everfire is."

A laugh erupted out of Ember. "Really deep down there. I don't know that I'd want to see it. If this stone can contain it, a fire that can consume everything, I say we just let it be."

Aunt Monte had walked a bit further down into the cave. "Look at this. It looks like someone else has come and chipped away at this wall. Do you see these marks? They weren't here when I came with Nuri. Why would someone excavate some of this stone? There are pieces of it lying near the entrance. Since there are scraps like you have ... I wonder what the phoenixes are up to."

Ember and Felix shook their heads. He said, "No idea. That's just weird. Not to mention, who would be out here? This isn't a place you just happen on. It's way off the beaten path. It's probably the phoenixes—they can fly over all the obstacles."

Another shiver down Ember's spine had them backing away from the end of the cave. "I think we should leave. We have what we came for. Let's go."

"You really don't like being here, do you?" Felix rubbed their back, trying to calm them.

"I don't know, at first I did, but now ... maybe it's the Everfire. It just doesn't feel right here." Ember's heart started thundering in their chest.

Aunt Monte came over and slipped her hand in theirs. "Okay, we can go. We got what we wanted. I have your stone. Let's head out."

They started back down the path and Ember finally felt like they could breathe. They saw the acorns littered on the path about a mile from the mouth of the cave. Heading out, it made Ember smile. Once they were clear of the projectiles, Felix said, "Why don't we go about an hour, then stop for lunch?"

"Sounds perfect." Aunt Monte's good cheer helped Ember to relax more.

The group's hike to a stopping point was easy. While Felix set up lunch, Ember shot up to their feet. "My dad! I should get a stone for him. I don't know why I didn't think of this before. We're so close. I don't know if he wants one, but it'd be so easy to have one for him."

"That sounds like a lovely idea. The trip out here isn't horrible, but it isn't simple. Grabbing another stone should be fast," Aunt Monte agreed.

Felix's head tilted. "Just think, it could be your next gift for him. One less thing to shop for. I know you hate shopping."

Ember snorted. "Okay, I'm going back."

"We're all going back," Aunt Monte corrected.

"No, you two stay here. We're an hour away. I have fire, I can protect myself in these woods. Not to mention, everything here is against witches, not phoenixes. Since I'm a phoenix, it should be easier if I go alone. I'll be quick, and when I get back, lunch will be ready." They waggled their eyebrows at them.

Felix rolled his eyes. "It doesn't take two hours to make lunch."

"Fine, wait an hour and a half to start then. I just know the forest will let me through faster if I go alone. I may even get back in less than two hours. Trust me, this makes sense."

"I don't like this, Ember. I know this is the Phoenix Forest, and I've let you take lead, but I'm the adult supervising the two of you. Your dad agreed because of the mix of magics." Aunt Monte pursed her mouth in disapproval.

"I know, but we've cleared this path, and we're close."

"Just put it on record. I think this is an awful idea," she grumbled.

Ember beamed. "But my logic is great, right?"

Monte's eyebrow rose. "What about flying? It would be faster."

"I don't know." Ember bit their lip. "We know Declan is out there, but there are others as well. Phoenixes and other shifters. I've mostly only flown with my Dad. I think I'd rather explore these woods with him or Aunt Nuri before flying on my own. Not to mention, I'm not sure I could hold the stone in my talons, and I don't want to be in the cave naked. It sounds ... just no."

Both Aunt Monte and Felix nodded. Felix gave them a hug. "Do what you're comfortable doing."

"I'm glad you're seeing my reason." They smiled.

They darted off, heading back to the cave. They were right that the path seemed to open up more easily and the cave seemed to be closer than it should've been.

Before they knew it, they stood in the rocky entrance, the sight bright and welcoming. The overwhelming sense of history weighed down on them. Steeling themself, they darted in and found another smooth piece of moonstone just inside the entrance. Again it felt weird, so Ember slipped it into their pocket. Not touching their skin, it wasn't as bad. The cave still resonated strangely, not a place they wanted to linger.

Just as they were about to turn to head back, a pain blossomed in the back of their head. The ground came up to meet them and their vision went black.

Chapter 28 - A Lost Friend

Felix

"It's been three hours. I'm worried." Felix paced back and forth in front of where their bags sat. He'd wanted to go after Ember after the two-hour mark came and went, but Monte had said no.

"I know you're worried. I'm concerned, too. Let's think about this. Maybe Ember decided to explore the cave. Us running in after them won't help the situation."

Though she counseled patience, her voice was tight with worry.

"I have a bad feeling about this. They said two hours. They'd go in and come back. I just don't think they'd hang out in there for an hour. It isn't like Ember to do something like that."

Monte searched the woods. "Felix, think. What do you think would happen? We're in an area patrolled by phoenixes. Ember *is* a phoenix. This is one of the safest places for them to be. I worry that we're allowed in the woods only because we're traveling with them. If we're heading out, all the creatures will be satisfied. If just the two of us head back towards the cave without Ember ... I don't know, I don't think it will go over well." Her face showed her concern. "I agree this isn't the best scenario, but at the same time I want to trust Ember."

He continued to pace, annoyance and worry vying for dominance. "Can we do something, anything? This waiting ... I just ... Maybe if we call Declan. Maybe he saw something. I just feel like something bad happened to Ember. When we called they didn't answer, nor when we texted."

"That's probably the cave interfering with the signal. It's lined in a powerful stone and filled with magical fire." Monte sighed. Their conversation had been going in circles for the better part of the last hour. It felt like they each had their lines that they were repeating.

"Please, can I call for Declan? I know he won't be happy to talk to us without Ember, but maybe one of his patrols saw something."

With a sigh of exasperation, Monte threw her hands into the air. "Fine. I just … remember, the phoenixes don't like outsiders. They don't like us knowing about them, they don't like us traipsing about their woods. We need to be careful."

Before Monte could change her mind, Felix gazed up at the sky. The trees seemed to stretch up forever, the tops disappearing into the cloud so high, they hid the small mountain that housed the phoenixes' Everfire. Taking a deep breath, he yelled, "Declan, if you can hear me, we could use your help!"

He watched, but there wasn't any movement above. Biting his lip, he waited a few minutes and then slumped. He'd hung so much hope on the phoenixes he couldn't see. In his imagination, he'd have seen Ember travel to the cave and … something. They would come swooping down, and everything would be okay. He wasn't sure what the shape of okay would take, but he needed them to be safe. Three hours of not knowing what happened to Ember wasn't weighing well on Felix's shoulders.

As he paced, he rubbed his temples, worry and stress causing a headache to start. He knew he could use meditation to help, but he had no calm within him to start that process. The hike to a spot to sleep would be hell, but once they had Ember back, he was sure everything else would get better.

A rustling behind him caught his attention and he spun. Declan stepped out, again only wearing a pair of jeans. His face was a mask showing no emotion. Short red-brown hair framed his face. He stood, staring at Felix.

Despite his relief at seeing the phoenix, Felix was terrified. He spoke fast, hoping the probably annoyed if not angry phoenix didn't throw a fireball at them. "Ember headed back to the cave three hours ago. They said they'd be back over an hour ago. We were just wondering if you or any of your people saw them. We just want to make sure Ember is okay."

A single hand lifted to Declan's nose as he pinched between his eyes. "Witch, stop talking." He snarled out the words, as if talking to Felix hurt. "Over the last few months people have invaded our land; it's why we've added protections." His jaw clenched as if every word hurt to say. "Some magic user found our cave and has been visiting regularly with friends. We don't know what he's been doing, how he gained access, or how he evades us, but he's found a way around our sentries. We didn't see Ember return to the cave, we saw no reason to monitor your group, but we saw the interlopers leave the cave two hours ago with a large bag. When we try to get close, they shoot at us with guns ... any bird, any animal, anyone." His eyes glowed with his anger. "We only let you two into the woods because you traveled with a phoenix. Now you tell me Ember is missing?"

Monte came up to stand by Felix while Declan spoke. "No, you've told *us* that Ember is missing. You never warned us other magic users had found their way onto these lands. If you had, we wouldn't have let Ember go back alone. Your arrogance has endangered a young phoenix and could've put all of us in harm's way. Holding this back was dangerous. You *knew* we weren't a threat or the people you worried about, yet despite that you said nothing."

His face hardened. "I assume you'll leave our lands now, witch."

Monte glared. "You need to worry about Ember's family. Just think what Ash Savita will do when he learns you let someone take his child. Or when Nuri Savita learns her brother's child was taken. You've angered the two most powerful phoenixes ... I want you to think about that Declan, witch-hater, and the one who endangered their young."

"We didn't harm a phoenix. No harm will come to me or mine." Before they could say anything else, he turned and walked away.

"I hope you're right," Monte said softly. But Declan's step faltered before he disappeared into the shadows.

Anger swelled in Felix, but there wasn't anything he could do. Declan was shifted and flying away without answering any of the questions Monte asked. They were essentially in Declan's house surrounded by his people. He and Monte weren't safe. Before anything else could befall them, he pulled out his phone and dialed Ember's mom.

"Felix? I didn't expect a call from you. Is everything okay?" She sounded distracted.

"No, I don't think things are." He explained everything that had happened as succinctly as he could. "I don't know if Declan told the truth about the bag ... he didn't maintain eye contact at that point. But there was nothing we could've done to get more from him. There was too much disdain."

When he finished, the line went quiet for a few moments. "Okay, we'll get this figured out." Her voice was tight and businesslike. He wasn't sure, but he thought someone was about to pay dearly for the harm to Ember. "Did Declan describe the people invading the cave?"

"No. I'm surprised he said as much as he did. The hate he felt towards us dripped from him."

"Okay, don't move."

"What do you mean, don't move? Monte and I could get a good three or four more hours of travel in today before we need to camp. Then we could probably get to the edge of the Phoenix Forest tomorrow. It may take one more day with our waiting here, but we'll move as fast as we can."

Mrs. Savita sighed. "No, don't move. Stay there. I can zero in on you, but not if you're moving. This may take a bit of time. I need to talk with Ash and Nuri. You'll have to give me about an hour. Don't move." She hung up.

Felix pulled his phone away from his ear and gaped at it. He wondered if he and Mrs. Savita were having the same conversation.

"Should we pack up the lunch detritus and head out? I heard you tell Sadie we could make it a few hours."

"Yeah ... no. We should just hunker down and wait."

One of Monte's eyebrows rose, and she tilted her head in confusion. "What do you mean, 'hunker down'?"

He shrugged, waving his hands to the side palms up. "That's what she said. Just wait. She didn't make it sound like a suggestion."

They packed up their stuff and made sure they hadn't left anything behind. About forty minutes after Mrs. Savita hung up on Felix, the air in front of him shimmered and Ember's mom walked through the distorted air with Vi. Their faces were stormy as if they were ready to fight.

Dumbfounded, Felix felt his jaw drop.

Mrs. Savita smiled tightly, then she shook her head. "Oh, sweetie, what do you think it means to have spatial magic? You control the boundaries of space. Moving people is a lot harder. I can only do that one more time, and then I'm done for the day. I don't practice this aspect of it enough."

"Can Ember do this?" *Maybe Ember will be able to save herself.*

"Not yet. She isn't strong enough."

Felix looked over at Monte. Her eyes were the size of saucers, mouth open wide. Felix felt a bit better knowing he wasn't the only one who was gob-smacked.

Monte looked crestfallen. "Gods above, I'm so sorry. You put me in charge, and I messed up big."

Mrs. Savita shook her head. "I'm livid someone took Ember. If I have my say, heads will roll. The patrol needs to do a better job. Letting people take from the cave! What are they thinking? Then there's the thieves. I'm not happy that Ember ran back to get another moonstone chip, but in the end, we are in the heart of phoenix territory. Something was bound to go wrong. I'm angry, but we will get them back."

Vi moved over and engulfed Monte in a hug. "Hey, love. I know you won't hear this, but don't feel guilty. It was a bad situation. Thanks for bringing the two teens out here. I heard some of the story. Who knew that the forest and the creatures had become so unwelcoming?"

Monte appeared to sink into the hug. "What are you doing here?"

Mrs. Savita took over. "I'm going to take you two home. The trip is over. We need to find Ember and bring them home, but to do that, we need answers. Nuri will see what answers she can get here. She can either call me to bring her home or fly back. Ash wanted to come, but with his exile, it would've been one more boundary to getting answers. He's home cooking enough food for an army—or magic users about to enter battle."

Felix licked his lips. "Is there more happening back home, or is Mr. Savita just worried about Ember?"

"It's Ember," Mrs. Savita said.

"Yeah, me too. The only phoenix we saw ... some teen named Declan, he may know something."

Vi narrowed her eyes. "He's a new pup. I haven't been back to the compound in years. I'll make sure he and the others all fill me in. Don't worry."

After Mrs. Savita and Vi explained the plan, Felix and Monte collected their bags. Mrs. Savita had them put their hands on her shoulders before she pulled up a small portal back home. All Felix could see was a hazy spot in the air in front of them.

"Hold on," Mrs. Savita warned as she stepped forward.

The air seemed to contract around Felix as he stepped through the shimmering spot to the point it was hard to breathe. His skin tingled as a tremble began deep in his gut. For a moment, he wondered if he'd become atoms spread across the area from the Phoenix Forest to Ember's living room, and then with a pop in his ears he stood in the warmth of the heated house, filled with the scent of enchiladas cooking.

He dropped the bags he held and collapsed into the closest seat. Mrs. Savita fell into the couch. Ember's dad raced to her, placing a hand on her forehead. "Out cold. I knew she'd push herself too far. I bet she won't wake until tomorrow. If this is really the start of war, she'll have to practice that. Now. Felix, Monte, tell me what you told her; tell me where my child is."

Chapter 29 - Welcome To Hotel Wells

Ember

Ember woke with a jerk. Their eyes opened to complete darkness. When they tried to stretch out their cramped muscles, they discovered their hands were bound behind their back. With a yank, Ember tried to adjust, but the binding cut into their wrists.

The arm under them was numb, and as they moved around the cool pins and needles bit into them from shoulder to hand. The pain distracted them from the pounding in their head from where they'd been hit.

The floor beneath them shifted erratically and they bounced, hitting the ceiling above them. Ember realized they could hear a hum, like wheels on a road, then gravity pushed them towards their feet as if they were tilting.

What in Hades? What happened? Where am I? Okay, I went to the cave, I collected a moonstone for Dad, and ... gods above! Someone must have knocked me out cold. Now I'm in a car? A trunk? Artemis, give me the strength of the hunt to survive this ordeal. I could use my fire, but not yet. If I let them know what I am, things could be worse.

Another bump and Ember went airborne for a moment, landing hard on their side. They yelped and tried to shift more to their back as blood flowed through their arm. Growling through the hurt, they thought back to the cave, trying to think of anything that would tell them who had taken them.

With a shake of their head, Ember mumbled, "Felix! And Aunt Monte! Gods above and below, what do they think happened to me? Are they still waiting?" Struggling, Ember tried to pull a hand from the ties. Though their hands were secured, they hadn't been tied very tight. It took some tugs and pulls, and their wrists grew slick with what they could smell was blood. The coppery tang started to fill the small space. But the important thing was Ember got their left hand out of the binding. The thought of fire flitted through their head, but they weren't sure what else was in the car ... who else was in the car.

Once one hand was free, they moved both shoulders and arms, trying to improve their circulation. Ember bumped into a box then rolled over and knocked their head against something solid. They rubbed their temple then their hands together, suffering the tingles as blood rushed to their fingers. Breathing hard, they finally regained feeling in all ten digits.

They patted down their jeans pockets. Nope. No phone. Ember wasn't surprised. They didn't expect such luck, but they'd hoped the people who'd taken them may have been in a hurry and forgotten. It would've been nice. They did find the moonstone they'd picked up for Dad. The people who took them probably decided the stone was a silly remembrance of the cave, nothing special. For all Ember knew, they were right.

I hope Aunt Nuri was right about what the moonstone does.

Ember rolled around the trunk as the car took a hard turn, and they slammed into the back of the vehicle. With a groan, they kneaded the spot on their head that hurt as if it had already been abused and was getting harmed again. As they tended to it, the car came to a sudden stop, and Ember's face struck the back of the car. They wanted to scream from the sudden pain in their nose but bit the sound back after a small cry.

They were cupping their nose when hinges groaned, and light cut into their eyes.

"She's awake," a deep, gruff male voice yelled. "Did Boss want her blindfolded and knocked out when she was dragged through the house?"

"Don't matter," a younger voice answered. He sounded like he just wanted to get the job over with. "It ain't like she's leaving. Just needed her that way to get her out of the woods quietly."

Rough hands pulled Ember from the trunk. Each man grabbed an arm. One put a hand over their mouth. They whimpered as the bigger one bumped their nose, the pain reverberating down their spine. The three were in a garage with several cars and trucks. It was huge but didn't look industrial. It looked like it belonged to someone with a collection of vehicles.

They yanked Ember through a building. It had high ceilings, fancy furniture that looked antique, and wall hangings that could be in a museum. *This place could be a palace.*

The hallway by the garage led past a large kitchen. Ember saw what could be a living room on the other side of the industrial-sized room.

There were a few people milling about. They all wore black suits and white ties. Even though they were dressed up, every one of them looked defeated. To Ember, they gave the impression of being staff, as if the suits were a uniform.

None of the staff looked at the men as they dragged Ember through their domain. Ember debated struggling, but suspected that none of the people paid to be there would react any more if they made noise than if they didn't. They didn't need more bruises. Or worse, to die and rise from the ashes. Ember knew they needed to survive despite what the goons had said about 'not leaving' in the garage.

Just as Ember caught a glimpse of a familiar face, the man at their arm tugged them onto an elevator. After a swift trip down, they were dragged past locked doors and wide windows. Ember didn't have time to look into any of the other rooms before they arrived at their destination.

The men heaved Ember onto a bed. The metal door shut with a clank and Ember looked around the small cell. A bed in a square room with one of the large windows that opened into the hall they'd been dragged through from the elevator. Off to the side was a room without a door. In it, Ember saw a small toilet and sink. Though the room was small, it smelled clean. It also couldn't be seen from the huge window, but they couldn't lock themself away and hide. *So much for privacy.*

It didn't take long for a familiar face to appear on the other side of the window: Cress, smiling at them like it was his birthday. *Of course it's him. Just the person I don't want to see.*

The lock clinked and the door swung open. Ambrose's dad—Ember recognized him from the ridiculous rally posters—and Tad Shade, the leader himself, walked in. *Should I feel honored? Or just annoyed?*

Ember debated showing their real abilities to escape, but with Cress watching and his ability to do mind magic, they worried about how far they'd get.

Ambrose's dad smiled. "Hello, Ember."

Ember narrowed their eyes. "How do you know me?"

"There are so few magic users with red hair; you're recognizable. Is it any wonder I would know one of my daughter's school companions? Not to mention, we did go to so much trouble to bring you here. Don't you think we made sure of your identity first?"

Ambrose told her dad about me? A shiver ran down Ember's back.

Before they could say anything else, the man continued. "I don't know that we've ever met. I'm Ambrose's father. You can call me Mr. Wells. This is Mr. Shade. We have a few questions for you. The first is: what were you doing at the cave in Phoenix Forest?"

Ember pushed back until their back was against the wall, then crossed their legs. They wanted to show the men in the room that they didn't scare them. "I could ask you the same thing. That cave was well hidden. It doesn't seem like something you'd just come upon randomly. It's also in a protected forest."

"Exactly; that's our point. So, tell me, what were you doing in that cave? Do you know what the cave is? It's in the Phoenix Forest, named from when the pesky fire birds still lived."

They gazed at the two men. Mr. Shade was tall and thin with sandy brown hair. He looked like the kind of guy who would disappear into the background. Mr. Wells, with his dark hair and dark eyes, was similar to Ambrose. He carried his charisma like a designer leather handbag, for everyone to see. There was something about the man that made you want to answer his questions. But his similarity to Ambrose also made them *not* want to answer any of his questions.

"Why am I here? Why did you knock me out and kidnap me? You could've just asked me by the cave if you wanted to know, or asked me at another time, but instead you hit me over the head and dragged me—" they made a point of looking around, "—to wherever it is I am now."

Mr. Shade's face contorted into an expression of anger. "Some of my men said they found you in a park and left you for dead. I want to know how you're still alive. I think if a person is left for dead, they should be good enough to stay that way. So, I asked them to find you and bring you back here. I want to see this miracle kid who defied their fire and lived on to annoy people another day. *That's* why you are here."

Ember licked their lips. "You brought me here to kill me?" Fear shot through them, despite the stone in their pocket. *Gods, what if it doesn't work? How am I going to get out of here? What if they see me rise from the ashes? I need to reach Dad!*

"Of course! But we're not the monsters you think we are. We'll inject you with this tranquilizer," he held up a hypodermic needle, "then bring in the man who said he used fire to burn you. We'll give him a second chance."

Before Ember could say another word, the two men who'd dragged them down to the basement held them to the bed. With a jovial smile, Mr. Shade approached and injected Ember with a needle. The injection was sharp, and then a heat flowed through their arm making them feel heavy.

Mr. Shade sighed. "Very good. You shouldn't be any trouble now."

All four men walked out, locking the door behind them.

If I'm drugged and they plan on burning me, I wonder why they locked the door?

Before the thought finished, the monster of a man glared at them from behind the large picture window. Ember could just see him from the corner of their eyes. As the flames erupted around them, trying to consume,

Ember's mind flitted from the moonstone in their pocket to the magic Felix had performed on their clothes. *Fire won't be enough to harm me ... it's just fire.*

Hopefully my clothes survive and I'm not naked.

Chapter 30 - Welcome To The Future

Ambrose

Ambrose sat at her vanity fixing her makeup. Father expected her to look her best tonight for dinner. The idea she would one day be paired with Mr. Shade caused bile to rise in the back of her throat, but Ambrose figured she'd deal with that another day. For now, she worried about building up her power base. To that end, she'd even put her hair up in wide rollers, so it would cascade in big waves past her shoulders, just like the men liked.

Once she felt her face looked just right, she sauntered to her closet. The light green dress, horrible in color and awful in cut, which she hated, wasn't anywhere to be found. Ambrose searched, knowing that Mr. Shade would love the monstrosity because it was his favorite shade of green. Her walk-in closet was spacious but crammed full of outfits, so she may have missed it. She searched again. No ugly green dress.

Pursing her lips to keep from scowling more, she walked from the closet. A young, human girl peeked into her room from the hallway. "Um, excuse me. May I come in? I was told to press your dress for tonight and I have it ready, but I don't want to disturb you."

Hands on her hips, Ambrose glared at the girl. "Well, me not having anything to wear is pretty disturbing, don't you think? How will I wear what you pressed if you don't bring it to me?" Great. Now she was taking her frustrations out on the help, not those who caused her anger. The girl was just following instructions, not well, but to the best of her ability. But Ambrose didn't have anyone else to complain to about how much everything sucked. All she could do was plaster on a smile and survive.

This habit Father recently adopted of switching out the help every few days was starting to piss her off. For most of her life, the Wells household staff—from the cooks, to the laundry maids—had been the same people. Ambrose knew them all by name, not that she used them often, but she could if she wanted. The old staff wouldn't have ever acted so meek. The dress would've been back in its rightful place by the time Ambrose had gone looking for it.

I miss the people I knew. I wonder what it would take to get them back. Are they quitting or is Father firing them? And if the latter, why?

In a snit, Ambrose grabbed the eyesore of an outfit. "You can go now."

The girl looked close to tears. "Yes, ma'am." She turned and ran.

Ambrose stepped into the outfit, a costume really, and found the side zipper. *At least I won't have to walk through the house exposing myself to find someone to zip me up.*

Moving back to the mirror, she flinched at her image in the dress, then sat to take the rollers out of her hair and brush out the waves. When it was done, at least from the neck up, she looked nice.

Another knock on the door and a second timid teen requested permission into her room. "I brought you some tea. There was a note in the kitchen that you were to get some at three."

Ambrose checked the clock. Four fifteen. "Well, you brought the tea, if not at the right time. Set it down on the table over there. Did you bring any sugar or milk?"

The servant blanched. "That wasn't part of the note. I'll bring it right away."

Ambrose wanted to rub her eyes in exasperation, but then she'd have to redo her makeup. The servant was back quickly enough, and Ambrose added sugar to her mug. She sat for a quick cup once the brew was to her liking. She'd have preferred the tea before she'd applied her makeup, but the soothing concoction would help relax her before she headed out to face her father and that horrible Mr. Shade. It was getting to the point that thinking about him sent shivers of disgust down her back.

Dressed and looking as good as she cared to make herself, Ambrose headed for her father's office. She found him sitting behind his large desk, reading something on his computer. "Father, we need to talk."

It took him a few moments to finish whatever it was before he turned from the monitor and gazed at her. "What do you want to speak about, dear? I'm a bit busy right now; these reports need to be filed before the weekend and it's already Thursday night."

"Why does the staff keep changing? For years we've had the same people who knew how the house ran, knew what we liked, when we wanted things, and how to prepare our requests. Now it seems every time I see someone, they're new and clueless."

"It's a bit of a long story." He spoke to her as if speaking to the help, not family. Though he'd always been busy, he usually gave her time when she asked for it. "A few of the members of staff haven't changed, and I plan on keeping them, but yes, we have several turnover positions."

"But I don't understand why. Can you explain it to me?" His avoidance of the subject irritated her.

"A few reasons. First of all, when a person signs on to work for us, they agree to a full smattering of conditions. Most don't read all of the small print. When they do, they often won't sign our contract. Second, they're only human, so does it really matter? The job they're doing is menial at best."

Anger filled her like the fire she wielded. What could the family possibly add to a contract that would scare people off? "It's menial, but that doesn't mean with time they don't improve and gain efficiency. The new people don't perform as well, and it's frustrating. But you're hiding something. I can tell. What is it, Father?" Though she hadn't raised her voice, it had gotten harder.

"You don't want to know." He said it with such authority, Ambrose wondered if he was right.

"I'm the only child you have. You've been treating Cress like a son, but he isn't your kid. I am! Tell me what's happening to all our staff."

His face fell and his mouth flattened. "This isn't anything you need to worry your pretty head about,

Ambrose." She clenched her jaw. *Since when is Father so condescending?*

One brow rose. "But does Cress know? Is he involved in our ever-changing staff?"

"Yes, he knows." It felt like a punch to her gut. *Is he replacing me? What is going on?*

"Then tell me, Father." Sitting tall, Ambrose was tired of being treated like an imbecile. She was more than a pretty face in a fancy dress. She was more intelligent than most of the people living under this roof, including her father.

"Fine, I'll tell you. But remember, I warned you. You won't like it. If you want, I'll have Cress remove the memory. He's gotten better at doing that."

"I wouldn't trust Cress in my mind in a million years. I can handle anything you show him. Gods above, I'm not a baby. When did you get to be so sexist?"

With a smirk, and a raised eyebrow, Father stood and came around his desk. "Very well, daughter, follow me." He led her to the elevators. While they waited, he sent off a text.

"What was that?" Paranoia began to replace her anger, but she didn't think it was misplaced.

"We need to meet Tad if you want to see what he's been working on. It isn't anything I'm leading."

The idea that Mr. Shade was ruling part of their home made Ambrose want to scream. Her jaw hurt from how tightly she clamped it shut. She didn't want to marry him one day, regardless of his power and influence. He was old and ugly ... and not very smart. She was young, beautiful, and brilliant. Why did his power, the leadership of this new movement he promised, have to come at the price of her?

It was only years of knowing how to act in all situations that kept her from saying something she shouldn't. He would bring them power, but at what cost?

Usually when they got into the elevator, Dad selected the first basement. Today he went for sublevel three, the lowest one. When the doors opened, she saw Mr. Shade standing in front of a large window. A shiver of disgust wormed its way through her. Her father strode over to join him, but Ambrose approached with trepidation. On the other side of the window, a human sat strapped to a chair. She looked unconscious. Ambrose recognized her from the laundry; she'd been part of the house staff for years. Her gut clenched seeing her trussed up like a criminal in a prison cell.

What possible reason could there be for her to be in this situation? She's never done anything wrong in the years she's worked for us.

"Why is Bianca in there? She's one of the best laundry workers we have in the house. The new workers don't hold a candle to her."

"The fact that you know the cattle's name is why she's in there," Father said, disappointment oozing from him. "They are the help, Ambrose, mere humans. Anyone can do what they do."

Did Father just call another person cattle? As if they aren't even worthy of being human?

Mr. Shade nodded. "Am I doing this demonstration, or not?"

"Yes." Ambrose turned to him. Despite her loathing of him, and the bad feeling she had about the situation, she needed whatever information he would give her. "I should know about anything that I'm representing, anything that Cress knows. I don't like being kept in the dark."

"Well, lovely girl," his finger gently rubbed her cheek, and it took every ounce of Ambrose's will to hold still, "if you don't like the dark, let me bring you into the light." He gave her a manic smile. "Years ago, while working at a human museum, I went out on a few archaeological digs. During one of my expeditions, I found it. It took years of searching, but perseverance paid off, and I found it!"

Ambrose listened to Mr. Shade as he went on about his prowess, overcoming working with humans, searching for ... something. It was worse than the worst of the teachers' lectures she'd ever heard. She hoped he'd get to the point soon and explain what "it" was.

"So, then I found the cave with the Everfire." Mr. Shade's eyes shone with his glee. "It was only my unsurpassed skills with void that let me in, but in I got, my dear. That's the secret, don't you know? Void. People think void is a worthless skill, but void's the key—that's what'll win us this war."

Shocked, Ambrose clamped her jaw before it dropped open. Once she knew she could speak calmly, she asked, "Everfire? You found the mythical location where the phoenixes stored their death fire so it wouldn't consume the world? I thought it was all just hearsay. Stories told to scare babies." She wanted to ignore the ranting about void for now. She worried he may do something dangerous.

"Oh, no, Ambrose. Everfire is quite real, and there are very few ways to destroy it. Phoenixes don't have magic, not like us witches; they can move their fire, but not destroy it. They found a way to contain the fire. That's it."

Something about the story troubled her. She narrowed her eyes and tilted her head. "What did finding their Everfire do to help you? It's a fire that is more dangerous than anything and everything. What can it do for you?"

He indicated the room beyond the window. "Do you see that box?"

Looking into the room, she saw a white iridescent box against the far wall, away from Bianca. It had a bit of blue and purple sheen that glowed in the light. "It's gorgeous.

Too bad it's in there. I wouldn't mind having it as a jewelry box."

Mr. Shade leaned towards the window, practically purring. "Not that box, my lovely girl. It's made of a stone sacred to the phoenixes. The one stone that apparently can contain their Everfire."

"What stone is it?"

"From everything I've read and studied at the museum," Mr. Shade said, turning from the window and smiling at her, even as he ignored her question, "I learned a lot, which wasn't easy. The information is a secret of that extinct bird, giving their life to save the worthless humans."

Again, he started on a rant, this time about phoenixes. Ambrose smiled at him as he went on. She worried if she interrupted him, he may get angry or violent. He didn't seem stable. She hoped if she was patient, she could learn the type of stone the box was made of.

"And then I read about the moonstone, the one substance that could contain Everfire. The journal I found stated that there was a cave in the Phoenix Forest where the phoenixes stored their death fire. The cave is lined in the moonstone. Not just any moonstone; this cave's stone has been altered by the fire it contains. Once I read that, I knew I had to find the forest, the cave, and the stone. Could you imagine what we could do if we could find a way to harness the fire? *Their* fire? I mean, I realized it could all be just folklore, but I had to know."

Ambrose realized she'd lost control of her jaw this time as she gaped at the man. Snapping her teeth together, she looked at the beautiful box and then back at Mr. Shade. "Are you telling me that that box is made of moonstone, and you have Everfire within it?"

Mr. Shade pulled a lever on the wall next to the window. A pulley attached to the top of the box lifted the top for a second before the box dropped back down. A lick of blue-white fire shot out.

Ambrose put out her hand. She had to stop this madness. She could feel the fire but couldn't control it. The power was beyond anything she could affect. Her arm trembled, but, unable to use her fire magic against the beauty on the other side of the window, she let her arm drop, and watched in horror as the fire began to eat its way through everything in the room.

Since the room had obviously been used before, the only things in it were the pulley, now dust, the box, shining in the light of the fire, and Bianca, sitting in her chair. Thankfully, they'd done something to knock her out. She was tied down, but fully unaware of what was happening around her.

The room was soundproof. Ambrose watched in horror, as if viewing a television on mute, as the fire consumed Bianca, her bindings, and the seat where she sat. The former laundress didn't react as, in mere moments, she was transformed from a human being into ash. The heat was so incredible, the destruction was quick.

Ambrose shook and her heart thumped in her chest. She'd stopped breathing, and she felt dizzy. *This is what they're doing? Killing humans as if they have no value at all? I knew they spoke about us versus them, but this is more than separation ...* Ambrose's mind couldn't comprehend the actions her father took in the name of power. This went far beyond putting on an ugly dress. "But why? If her service was inadequate, then why not just fire her?"

Mr. Shade chuckled low. "But we did fire her, my dear." His hands clamped down on her shoulders possessively.

"Beyond you being too familiar with her, dear," Father said, "she saw some of the papers left in my jacket pocket when cleaning my suit. She said she hadn't read them, but you know humans. They lie about anything. We couldn't take the chance."

"But—"

"Ambrose," Father snapped out. "Either you let the men lead, or I'll tell Cress to wipe this memory from your mind."

But Cress's ability to wipe memories was exactly what they needed to solve the Bianca problem. Why couldn't he have done that to her? But then she knew the answer. Bianca was merely human.

Gaping at the now empty room, Ambrose fought the tears that threatened to fall. She wasn't sure if they were over the death of the laundress or her own innocence. Then again, it could be anger over her father's flippant ease around death.

She wondered if she could continue representing a group that did this to living people. Then a more worrying question sprang to mind: *Would they allow me to stop?*

Chapter 31 - When Bad Guys Are Considerate

Ember

Ember snapped awake. Ember realized their bumps and bruises from the forest and the abduction were gone. Not only that, they'd died and kept their female parts. *It worked. Everything worked. Oh, my gods, I can't believe it, Nuri's a genius.* They patted themself down and realized they were still wearing clothes.

Thank you, Felix ... wherever you are. Gods above, I hope you and Aunt Monte made it out of Phoenix Forest okay. Felix is amazing.

Ember's heart thundered in their chest. *Okay, now to figure out what to do next. Survival isn't the same as surviving.*

Pushing themself up, they tried to steady themself. Ember itched. They headed to the small bathroom and found ash under their clothes. With a snort, they recalled having Felix fireproof their shirts and jeans, but not their underclothes.

They quickly stripped, wiped away the ash, shook out their clothing, and flushed the bigger chunks before redressing. Next time they were fireproofing clothes, they'd be more thorough.

Once dressed, they washed their face. They felt better afterward. They'd escaped death—this time. If this group wanted them dead, they'd find a way.

They reached into their pocket and rubbed the moonstone. A tingle shot through their body, and they released it quickly. The stone should maintain their body's sex. The fireproofing kept them clothed. Looking around the room, they wondered how long they'd been locked in this prison. No clock hung on the wall and their watch hadn't survived the ordeal.

Well, I'm supposed to be dead. They headed to the door and gave it a tug. Nothing. They sighed and flopped onto the bed. Someone would be around soon enough, and they'd have questions. Why had Ember been in the cave? Why were they still alive? And the biggest issue, would the jailers try to kill them again? The answer to that last one was probably the easiest one to answer, of course.

While they waited, they lay down on the bed and stared at the ceiling. They tried to meditate but weren't sure they could turn their mind off. *Dad? Aunt Nuri? Can you hear me? Help me if you can.* They tried calling out. There was no response. Ember wasn't surprised, but they figured they'd try periodically, just in case. It wasn't like they had anything better to do.

They opened their eyes and looked around. The room was a metal box. They shut their eyes and pushed out to see if they could feel for anything they could bring in that would help. The walls and floor of the room were lined in something impermeable to their magic. They stood and touched the wall. A tremor ran through their body, and they felt like when they'd been in the cave or first felt the moonstone pendant. *Did they crush up moonstone and paint the room with it? Can the stone stop magic the same way it stops Everfire?*

Ember walked to the window and searched the hall. It looked empty. They tried to form a fireball near the ceiling in the hall. An alarm went off and water erupted from a sprinkler. Snorting, Ember backed up and sat on the bed.

Okay, I can force my fire outside of the room, through the window. I can do magic in the room. I just don't know if I can do magic through the walls.

The door slammed open and one of the men from the day before—was it the day before?—came in. "What did you do?"

"What did *I* do? What do you mean?"

"The sprinklers," he snarled. "What did you do?"

They scoffed. "I'm locked in a room. How could I make it rain outside the window?" Then Ember waggled their brows. "Is it raining outside too? A stormy day for everyone?"

His face scrunched up. "We have other questions for you, girly. You're supposed to be dead ... again. Now it's raining outside your room. We'll figure you out, you know. The question is, will you be alive or dead when that happens?"

Ember wondered how they'd try to kill them next. They worried, but not too much. They shrugged. "How about you? Will *you* be dead or alive? Your fire seems to be faulty. Can't seem to burn a fly, can you? Maybe *you* caused the rain, trying to blame it on me. Are you so afraid of a young teen in secondary school?"

"I didn't do it!" he snarled. "You can't blame me for that."

"So, you are on guard duty, a magic user with fire, and you're going to tell your boss that me, a kid with air magic, somehow set off the sprinklers?" They raised their eyebrows.

His face hardened. "What did you do? How did you set off the alarms?"

As he finished his question, the alarms finally stopped, and Tad Shade entered the room with Mr. Wells. They both looked exasperated.

"Why were the sprinklers going off on this level?" Mr. Wells asked.

"It was her." The guard pointed a meaty finger at Ember.

Mr. Wells sighed. "We've explained to everyone working, the prisoner isn't a 'her' or a 'him,' so please be considerate until we kill them. We know you're limited in intelligence as a guard, but this is your last chance. Use this as a litmus test on employability. Now, you're telling me a guest without fire magic burned out the sprinkler indicator? After failing to burn Ember twice, you now say they caused the fire outside of a magic proof room?"

Ember wondered if they could call air magic outside of the room. Maybe their half-phoenix nature allowed them to call the fire outside the magic proofing, though they weren't able to use spatial magic. Once they were alone again, they'd test whether they could use air.

"Since you can't seem to use fire with any skill, maybe you can go get Ember food from the kitchen. If they're going to be a guest for another day, there's no reason for us to be inhospitable."

It took work for Ember to keep their face blank. *Why bother with food if their next plan will be to try to off me again? Then again, I am rather hungry. I guess I won't remind them that their end game is my demise.*

Several minutes later, they heard the elevator doors open and close, and the guard returned with a tray. He dropped it on the bed while Mr. Shade stood at the door with a genial smile.

Ember sat warily, not trusting any of the people in this prison.

Tad Shade's mouth twitched in a semblance of a smile. "Now, eat up. We'll be back in a few hours to talk. We're busy; we have a meeting starting up in a couple of minutes, but we do have some questions we need you to answer."

The group left and Ember heard the lock click. The tray held a bowl of chili, a plate with cornbread, and some corn on the cob. It smelled good, and they salivated. They debated not eating, but they needed their energy if they were going to use magic, and Mr. Shade did say he wanted to question them.

The food tasted as good as it smelled. It wasn't as good as Mom's chili, but it filled the belly.

Less than an hour after they finished, their stomach cramped. Knocking the tray to the floor, Ember wanted to kick themself for their idiocy. Of course they'd poisoned the food. The whole goal was to kill them. The questioning wasn't important. It wasn't that Ember cared about the murder attempt, it was the pain while the poison ran its course until Ember lost consciousness that really pissed them off.

Chapter 32 - Finding Hurt Friends

Felix

It had been two days. Each morning, Felix drove over to Ember's house to help their parents and Monte try to figure out where Ember had been taken. Part of him wondered if they—he—should contact Daisy and bring her into the task force. In the end, he knew he couldn't. She didn't know about phoenixes, so she had to be kept in the dark.

With a sigh, he looked at the house. If they'd let him, he'd sleep there. Or, more likely, not sleep, and spend the night searching more.

Vi was still with the phoenixes trying to work that angle.

Felix was convinced Ember was somewhere in Ambrose's house. Her family was working for Tad Shade. More than that, the palatial mansion he'd visited when he was friends with her was more than big enough to hide holding cells. There was no way for them to get in and search, so no matter how convinced he was, there was nothing he could do about it.

He parked his old Toyota Camry in front of Ember's family's house and rang the bell. Inside, Mrs. Savita, looking tired and drawn, offered him bacon and eggs with toast and coffee.

After he'd eaten, Mr. Savita wandered into the kitchen looking harried. Felix wondered when he'd last slept. "Have you done any searches on reputable sites on that computer of yours? Maybe there's something on there that will give us some information."

Felix shook his head. "No. Yesterday I focused on social media. I have my personal accounts, but I have a fake student account that follows Ambrose, Josie, and Cress. I stuck to that account, checking if any of them had done any bragging."

"Hmm." Mr. Savita sipped his coffee. "Maybe check out some other sites, get some information from adults today. I'm going to go out flying."

Gods ... I'm working with phoenixes! I wish I could go out flying with him. He shook his head. *No, focus. Ember.*

Mrs. Savita pursed her lips. "Is that safe? There's a reason you don't do that, even invisible."

"Ember spoke to me when I was in phoenix form. I'm going to go out flying. If I can get through to them, then we can put together a plan."

"But, Ash, wasn't their range short? You'll have to be just over Ember to get through to them."

"Sadie, it's what I can do today. I have to do something," he snapped back. "I can't stay indoors any longer. I need to move. Flying will be the best way to expend my nervous energy. I have to do this."

Mrs. Savita nodded tightly. "Okay, fine. I get it. There isn't a lot we can do in the house. Please check in every hour or so. I can't easily get a hold of you outside of throwing air drafts at you or randomly having mugs pop in front of you."

Mr. Savita smirked. "Deal."

As Mr. Savita finished his meal, Felix headed into the living room and pulled out his laptop. He decided to start with the FB Coalition site. The committees were keeping the site up to date and had very good researchers working for them.

He started with the articles and politics. None of the titles concentrated on missing people. *Maybe we'd have to report Ember missing before there was an article about it. I wonder if the people who do this research could help?*

Felix thought about the good people working to keep the site up and running with current information. They were top notch; professors, teachers, lawyers, smart and industrious workers who knew how to find the facts. "Mrs. Savita, Mr. Savita, what do you think about contacting the FB Coalition and telling them about Ember going missing? They have a few investigative teams who may be able to find something."

Ember's dad paused with his mug almost to his mouth, then tilted his head to the side and stared at Felix. "My instinct is to say no, but that comes from my years of hiding. This isn't about keeping our secrets. It's about finding our child." He turned to his wife. "Sadie, what do you think?"

"Honestly, if we can get a bigger group helping us with this, I'm all for it. I'll call Monte now. She'll know the best people to contact. She said she'd be over to help, but not until later. With Nuri out in the Phoenix Forest, she's stuck running FB alone."

With a final nod, Mr. Savita said, "Call her. I just want Ember back. Good thinking, Felix. Does that site have any other interesting tidbits?"

Felix shrugged and went back to his search. He clicked over to the hospital link. Maybe, if Ember was hurt, their abductors would've dropped them off where they could've been picked up by an ambulance. Felix hoped their parents would've been called, but if Ember's ID had been taken, the first responders may not have known who to call. Whoever posted to the medical page would know they were a witch, and a picture would be included.

He wasn't sure if he wanted to see a 'Jane Doe' picture or not, but knowing where Ember was would settle something in him.

The lists of names kept growing. There were a lot of people who had minor injuries, but without a lot of healers, people who should have been released quickly ended up staying longer. Combing the lists, he startled when he saw Mr. Elias, his history teacher, on the list of people who'd been hurt long enough to be hospitalized for several days. Apparently he'd been released the day before.

The column before the one showing people who had died listed witches in serious condition. Once they'd been healed, they'd move to the column Mr. Elias was in: they had been critically injured but were now released. Scanning the names, searching for the capital 'E' that would signal Ember, Felix's body went cold, and he gasped.

"What is it? Did you find Ember?" Mr. Savita suddenly stood behind him.

"N-N-No." He raised his trembling hand and pointed.

Less concerned about people who weren't his child, Mr. Savita turned away. Mrs. Savita took his place and gave a strangled sound when she read the name he pointed at. 'Daisy Autumn' Condition, 'Severe'. Admitted, 'Wednesday.'

"She's been in there for two days. It doesn't look like anyone has been able to do much for her. There are so many people who are hurt. Ash, call Monte, Felix can take her in to visit the girl."

He grunted. "What about Ember?"

"Ash Savita." She slapped her hand on the table. "Daisy is family. Monte can call someone to start the search for Ember, then she and Felix will go and visit Daisy. This isn't negotiable. Ember would never forgive you if you helped them and ignored their best friend."

He pulled out his phone. "You're right. Fine. I'll make the call, then I'm hitting the sky. I need to be around fewer people; this is getting ridiculous."

Felix listened while Mr. Savita spoke tersely on the phone, then he dropped his device and walked out the back door. He saw a flash of white flame, and then nothing where the man had stood a moment before.

As awful as everything was, he marveled yet again how his life had landed him where he was.

Chapter 33 - An Old Friend

Ember

Ember woke up, their body quivering. Poison may have been the worst way to die, especially without the purification of the fire. They debated tossing the moonstone, but what would the people of the house do when they turned to ash? They shivered at the thought.

Finally relaxed, lying on the edge of the bed, it hit them, they survived the poison and the moonstone *still* worked.

Their belly churned, and they headed to the bathroom. Apparently there was still some gunk in their system they needed to get out. Sitting in discomfort, Ember swore they'd get back at the people who'd prepared the spicy chili that fought back. *And apparently won.*

They brushed their teeth with a finger and debated a shower. They felt gross, but putting on dirty clothes after the shower would be worse. This "hospitable" family had left clothes, but once they tried their daily murder-by-fire routine, the clothes would burn up, and that wasn't something Ember wanted to experience with the guards. If they realized everything on them burned except the moonstone, they may take it away, and then what?

Despite the chili and the poison, I felt physically great.

Ember bit back a cheer, not wanting to get the guard's attention. Then they thought about their options for escape. They could try to burn their way out. The problem was it would be obvious what they were doing. They could transform and fly out, but again, obvious. And phoenixes would be exposed. That wasn't an option.

I wish I could ask Dad. Dad! Can you hear me? Tell me what to do! Gods above and below, it would be nice if you heard me right now. All I want is for you to give me a plan of attack. That's not too much to ask for, right?

Anxiety thrummed through them. They needed to get out but couldn't reveal their phoenix nature. How could they escape without letting everyone know phoenixes were still alive? *Help me, Dad, tell me what to do.* Their plea was a continuous echo in the back of their mind.

If they couldn't escape when alone, they'd have to do it when visited by their captors. The first option was to kill whoever came to visit. A shiver of horror and disgust traveled through them at the thought. It was a last resort option, but if it was life or death they'd consider it.

Ember could accomplish it in several ways. Fire was easy enough. Their control was good enough that they could put a tiny fireball within the people, and figuring out the cause of death would be very difficult. They could use spatial magic, pulling out a vital piece of ... something.

Their spatial magic wasn't as strong as they'd like. If they moved internal organs around, it would get messy, and possibly Ember would get caught before everyone was killed. If they used fire on the people, they could do everyone at once, but Ember hadn't ever killed before, and the thought had bile rising in the back of their throat. A shudder of disgust rocked through their body at the idea.

Come on, Ember, they're trying to off you every day. They've done two attempts so far ... three if you count the park. How many are you going to let them do before you start fighting back?

The real problem was, if they got past whoever guarded the door here, they still had to get out of the house. How many people, innocent people, would die if Ember attempted to escape?

But Ember, a part of their mind argued. *If they work for the people who are imprisoning you, trying to kill you, are they really innocent?*

Yes! They snarled back to themself, wondering if they'd completely lost it. *Some of the people working for the Wells family just needed a job. They have no idea that the people they're working for are monsters.*

That's malarkey, and you know it. You're just trying to justify your cowardice.

Gah! I am not! Servants who work for this family are humans who are just looking for employment, how *could they know what their evil overlord of a boss does for fun?*

Fine, whatever. I still say you're being a coward.

And with that, Ember stopped fighting with themself, though they began debating their own sanity even harder ... mostly because they thought they'd brought up some good points in their own debate, on both sides. They were being a bit scared in a fight that could mean their life, but these people were systemic of a larger issue. Harming them could mean pain and embarrassment being taken out on those weaker and not deserving of such punishment.

"Are you still alive?" Cress's grating voice came to Ember. They rolled their head to stare at their classmate through the window. He stood beside Tad Shade.

"Were you worried about me? How sweet." Ember's voice was flat and bored.

"No, I just want you to die and to stay dead. Did you know Mr. Shade had a medical examiner enter the room and check on you a few hours ago, right after your death. He said you were good and dead. This time no one did anything with your dead body. You were examined every few hours, and, sure enough, eventually you were just sleeping. What the hell are you, Ember?"

"I think you've been watching too many shows on TV. That isn't how things work." Ember wasn't sure how to play this off. They figured they'd do something like this eventually, but this was faster than expected.

Mr. Shade gave Ember the same slick smile. It made them feel dirty. "I'm very good at doing research, you know. You can ask your mother. When you arrived I was informed that your name was Ember. It wasn't until later that someone let slip it was Ember Savita. That name, how could I forget such a lovely lady as Sadie Savita, my old Air Magic instructor from University. "

He paused, as if waiting for Ember to react. Maybe leap up and deny it was possible. Exclaim there was no way this man of sixty could've ever been taught by their young, beautiful, nice mother. But no, Ember had heard enough of the story to know the truth. So, they just stared at Tad Shade, waiting for them to continue.

His face tightened before he said, "Do you think your mother was my instructor? From the descriptions I got from a kid named Simon, it sounds like the same person."

Ember shrugged. "It could also be my grandma or my great aunt. So many people with that name, it's really hard to tell."

"I think I know what you are, Ember Savita. I have a way to test it."

"What do you think I am?"

"Oh, I'm not telling, but I left a big orange spider in that room to test my theory. If I'm right, we may finally have found a way to rid ourselves of you."

Ember's gut action was to jerk and look around. They tensed their muscles and continued to keep a blank face. It took a moment to relax and think through just how dumb Tad Shade was. Even Felix knew the spider killed a phoenix, but not to true death.

"You think I'm a phoenix? So, if that, what, camel spider bites me and I die, you'll have proven that I'm a shifter animal that's gone extinct. But then what? I burst into Everfire and consume this house and burn the city down. Great plan!"

His smile turned mocking. "Well, if you are a phoenix, you aren't very smart, are you? Everfire morphs into regular fire under a void bubble, then anyone with fire magic can—poof," he snapped his fingers, "snuff it out."

"You've tested this little theory of yours, I take it?"

"Of course, I have, you moronic brat!" he bellowed. His face was contorted in fury, eyes narrowed and mouth small and tight. "Why does everyone question me? I'm a genius!"

Ember rubbed their eyes. "Sorry, didn't realize I basked in the aura of someone so superior. So, the plan is, wait for the spider to dispatch me, and then ..."

"Collect the fire, of course. How else are we going to win this fight? Now, that's enough of this discussion. We'll be back tomorrow morning. I don't care to watch you die. The floor, ceiling, and walls are covered in moonstone paint, so if there's an issue, which I'm not planning on, someone will get me. Good night, spider bait. I await the call that the room is ablaze in fire, and I'm needed to come and collect my bounty."

Terror gripped Ember. They knew they'd survive the bite, they already had, but their phobia of the large, scorpion-like orange beasts was real. They didn't want to spend the next several hours with the creature, especially dead. Who knew what that creature did after it killed its prey.

Ember leapt up and began to pace their room. It wasn't that big, but they needed to move. The orange creature was somewhere, and they had to survive it. Maybe they could burn it. If no one was coming for hours, it may just be their best plan.

On their fourth circuit of the room, they saw it, a glass box under a small table with rocks and dirt. The creature nested in the center. Now that they knew where it was, all they had to do was avoid it. Sitting back on the bed, they watched as it hung, ignoring them, swaying in whatever air currents apparently existed in the room.

They grabbed a folded up blanket from the foot of the bed, ready to sit and wait out the night. They were young, they could go a night without sleep. As the blanket draped over their legs, they felt it, a second orange beast, just as it landed on their leg and scurried to their hand. As quickly as Ember jerked their hand away, the spider was faster. Their whole body trembled as they saw the creature that had bitten them splat on the window across the room with a meaty crunch.

Head dizzy and stomach churning with bile and nausea, Ember lay down and waited to die.

Chapter 34 - The Healing Touch

Daisy

Daisy hurt. The healer had come in to sedate her after she woke up on Thursday, but they'd told her there wasn't anything they could do to help her until the critical cases were healed. She wanted the critical cases cared for. Of course she did. She just wished it hadn't taken days to get to her.

Part of her felt she deserved the pain. As the TV played in the background, she focused on the news. The *World Wizard Network* showed updates of local campaigns under Infinite WISDOM's platform. The newscasters were all smiles and positive feel-good anecdotes. When she switched to the human stations, the news recorded missing people, deaths, and the overcrowding in the hospitals. Anger boiled in Daisy's belly at how different the stories were.

If only I'd listened to Ember and Felix. They were her friends, were smart, and had never led her wrong. Why did she think they'd dislike an organization only because it was represented by Ambrose and Cress? Even her parents didn't seem to like Infinite WISDOM. Despite it all, Daisy kept pushing. She could've done research at any time over the last several weeks, but no, she blindly followed.

I never do that! Why was I so caught up in it all? Such an imbecile? I bet Ember hates me for being so dumb; it's why they haven't visited or called. They probably figure I have new friends to support me.

Daisy knew she wasn't being fair, but she had little distraction from the pain, and she was lonely and just plain bored.

The doctors kept her medicated, but the pain kept breaking through the drugs. When that happened, she had a lot of time to think about her actions since Infinite WISDOM came into her life.

The human doctors had come in and offered their help. She'd heard her parents speaking in low voices. Waking up, she knew they'd accepted the offer because there were casts on every limb. Daisy couldn't bend either leg or arm. It was annoying but helped her to not move. She was scheduled for her first round of healing spells tomorrow morning.

When the medical professionals had first given her the rundown of injuries, it had included more broken bones than she wanted to think about. *Can someone survive so much trauma?* One of her ribs had even punctured a lung, but that had been healed right away. Apparently internal injuries were considered critical.

At first she wanted to freak, but over the minutes, hours, and days, she'd become desensitized to being in the hospital. She was so bored, and she couldn't even read a book, because her fingers couldn't hold anything.

Her parents had offered to read to her, but it just wasn't the same. Not to mention, it made her feel even more helpless. Daisy really wanted Ember to visit, but their phone had gone straight to voicemail when her parents had tried calling. If she couldn't get a hold of them today, Daisy would break down and try first Felix, and then Ember's parents. She didn't want to worry either party, however, she was getting lonely, and missed her friend. *Ember can't really hate me, can they?*

A nurse came in. "Who's ready for lunch?"

Daisy groaned at how chipper the woman was. "Do I have to drink it again?"

"Unless you can feed yourself, a chocolate protein smoothie is what you get. Come on, it's your favorite flavor. I'll get this set up so you can just turn your head and sip at your leisure."

She wanted to scream: *All I've had is leisure!* If they'd spent a bit of time just fixing the bones in one of her arms, she could feed herself, then they'd bring her real food, but her arm wasn't considered critical. When her parents came, they brought real food and fed her, but the nurses didn't have time for that. They were lovely people but busy. And as much as she loved chocolate, she would give almost anything for something savory and some coffee.

Gods above! I miss coffee.

The rooms were filling fast, and Daisy feared she knew why. She couldn't turn a blind eye to what was going on anymore.

A soft knock came at her door. She slowly rolled her head to see who might be visiting. She couldn't imagine anyone but her parents, but they didn't knock. She saw Felix, and a lightness filled her. He wasn't Ember, but he was still a friend. It occurred to her that she should've called him sooner.

He was with an older woman with wavy brown hair. She wore a dark purple dress and off-white shawl. Her hair was pinned back and on one side a yellow flower, that perfectly complimented her outfit, was in her hair. She looked amazing. Daisy wished she could be as put together and elegant as this person. Considering how well Felix dressed, she figured it must be some relative of his.

Wishing she didn't look so bad, but excited to finally see someone, she forced herself to give at least a semblance of a smile. "Hiya, Felix, come in. Is this a relative of yours?"

The two entered the room, and the woman checked the hallway before shutting the door. Felix came up and his hand hovered over her shoulder. "Gods above and below, Daisy! Why hasn't anyone done anything for you?"

"I'm not in critical condition. They're helping those people first. They did the insides but are leaving the bones until later. I just want to be able to bend one arm, so I can eat solid foods again. I think I'd be okay if I could do that." She was whining, but she couldn't help it. "Or drink coffee. I may give up a magical proficiency for coffee."

Felix laughed. "I brought you a coffee. Wouldn't come without it. But let's do this first." He waved at his friend.

The woman came up beside the bed. "Hi. My name is Monte. In a previous life, I was a healer. If you'll let me, I'd like to mend some bones, maybe get you to a point where you can move your arms ... both of them. I don't know how bad you are, but I'm guessing I can improve matters."

Excitement flashed through Daisy, before reality crashed in. "Wait, why would you come to help me? There are so many other people who need help. Who am I?"

The woman, Monte, smiled. "You are a person who shouldn't be here. From what we read, you were heading home from a coffee shop when you were attacked by strangers. Also ... Well, I guess I'm Ember's aunt. Aunt-in-law? Something like that. I don't usually work in healing, but I'd like to do this for you. From what I understand, you're practically family."

For a moment Daisy gazed over the woman's shoulder, expecting Ember to pop out, but her friend wasn't there. She'd have to figure that out later. Her pain was too overwhelming to focus on much more than the conversation. *What had she said? Strangers?*

"They weren't all strangers." She turned to Felix. "Cress. He's the one who stopped me. He brought the other two who grabbed me and—gods above! Why was I so blind?"

Felix sandwiched her fingers between his hands, maybe the only part of her not broken. "You always want to see the best in people. It's what we all love in you, Daisy. You weren't blind, you were just seeing the good in what they said. We all love the idea of magic users supporting each other. But when you step back and hear their whole message, it gets dark ... and dangerous." He smiled. "Now, will you let Monte help you?"

Tears burned Daisy's cheeks. "I didn't want to learn this lesson this way. Gods above, it hurts."

Monte came over and placed a hand on her forehead. Coolness washed through her. Monte whistled. "You are a mess, girl."

Daisy felt a push of magic. It had an icy flavor she'd never tasted before. She closed her eyes, and let the cool waves flow like lying in the ocean as the tide came in. The waves crashed, water knocking through Daisy over and over. For a few moments she forgot to breathe. She was so lost in her imagination that she feared she'd drown.

A soft voice spoke to her. "Breathe, Daisy. I'd hate to fix you up, only to have you suffocate."

A final shiver ran through Daisy from head to toe, and then she realized the background of pain she'd been feeling since she woke was gone. "What did you do to me?"

Monte smiled. "I fixed you, like I promised."

"I was told it would take two or three sessions with a healer to fix all my broken bones, but I'm not hurting. So, what did you do?"

The woman rubbed her face. "I don't know what they're teaching the medical witches, or if who they have working here is just that low in power, but all I did was fix you up, friend of my nibling. Felix, we need to get these casts off her. Keeping her from moving at this point will do harm."

"Do we let the medical staff know what we did?" He looked concerned, then started towards the door.

"Wait," Monte said as Felix reached the door. "I know a nurse who works here. Do you know Daisy's parents' number?"

Daisy listened as they each made their calls. Her mind reeled as she realized the wonder of movement and living a pain-free life were within moments of being hers again. Her cheeks hurt from smiling, and she couldn't wait to be able to move around.

It took about a quarter-hour for the nurse to show up. She hugged Monte and, after checking Daisy over, cut away the casts. "I didn't know you were a healer, Monte. You did all this?"

Once she was free, Felix handed Daisy a coffee. As the other two spoke, he whispered, "Enjoy."

Her first sip tasted of hopes and dreams.

Monte replied to the nurse, "Yes. I haven't practiced healing in a while; I'm busy doing other things. I may get back into the business, though. Three shots to heal this dear girl! It's a travesty."

The nurse left to get Daisy's discharge paperwork started. Her parents showed up soon after and engulfed her in a hug.

Once they were sure all her injuries were healed, they hugged Felix as well. "Thank you for bringing your friend."

He smiled. "If I'd known yesterday, I would've brought her then. Monte Doyle, these are Daisy's parents, Winnie and Santos Autumn."

"It's a pleasure to meet you both."

Daisy's mom helped her to stand. Her legs were a bit wobbly but getting out of bed felt divine. Mom asked Monte, "I don't mean to sound ungrateful, but why help Daisy when there are so many people who need healing?"

Monte laughed. "You sound just like your daughter. I'm Ember's aunt. I heard their best friend needed help, so I came as quickly as I could. Now, let's get out of here before someone else comes to ask the same thing."

As they walked to the elevator, Daisy asked, "Where's Ember?"

Felix stiffened. "It's a long story. I can't tell you here. Not in the hospital."

Worry slammed into Daisy as she imagined the worst. Was Ember mad at her? They wanted Daisy healed, but they weren't ready to talk? Or worse, did Infinite WISDOM get to them? Was that why her best friend wasn't there, and Monte was at the hospital? A lump formed in Daisy's throat. The possible reasons why Ember wasn't there terrified her.

Then she remembered something else she wanted to tell Felix about that awful group. She reached for his arm to hold him back. He tilted his head. "What's up?"

"Before I got attacked. I had been out having coffee—well, hot chocolate—with Simon. He's the one providing the 'evidence' for Infinite WISDOM. Everything about their website is a sham."

Felix looked at her, brows knit, as if in thought. When they all filed into the elevator, Daisy realized Monte, too, seemed to be considering her words.

Chapter 35 - Midnight Visitors

Ember

Ember's body felt heavy with fatigue. *Maybe I woke up before the healing finished.* They'd woken up feeling tired and sore. Rising from the ashes healed all wounds but dying each day ... each night ... Time lost all meaning in a windowless cell. Although the moonstone kept their body from changing, it also seemed to mess up part of the recuperative properties of the phoenix.

Their injuries were mended, but Ember didn't feel like a million bucks. Maybe five ninety-five. After their first death with the moonstone, they'd woken up feeling good. Possibly, it was the fact that they were trying to kill them every day. There was only so much the body could take.

They rolled to their back, then pushed to sitting. The spider in its box still sat in the corner. Ember recoiled with a shudder, wanting to move as far away from the creature as they could. Checking the window and the floor, they saw the second spider where they'd thrown it—a splat of orange against the seam where the wall and floor met. They weren't about to check if the second beast was dead or alive.

Every instinct told Ember to create tiny balls of fire within their enemy, to kill them now before they had a chance to attack again, but if they did that, there was a small chance someone in this organization would figure out what Ember was. They needed to oust the spiders without killing them.

What do you think, Dad? Let the spider live? Use fire? Can you hear me? When will you save me? Burn this house down, Dad. If anyone can do it, it's you. But try to save the blameless. Gods above, they were asking for so much from someone who obviously couldn't hear them.

A creaking alerted them that someone had opened the lock. They closed their eyes, hoping their thick blanket hid that they'd woken up.

"Be careful," a low, gruff voice came from the hallway.

"We were told to wait three to four hours and check if the prisoner appeared dead. Every night between midnight and three in the morning, this kid has had no pulse, hasn't been breathing, nothing. If I didn't know better, I'd say we had a vampire. Why do I have to be so careful of a dead teen? It's two in the morning for crying out loud." The second man had a low voice, but higher than his partner's.

The gruff voice grunted. "So, you want me to leave the door open?"

"Yeah but stay on guard."

Ember's mind felt like Jell-o, but their fear of the spiders cleared some of the cotton away. If the door was open, they should be able to move their enemy away. Keeping their eyes closed, they pushed their magic out, trying to find the spiders.

The sound of the footsteps approaching distracted them, but they only had a moment to rid their cell of the camel spiders and they had to take advantage. They found the devil in the box first. Holding themself as still as they could, they used their spatial magic to move the spider ... anywhere that wasn't in their cell.

A warm hand landed on their neck. "There's a pulse." The hand moved down to their chest. "Yeah, their heart is beating."

"Get out. We ain't supposed to be in there if the prisoner ain't dead."

"We're supposed to find the spiders. See if they did their job and bit them."

The man at the door snarled. "Is that one of them on the floor, over there under the window?"

Ember heard footsteps walk away. "Gods above, this one's dead. It looks like it was thrown against the window. Wonder if it was out of fear or pain." Footsteps. The blanket was pulled away. "I don't see a bite, but it may not leave a mark." Footsteps, the door shut, and a click of the lock.

They cracked their eyes and tried to look out the window. The hallway was dark and there was a small light left on in their prison room. There was no way to see out of the room. With a sigh, Ember gave up. They wanted to sleep, but it was too cold without the blanket, and they felt too exposed. They reached for the flipped blanket, pulled it up, and rolled over to their side, giving their back to the window. If they didn't get sleep, they wouldn't be able to battle their enemy tomorrow.

Chapter 36 - Decision Made

Felix

Felix sat in Ember's family's living room. He contemplated the past week. It started so innocently with a trip to the woods with friends. Who would've expected it would end with Ember kidnapped?

Guilt had been a constant companion since he'd realized Ember hadn't returned from the cave. How could they have been so dumb as to separate in the woods? That was the biggest horror movie cliché ever.

Mrs. Savita came into the living room. She stood tall and was well-dressed in an eggplant pant suit with a white button-down. Despite the outfit looking like she was ready to face the world, her eyes were puffy and tired-looking. *I wonder if she's slept at all. I haven't.* "Monte will be here in a few minutes. We're going to discuss our plans for this afternoon over tacos, which she's bringing."

He nodded. "Sounds good. I can't imagine what they're doing with Ember. It frustrates me. I want to storm the castle, so to speak."

"Trust me, you aren't the only one." The fierce determination matched his own feelings. "I'd love to pull her out, but I can't use my magic if I don't know where to connect. I either need a visual or a strong sense of the person. Ember is ... blocked. I can't quite explain it."

The front door opened, and Monte walked in with Vi. Mrs. Savita leapt up with a gasp, then yelled for her husband. She ran to Vi and engulfed her in a hug. "You're back! Tell us what happened. Did you find any clues about Ember?"

Vi forced a smile, then pulled back as Mr. Savita pounded out from his office. "Nuri! What did the others tell you? Did they see the cretins take my child and do nothing about it? Tell me heads rolled after you were done with them."

Her face hardened. "They saw. They said they thought Ember went willingly, though they admitted after a bit of persuasion that Ember may have been unconscious. I questioned them, 'how was that willing?' They didn't have a good answer. They just said, 'the way of witches confused them.' Apparently Ember was tossed into the trunk of a car and driven off."

A shiver ran down Felix's back. They'd put Ember in the trunk of a car. He thought about their two-day journey to the cave. "How did they get out of the woods with Ember? It took us two days of heavy traveling to get to the cave."

"According to the watchers, they created a piece of earth that acted like a platform. It zoomed them through the trees. The group has been back and forth enough that they have a bit of a path."

Felix's confusion gave way to anger. "We were stopped over and over, challenged, attacked, and questioned, and they let these jerks through. They see the goons take off with a known phoenix, and they still do nothing? Who are these watchers and what exactly is their function?"

Vi smiled at him. "Funny, you sound just like me when I reached the center of the phoenix compound. The difference: I knew a lot of the people there from my childhood. There haven't been many younglings over the last two hundred years. We're long-lived beings. We know if we're not careful we could overpopulate. But, as it goes, reproduction isn't easy within the phoenix community. Ember is one of four new phoenixes in the world to replace the two dozen that died in the last war. In all honesty, there are still over a hundred phoenixes living, most in the compound, but they like their anonymity."

Mr. Savita growled. "I'm going to fly back to Serafina Landing and tear it down, brick by brick. Those birds do not know what they've done, letting my child be captured by those creeps."

"Serafina Landing?" Felix asked.

Rubbing his face, Mr. Savita sat down at the table. "The name of the phoenix stronghold. It's been around for millennia. It's the place I was exiled from when we decided to help preserve the balance between the magic users and humans and asked the shifters to help. The elders thought getting in the mix exposed us too much. When we agreed to help propagate the myth that phoenixes had gone extinct, they downgraded the banishment to shunning. I don't really care what name they put on it. They ignored the larger picture. Magic users who could annihilate so many other beings wouldn't stop at witches and humans. They had to be stopped. I was not going to stymie my actions due to their short-sightedness."

"What happens if you expose phoenixes to the world?" Felix sat down after grabbing a few tacos, as did the rest of the adults. He wasn't sure if he could eat after everything he'd heard, but not eating would affect his ability to use magic. He needed all his strength to help save Ember.

Vi bit into her taco and shut her eyes in enjoyment. Taking a sip of soda, she leaned back. "If the world learns that phoenixes aren't extinct, then humans and witches will have to face the fact that they're living in a more dangerous time than they imagined. They will have to acknowledge there is a creature with stronger magical ability than theirs, even if only in fire. Then there is our immortality. Beyond that, I don't think it matters. The phoenix elders believe the mortals will try to hunt us, but besides that being foolish, there isn't much they can do if they find us. We're immortal. Our death, while annoying, isn't permanent."

Mr. Savita laughed. "And if they do manage to figure out how to trigger our final death, more danger to them, right? Only the phoenixes know how to control our Everfire."

Flabbergasted at the idea that people would hunt phoenixes, Felix leaned forward, resting on his elbows. "If the phoenixes aren't extinct, does that mean the other shifters people thought were gone—wolves, panthers, dragons, bears, and hyenas—are still somewhere in the world, too?"

Vi's eyes narrowed. "You are a bit too smart. Has anyone told you that?"

"Yes. Now answer my question." Felix smiled at her, hoping his quick response would work.

"Shifter dragons have never been extinct; there just aren't many of them. If we can get Ember back, maybe I'll introduce you to a family I know. The wolves and panthers are still out there causing havoc and mayhem as always. The bears ... I hadn't heard they'd gone extinct. We should ask the bears if they knew. But, unfortunately, the hyenas are gone. I believe they were the only race of shifters to actually not walk away from the last war."

"I could see a dragon? A real dragon? Is it safe?" Felix's arms and legs were beginning to feel numb just imagining standing in front of such a majestic beast.

"Not if you gape at them like that, but the family I know are rather nice. They're old-fashioned, and if you bring a gift, they're more likely to take kindly to you."

"What kind of gift?" Felix wanted to get out a pad of paper and take notes.

Mr. Savita smirked. "A maiden for sacrifice is always a nice present."

Felix felt his jaw drop.

All the adults laughed, and Monte patted his shoulder. "From what I remember, a book or wine works well."

Mr. Savita finished his plate of tacos. "Okay, I needed that break, thanks for that."

Monte stood to get more. "Vi, I forgot to ask. Did you go into the cave? Did you see the destruction? Did you ask the other phoenixes if they have a theory?"

"Gods above, the damn cave. Yes, I talked with some old friends—" she turned to Mr. Savita, "—Pat and Lesly Luz. They said that they've seen a bit of what's been going on. It appears that this group has been excavating some of the moonstone, not a lot, but enough to be noticed. They think they're trying to pull some of the Everfire out. The elders disagree. They think there's another reason for the desire for the stone."

A buzzing sound echoed in the dining room. Monte pulled out her phone and checked the display. She started scrolling and reading what looked like a long text.

Mr. Savita snarled. "On my earlier flight I thought I felt Ember at that mansion where Shade is holed up. Idiots! The elders. Shade. All of them! We need to focus on Ember first and getting them out, then we can determine their asinine plan with moonstone. Now, Nuri, like I said, I think I know where Ember is, but when I went to reach them, I couldn't. If they're not awake, that could be the reason. Why don't we do a fly-over and both try to call? If we can tell them that we don't care if they shift, maybe they can save themself."

Felix's jaw dropped. "You're willing to let Ember expose the phoenixes?"

Mrs. Savita's face hardened. "I, for one, am glad. We've played their game for centuries and where has it gotten us? Let's save our child!"

Monte looked up from her phone. "It's confirmation from the researchers we asked to search for Ember. She's at the Wells's estate."

Hope and fear mingled within Felix. He knew that estate. It was large, well secured, and getting Ember out wouldn't be easy. But he knew the people he stood with were formidable.

Mr. Savita's jaw clenched, and he leaned forward, fire glowing in his eyes. "At this point, secrecy and hiding may be too late. I'm pretty sure the group is trying to kill Ember. When they can't, what other conclusion will they come to? If they do succeed, not only will they create Everfire—a dead giveaway—I'll destroy them all ... in my bird form. Come on, Nuri, we have my child to rescue."

Chapter 37 - A Long Distance Call

Ember

Ember woke up feeling better. They weren't sure how long they'd been in their cell. The light was on, but it was often on, so they didn't know what time of day it was. All they knew was, eventually, someone would try to kill them again. *Another day, another death.*

Sighing, they headed to the bathroom, then paced their cell. After days of captivity, they needed to move ...

walk, run—gods above—fly! Not trusting their jailors, Ember searched through everything in the room to make sure there weren't any surprises this time. They didn't find anything.

By the door, a small table held a tray of food: A banana, a bag of beef jerky, and a bag of chips. When they squeezed the two bags, there weren't any holes, so nothing had been poked in. It was as close to safe as they could detect. Starving and knowing they needed energy to fight, they decided to eat.

They carried the tray to the bed and opened the protein first. It took time to chew through each piece, but even after the bag lay empty on the tray, Ember's belly grumbled and cramped, demanding more. It hadn't been enough. Next, they ate the chips. They didn't trust the banana and left it untouched.

Ember headed into the bathroom and cupped their hands to get water from the sink. They doubted they'd poison everyone to get to them.

Then they went back to sitting on the bed.

There has to be a way out. Something I'm missing.

Hunger bit back at their center. The food helped some, but also mocked Ember in its sparseness. Feeling dizzy from lack of calories, they flopped down on their back with their arm over their eyes. They craved a dark room and a few hours of peace.

Dad, come and save me. Burn this place down! They started up their daily mental call. They needed someone to talk to, and he'd become their person of choice.

'Ember! You heard me?'

Sitting up, Ember searched the room to see if anyone was around, not that they could hear in their head. *'Dad? Is that really you?'*

'Thank all the gods, above and below. You're still alive.'

Ember snorted. *'Not for lack of them trying to kill me. Every day and night, I think. They're trying to figure out what I am. What day is it?'*

'Saturday.'

'So this is my fourth day. I have to get out before they do something more extreme.'

Ember sat and waited for Dad to respond. They looked around the room, half expecting their dad to appear, but knew that wasn't possible.

'Dad! Are you still there? Hello? Please don't leave me.' Fear wracked them. The moment of connection released hope, and now they were scared of being alone.

Their breath came in and out in a ragged tempo. They gulped in a large amount of air and held it, hoping to even out their system. Then they closed their eyes and focused up to the sky. *'Dad, please hear me. Don't leave me here.'*

'We're trying, hon.' Aunt Nuri's voice rang clearly into Ember's head, and they let out a small gasp of relief. *'Tell me you can hear me.'* Aunt Nuri kept repeating her words.

'Aunt Nuri! Thank the gods above. Help me.' They felt like they could hug the words in their head. Warmth surged from their gut.

'Ember. Okay, I don't know how long you'll hear me. Use your fire. Escape. Don't stay. We'll work to get you out as well.'

'Give away our secret?'

Nothing came back to them. They kept trying to reach out to Aunt Nuri or their dad, but they didn't hear anything else. *Use my fire? Should I fly out? I wish I'd gotten just a bit more information from them.*

They sat up and pulled their knees up to their chest. Resting their forehead on their knees, they tried to reach out with their mind, their magic, anything, but the more they tried to connect with their family, the more they knew they were alone in this cell underground.

Gods, I want to get out of here and fly ... but what if I'm wrong? I can't be the reason phoenixes are outed. My whole life I've been told this is my biggest secret. Do I have the right to out us all?

Chapter 38 - A Dangerous Story

Daisy

Sunday morning, Daisy woke up feeling great. All her injuries were not only healed, but the body memory of them was gone. She'd spent Saturday on the computer doing more research. After weeks of supporting Infinite WISDOM, she knew the organization wasn't what it claimed, but now she needed to know what to do. She'd spoken to her parents, and they seemed happy with her change of heart.

In all her research, she kept coming back to the site that compiled the evidence against Infinite WISDOM: FB Coalition. She'd tried to find out who ran the site, but there wasn't any contact information or a page about the leaders of the group. She did find a place to email for more information, and she'd decided, if she couldn't find anything else today, she'd send that email.

Biting her lip, she thought she'd start with Felix. At the hospital the day before, Felix said he'd explain later, but she'd been whisked away by her parents before he or his friend, Ember's Aunt Monte, could explain. Last night, her parents wanted to celebrate with a nice dinner.

Now she needed to get a hold of Felix and get answers. She needed to find out why her best friend wasn't answering her calls. She had several questions for Felix, and though she'd never called him, she had his number and decided it was time to use it.

Her finger hovered over his name for a few seconds before she finally went ahead and let the phone dial his number. She hoped it wasn't too early. She was up, so she hoped he would be too.

"Hello? Daisy? Is that you?" He sounded distracted, but not unhappy to hear from her. She berated herself for thinking he would be. He was her friend as well as

Ember's boyfriend. Why did she always assume he wasn't?

"Hi, Felix. Yeah, it's me."

"Everything okay? Did your healing Friday get everything?" His focus seemed to now be on her. Maybe he'd been finishing up something on the computer or playing a game with his family. Maybe he was busy right now. That said, he sounded really concerned, like maybe she was calling because she needed to head back to the hospital.

"Yeah, everything's great. That isn't why I was calling. I had a few things I wanted to talk with you about, if you have a few minutes. Or are you busy?"

"Um, sure. Yes. I can talk. What's up?"

She bit her lip. He sounded distracted again, but this was too important to her. "Well, you know I had been a supporter of Infinite WISDOM—" She took a breath. She felt foolish even saying that, especially to a friend who supported her without supporting the movement. All her friends had opposed the organization. They'd been nice to her despite her gung-ho following of the gang that did awful things. "—anyway, I've been doing a lot of research into how to fight them. There's a lot out there, but I feel like a leaf in the wind. I know that you've been against them from the start. Do you ... I dunno, do you know a place I can get more direction? I mean, I found an amazing website, but I don't know how to find the creators. They don't have any contact information." She bit her lip again. "Sorry if this sounds silly."

She heard him sigh. "No, not silly. I'm glad you've come to this conclusion, and I'd be happy to help you figure out how to fight the group, if that's what you're looking for. I just ... Daisy, is that really what you want? This is a real one-eighty for you."

"Yes, I promise this is what I want. I had come to that conclusion before the hospital—it may be what landed me in there. I had been questioning things with Simon ... I was overheard. I guess I chose the wrong person to speak with."

Anger built in her gut when she remembered how proud Simon had been of fabricating the site and the nonsense the organization used as proof. It made her want to scream.

"Yeah, probably. But Ember and I were out of town. You didn't have a lot of choices. Maybe Tansy and Olivia ... but I don't know if you know them as well as Ember and I do."

"Not yet. Before secondary school I was never in classes with them. Then when Ember moved to town ... well, you know." Daisy took in a deep breath to center herself. "Which brings me to my second, or really my first question. Why is Ember avoiding me? Did I do something to make them mad at me?"

The line got really quiet. "They're not avoiding you. Look, can I put you on mute for a few minutes? This is a bigger question than I can answer on my own."

Daisy's heart dropped into her gut. "Yeah, that's fine." Though Felix said Ember wasn't avoiding her, Daisy wondered. Was Felix spending time with Ember now?

Daisy sat on the couch as she waited for the news that told her she'd done something to lose her best friend. She knew she'd been acting the fool, but she wasn't sure which thing had been the last straw for Ember. A tear ran down her cheek imagining school without her friend by her side. Walking the halls, making jokes, being goofy, movie nights, everything. She'd do anything to fix what she'd broken.

The few minutes turned into almost fifteen. Daisy tried to swallow past a lump in her throat, but her mouth was dry and her hands trembled. She fought to keep herself from crying. She had to know what she'd done so she could fix it. Clamping her jaw, she decided she was a warrior and would fight to get her friend back.

When the sound returned to the line, her breath hitched. "Sorry that took so long, Daisy, I had to talk to a few people. It's a rather tense day where I am. Look, if you're free, can I come and pick you up? This would be easier to explain in person."

"Yeah, of course." Her hand shook as she hung up and got her coat on.

What is so bad that he has to tell me in person? And why did he have to talk to several people? Daisy's mind swirled with confusion.

Twenty minutes later, Daisy sat in the front seat of Felix's Toyota Camry. They headed towards the rich part of town. He started telling a story she couldn't quite understand, about phoenixes, kidnappings, and an organization so much worse than she'd thought could exist.

"Wait, Ember is a phoenix?"

Felix looked pained. "Yes."

"And they told you, but not me? Their best friend for three years."

"It isn't that they told me. I figured it out." Felix navigated through traffic, though he stayed calm, his face was tight, and his hands were white from grasping the steering wheel.

I'm Ember's best friend. Why didn't they trust me?

Daisy shook her head, and there was a bite to her tone. "When? How? How did you determine Ember was the mythical extinct phoenix? I mean, I knew you were obsessed, but that is quite a leap."

"The camping trip we went on for school."

Daisy's jaw dropped and her eyes widened. "The fire. The one that burned the tent down. The spider ... that orange monstrosity. Gods, Felix. Ember died that day, didn't they?"

He just nodded.

"How could I have left the park not know—" She glared at Felix. "It was you, wasn't it? You messed with my mind."

Again, he nodded.

Gods above! These are my friends and none of them trust me. Daisy's fists were clenched so tight, her nails bit into her palms. *How could Felix do that to me?* Her eyes burned with the tears she refused to shed. "Felix! Say something. You could get into a lot of trouble if I report this."

He pulled his car over and parked. She saw his whole body tremble and his face had lost all its color. "I know. And I hope you don't, but I wouldn't blame you if you did. I just ... Daisy, I panicked." Still gripping the steering wheel, he finally faced her, his eyes wide and full of fear. "Ember had just burned to ash. I knew it had to remain a secret. You were freaking out. I just ... I didn't know what to do. I'm so sorry."

"Are you?" Daisy snapped out.

He took a slow breath. "Yes. I truly am. Knowing you and Ember and your friendship ... I should've just waited, let you calm down."

Daisy scoffed. "Yes, you should've. I know how to keep a secret, believe it or not."

He nodded, just watching her. It looked like he wanted to say something, his mouth opening then shutting, but he just watched her, looking miserable.

Daisy tried to keep her tears from Felix. Then she made a disgruntled noise. "I am so mad at you, but we have such bigger issues. Ember is being held prisoner?"

"Yes."

"By these same monsters?"

"Yes."

She sniffled, wiping away her tears. "Then drive. We will figure this out later."

"I'm really sorry, Daisy. I wish I could take it back," he whispered, then pulled back into traffic. It didn't take long to get near a mansion with other cars parked along the street. Once the car stopped, Felix didn't move to get out. "Look, what's happening with Ember is really important, but so are you. You're a dear friend, and someone I care about. There are things I want to tell you, but can't, but mostly ... I'm sorry for what I did. I hope that one day you'll forgive me."

The anger still burned. He'd violated her mind. Daisy wondered if it'd been the other way around if she'd have done something different. She hadn't been given a chance. "Promise me you'll trust me moving forward and never do anything like that again ... to anyone."

"I do trust you. That's why you're here. And I won't." He slumped. "This is a sensitive mission, but Ember needs you here as much as me and their parents. If they get out ... *when* they get out, it'll mean the world to them to see you, to know you're here for them. It's ... it's important."

Daisy nodded. "I agree and considering what that organization and their cronies ... and Cress ... did to me, there is no telling what they'll do to Ember."

Chapter 39 - Today Is Not A Good Day To Die

Ember

Ember wondered if Tad Shade was trying to kill them with boredom. They'd gone the full morning without seeing or hearing anyone, and they'd only received a banana that morning. Their mind played tricks on them with the monotony of their time and surroundings. They started counting the small tiles on the floor and ceiling. It was all useless. They just needed to escape.

Ember ended up napping a lot, or as much as they could convince their body to rest. They interspersed their awake time trying to reach out to their dad or Aunt Nuri. They hadn't been successful after that one time ... yesterday? It felt like a day had gone by. With the light in the room always on and no windows, time was a bit of a blur.

Every time they nodded off, food appeared on the small table next to the door. Besides the food appearing, they didn't see or hear anyone in or around their cell. Each meal was less than they wanted to eat but all the food was stuff that Ember could tell was not poisoned. They weren't sure if they'd be able to do enough magic to escape, though they figured fire was who they were.

Why don't you just escape? Dad told you to fly away.

But did he? Maybe I was imagining it with wishful thinking. I barely heard anything. And no matter what I've tried, I haven't gotten any more information.

But you can't stay here. They'll figure out a way to end you eventually.

Ember clenched their jaw at their internal battle. *I can't be the cause of revealing phoenixes to the world, not if I'm not certain.*

After they woke up from their last nap, Ember started to pace and noticed a box by the wall perpendicular to the window. It sat on a second table they had also brought in. The box looked like it was made from moonstone. *No wonder the cave appeared to have been looted. They chiseled away to get the stone. But what's in the box?* Despite their curiosity, the last thing brought into the room had been camel spiders, and Ember wasn't in that much of a hurry to learn what new threat their jailers had gifted them.

The amount of moonstone in the box resonated in Ember, making them feel a weird vibration in their chest and gut. A second reason to avoid not only the box, but that side of the room. Everything about it felt off.

Should I try to burn my way out? Would there be anyone else around to help me? Would I have to kill everyone between me and escape? Can I do that much killing?

In the end, Ember decided to wait. They needed more information.

They opened the bottled water that appeared on the tray and drank it down. They fantasized about coffee. Dreamed about almost any source of caffeine. They wouldn't drink freshly made coffee from their captors, but most stores had cans of coffee, soda, or energy drinks. Anything with caffeine right now would be glorious. *Oh! Maybe they planned on killing me by denying me caffeine, the test of what extremes a teenager can really survive.*

Ember laughed at their own thoughts as they finished off the water. Once again, just enough for survival, but not enough to satiate them.

Sliding back on the bed, they debated what to do next. They weren't tired. They'd paced the room enough to know the twelve steps back and forth were getting tedious. They could shower, maybe with their clothes on and sit with wet clothes that weren't as dirty, but that left the room cold. They did have a way to dry their clothes; that wasn't difficult. Dad did say to use fire and to no longer hide. Maybe ...

Decision made, they started to move to the edge of the bed to get up. Just before they stood, a voice stopped them. "And where are you off to?"

Ember relaxed their arms and fell back onto the bed. Gazing at the large window, they saw Tad Shade, Mr. Wells, and Cress. *I wonder where the fire princess, Ambrose, is during all these tests? Is she above it all or does she not know?*

"You know," Ember said with a wry smile. "Errands to run, people to see. If you'd just open the door, I'll be off."

Mr. Wells's face didn't even twitch. "We grow tired of you. It's time we end your stay as our guest."

Ember guffawed. "If this is how you treat guests, I'd hate to see how you treat someone you don't like."

"Do you see that box, Ember Savita?" he went on, ignoring them.

"The one made of moonstone? Of course, I do. There's nothing else in this room. Every time you change something, I notice."

"My daughter and Cress, here, tell me that you're a powerful air witch. In all my research, shifters and witches can't mate, which tells me, if you can wield air magic, you are a witch. I'll be glad to see if this fire is as good with witches as it is with humans." Mr. Well's smile turned predatory. "I wonder, how will you respond to fire?" he asked, a sneer finally changing the smile on his face to something less creepy.

Ember cut their eyes to the moonstone box. Most fire would be smothered in a closed box like that. They could only think of one fire that would survive in a closed container, but how could they transport phoenix death fire? Sighing, they looked back at the trio of men watching them. Cress had a hunger in his eyes. Mr. Wells's had a calculating interest. Mr. Shade's held a gleam of superiority and arrogance.

A cold tranquility took over Ember's body as they waited for what would happen next.

"What, nothing smart to say?" Mr. Wells asked, almost sounding disappointed.

Ember raised an eyebrow. "I'm tired, Mr. Wells. What more do you want me to say? You've all kept me in here for ... how long has it been? Just do what you want to do and let's move on with our day."

Tad Shade reached up with a remote in his hand. A moment later, the top of the moonstone box lifted. The chill in the room dissipated as the heat of the fire filled the small space. Ember gaped as they realized what they faced. Everfire. Though they'd considered it, the idea that this witch had secured it terrified them.

At first, the fire looked like any other. But the presence of a phoenix emanated from it, old and heavy. Ember could almost feel a story coming from it. The life of the phoenix the fire came from wanted to whisper its story to them. The more Ember gazed at the flames, the more they could almost see the shape of the bird, the color of its feathers, the heart of the person who'd lived the life that burned in front of them.

It took an effort for Ember to pull their focus from that life that had been and remember that they were being watched by the enemy.

I can't put this fire out. That isn't an ability I have. Even if I did, I wouldn't want to ... it still has something to give, a story to tell. But if it's free from the cave, it'll consume everything in this room. It may even consume me ... though probably not. They closed their eyes and felt for the fire. The heart of the flame sang into their soul. Ember tried to put it out, but it sounded like the music laughed at them, a cheerful ditty, letting them know that extinguishing the flames was not in the picture, but it would happily entertain them.

They heard a loud crash and their eyes snapped open. The box had fallen to the floor after the fire had destroyed the table.

Ember knew they couldn't put out the fire. They didn't have that power. *Does any phoenix have that power?*

That wasn't the only option available. They held up their hand and felt for the soul of the flame. They moved it towards the wall with the window. When it reached the thick material, they continued to push, feeding the fire into the one non-moonstone part of their cell.

"Gods below, how are they doing that?" Mr. Wells's voice rang out in fear.

"I don't know." Cress's voice was hesitant. "They've never been in any classes for fire magic. They don't have that proficiency. This isn't possible."

"I knew it!" yelled Tad Shade. "They're a phoenix. That's the only answer that makes any sense."

"Don't be an idiot," Mr. Well's snarled. "There hasn't been any indication of ash, they haven't really died, or if they did, there hasn't been any fire and ash that they've risen from. And to top it off, phoenixes are extinct. Add to all that, both Cress and Ambrose have confirmed that Ember has magic. You even said their mother, *your magic teacher,* was a witch. There's no way that person is a phoenix." Mr. Well's glare bounced from Mr. Shade to Ember and back. "I know you want this to be the case, but you can't change facts. You heard the stories and have seen the evidence. They can use air magic. That's probably what they're doing right now. They're the top air witch the school has seen in years. This is probably a manipulation of air waves. Don't be naive."

Ember heard before they saw the cracks in the window. They felt when their magic expanded and knew a hole had melted in the thick glass. They breathed a sigh of relief. They could escape through that hole once they were alone.

The air around them became thick, like they were inside sticky water. The analogy barely made sense to themself, except that's how it felt. The Everfire's song died, and Ember knew they faced regular fire. A shimmering dome sparkled around them. When they gazed at the fire, they knew they could've put it out, but they weren't scared of regular fire, and it still headed towards their enemy.

It took a few moments for Ember to realize the three males had been speaking.

"—do?" Mr. Wells was saying.

"I put up a void bubble. What else could I do to contain the fire that was attacking us? I put it over the witch as well. If they're using air magic, then that will stop them.

They can't use their magic within the bubble, though we can from outside." Tad Shade sounded smug.

Ember thought about expanding the fire to see what the three idiots did. Maybe they'd run off in terror.

"What do we do now? Once your bubble is dropped, it converts back into Everfire. We usually don't release all of it." Mr. Wells's voice sounded strained.

"Cress," Tad Shade snapped out. "Go get your girlfriend. She has fire magic. She can put the flame out, as long as I hold it in the void. Hurry now."

Ember heard the pounding of feet. *Why don't they all just leave? I'm ready for the end of this captivity.*

Mr. Wells turned to the taller man. "My daughter has been kept from all of this since she saw the example made of the one servant. I don't like the idea of her seeing a school mate, an actual witch, being held in captivity. She'll make a fuss." The frustration in Mr. Wells was mirrored in his clenched jaw.

Or maybe cheer you on? We've never gotten along, bucko.

With a wave of his hand, Mr. Shade said breezily, "If she's that obnoxious, have the boy alter her memories."

Ember balked at that. Had they been playing around in Ambrose's mind all along?

"If Cress is found doing that, he'll get arrested," Mr. Wells hissed out.

That's what you're worried about? Not that your daughter's mind is getting messed with? Wow, parent of the year, you are not.

"He's underage; he'll only get a slap on the wrist. You don't have to worry about messing with another person's mind until you've graduated secondary school. That's why we're using him." The condescension dripped from Tad Shade's voice, as if he spoke to a toddler.

Maybe Cress will get caught and go to juvie. Like I could be so lucky.

"I know that," snapped Mr. Wells. "I just don't like it when it's my daughter's mind you're talking about altering."

There it is ... he does care about Ambrose ... a little, maybe. So much love in this home.

The sound of the elevator door stopped the two of them from talking. Mr. Wells's face contorted into something ... friendly? "Ambrose, sweetie, we have a request. Can you put out that fire?"

Ember saw Ambrose take in the tableau. Her jaw started to drop before she snapped it shut. "Father, that's Ember in there. They're a witch. Why is there a witch in the holding cell?"

"Ambrose! Just put out the fire. You can ask questions later."

She flicked her hand and the fire dissipated some. Face tightening, she spun to glare at the offending heat source. She put out her hand and Ember felt the push of power that flowed out of Ambrose until the fire finally went out. Everfire, even in plain fire form, was aggressive.

I wonder if I could've put it out more easily.

Tad Shade flicked his hand. "Lovely." The void bubble released, and Ember sighed. The stickiness that felt like swimming in air evaporated, and they slumped.

Ember debated what to do next—*could Ambrose be an ally?*—when they felt a rattling in the building around them.

Tad Shade looked at Mr. Wells. "Something's happening. The guards won't be available for another thirty minutes. We need to see who's attacking us." He faced Cress. "You and the girl need to make sure the ... guest doesn't leave this room. We'll send some guards to move them to a more secure location as soon as we can."

Ambrose's face contorted with fury. "But they're a classmate. Why are you locking up a witch?"

Cress placed his hands on Ambrose's upper arms. "We'll do what you ask of us, Mr. Shade."

As the two older men darted off, Ember stood. They knew it was the beginning of the end. *Now's my chance!* "Ambrose, be wary of asking questions. Your dad and Mr. Shade are planning on having Cress play with your memories. He may have done it already in the past." Ember didn't think she'd believe them, but any warning was better than nothing. "I don't know about you, but he's the last person I'd want in my mind."

Cress glared. "Don't listen to the human-lover. They're just trying to get us to fight."

Ambrose's right hand lifted to touch her forehead. She watched Ember as she said, "I trust you." Then she shifted to look at her partner, face hard. "Cress."

Ember opened their mouth to say more, when a buzzing started in her head.

'Ember! Can you hear us?'

'Dad?'

'Gods above, it's about time.'

'What's happening?'

'We're here. Be ready to fly.'

Chapter 40 – Rescue

Felix

Felix stood outside his car with Daisy. Four other vehicles filled with people from FB Coalition were parked outside the gate of the Wells's mansion, including Ember's mom. Though there were other mansions nearby, every estate's home was a good quarter to half-mile back behind a gate. There was a sense of privacy to this mission.

The plan was to get in and try to help the innocent bystanders exit in case fire consumed the house while extracting Ember. Felix wasn't sure if that would be possible. Fire was destructive, after all.

Mr. Savita and Vi were planning on rescuing Ember in bird form; there was no way of hiding who they were. He remembered the power of the mind magic attached to when they turned invisible, that he knew it would be enough to cast enough doubt to hide their return, however, the issue was technology. If anyone recorded any part of the rescue, the truth would come out regardless of the suggestion that phoenixes were extinct contained in their invisibility. The twin birds decided they would embrace their truth.

Words appeared, in fire, on the far side of the gate, thanks to Mr. Savita. *It's time. Everyone be ready'.*

Daisy gasped. "Did ... how ... what?"

Fire and smoke erupted in different areas of the gate, cutting off her words, and then the whole thing fell to the ground with a crash, followed by a grand exodus of all the birds within the vicinity. There was rustling from the scurrying of ground animals, squirrels and rabbits and the like. The site and sound of all the wildlife fleeing caused half the group to jump.

The volunteers moved towards the house. Felix stayed by Daisy's side, just behind his parents. It didn't take long to reach the front door.

Between the fallen gate and the front door of Ambrose's palatial mansion was an expanse of manicured gardens, pathways, hedges, and a driveway. Because of the fallen wrought iron gate, they couldn't just drive the cars, they had to go on foot.

The phoenixes appeared above the roof, white fire in the form of flame and feathers. Fire shot from their mouths and burned an opening through the roof. They disappeared into the house. Screams arose from within.

Felix and Daisy were in the middle of the pack, heading along the driveway, watchful of any movement. Fire popping and crackling covered any softer sounds that may have come from around them.

"Come on!" Felix said. "We need to move."

The group, almost fifteen strong, didn't waste time getting to the large house. Felix had spent time in his youth here, when he'd been friends with Ambrose. He wasn't sure when she'd stopped being a decent person, but he knew he'd stayed friends with her for too long after that.

He'd given a basic layout to the members helping to save anyone inside. The doors were shut despite the fire raging from the roof.

He shut his eyes and did a mental sweep with his magic. "I don't sense anyone awake in there. My guess is they used a mental blast to knock them all out." His mouth twisted with his disgust. "I guess it's better than just killing everyone."

Three phoenixes burst out of the roof, ascending in a spiral. A sense of relief and awe flooded Felix as he gazed at the fire birds. *I wonder if I'll ever get used to seeing them.* He pointed out Ember to Daisy. Her jaw dropped in astonishment. Then the phoenixes flew towards the cars as all the fires went out in the house.

Felix whispered to Daisy, "That was probably Ember's dad who put out the fires. He's really powerful, but then again, so is their aunt. You'll like her."

"Can anyone get this door open? There are still people in there, just not conscious." Felix faced the group that had joined them from FB Coalition. Everyone had their back to the house, mouths and eyes wide, gaping at the point where the phoenixes disappeared. "People! We have a job to do. We don't know how long we have!" He heard the snarl in his voice. He wished the three had been invisible the entire time, if for no other reason than to avoid his helpers being distracted.

Ronny, a FB Coalition member from before Felix's time, approached. "I can get that lock melted off with a bit of fire, then blow the door open with air. I agree with your assessment of the state of affairs." He tapped the side of his head.

"Thanks. Let's do this."

Daisy stepped up. "If you want, I can blow the door open with air magic. It sounds like you've done quite a few things already."

"Sure," Ronny said. "Sounds great. I'll give you the signal when I'm done with the locks."

Felix watched as smoke blossomed on the door. An acidic stench followed, then Ronny waved his hand. Daisy waved both her hands as if shooing away a pesky dog and a strong breeze attacked the door. After a few seconds, the door swung open, slamming against the inside wall.

They moved in. Since he knew the house, Felix assigned floors and wings to the volunteers. He and Daisy took the main floor, searching the living room, dining room, and kitchen. Since he and Daisy were the weakest—magically—the two of them stayed in the areas least likely to run into trouble.

The first two areas were clear of anything. When they reached the kitchen, they found two people on the ground, either dead, knocked out, or asleep. A quick check told Felix they weren't dead. He took out his phone and texted Mrs. Savita that there were two people in the kitchen.

They moved out to check the closets and restrooms.

Daisy stood in the doorway between the kitchen and dining room. "This is insane. What happened to them? How can they just be crumpled on the floor?"

Felix finished checking the last closet but couldn't find anyone else in their area. "If they have a powerful mind mage, or a few of them, they could've knocked everyone out. As to where the magic users are, that's what I want to know." Frustration boiled in him that they had all got away. He couldn't believe they'd done all this injury to magic users and non-magic users alike and were going to get away. It made him want to scream. Taking a breath, he reminded himself that Ember had survived. He'd seen them fly away to safety. "They didn't escape out the front door, through the garage, or fly out. The two in the kitchen are servants, which makes them human."

Mr. Savita came through the front door with Vi and Ember. Jaw dropping, Ember's eyes grew to saucers as they gaped at Daisy. They paused for a moment before they ran to their best friend and nearly knocked them both to the ground. "Gods above, you're here. How are you here? I'm so glad to see you, I've missed you. But how are you here?"

Felix heard the two laughing as he followed the adults into the kitchen to collect the humans who'd been left behind. Warmth filled him at the reunion of the two friends.

Chapter 41 - Ice Cream To Soothe Your Soul

Ember

Ember sat in their cell, wanting nothing more than to escape. Dad said to burn their way out, shift, become a phoenix ... but when? Should they join in the fight now?

They watched Ambrose and Cress as they paced the hallway. Loud crashes came from above. They could feel the fire, and wondered if Ambrose could too.

Be ready to fly, their dad said. They'd been wanting to fly away since they got into this place. Well, if now was the time, it couldn't be soon enough.

Ember looked over at the opening to the restroom. They could head in there. It wasn't like the two watchers would follow them, would they?

'Ember, we're coming now. Put on your feathers.' Dad's words reverberated through their body. Excitement filling them, they shot up. A smile blossomed on Ember's face. There was no more putting this off.

Cress's eyes locked on them. "And where do you think you're going?"

"To the restroom. Is that allowed? Or are you going to follow and watch me tinkle?" Ember's smile fell away as they sneered at Cress.

His lip twitched. "You disgust me, you know that, right?"

"Feeling's mutual, buster." Halfway to the small room, the sound of the elevator doors opening stopped them.

"Cress, Ambrose, to door D. The house is under attack. Cress, plan B. You're in charge of this floor. Humans only. Well, prisoners only. Get that one too." As Mr. Wells ran by, his thumb pointed to Ember. He was closely followed by Tad Shade and a group of a half dozen others.

Cress's eyes widened for a moment as he nodded slowly. "There are five humans on this floor, so six total?"

Mr. Wells returned and pushed his face into Cress's. His voice lowered, he snarled, "You can handle that, can't you, boy?"

Though Mr. Shade led the movement, right now Mr. Wells was in charge. Ember could tell he was the one with the escape plans in place and in charge of personnel.

I wonder if Mr. Shade knows that he's only partially in charge of this organization?

"Ah ... yes. Of course. Six. I can do it." His face scrunched up and his breathing got faster. His body began to shake as he focused.

Ambrose put her hand on his arm. "Do what?"

Ember backed into the bathroom. They weren't sure what was being discussed, but they knew they were running out of time.

Face softer, Mr. Wells pulled his daughter's hand from Cress. "Don't worry your pretty little head, daughter. We need to leave. The house is burning down, and it isn't salvageable."

She pulled away. "What about the staff? All us witches are here ... but the staff?"

Tad Shade snorted. "They're human. What do we care about them? They're replaceable."

Holding her face and body stiff, Ambrose nodded. "Fine. And Ember?"

"Live or die," Mr. Shade spun and marched off. "It's up to the people out there." He waved his hand out to the side. "Now, go. Or you can stay and die with your classmate, little lamb."

Cress's face, a mask of concentration, turned a fine shade of red. "Okay, I'm pushing out my magic ... now!"

Just as Ember was about to strip to shift, everything went dark.

'Ember! You have to wake up now! Aunt Nuri sounded annoyed. *Gods above, burn out the mind magic. You're a phoenix. They have nothing on you. Their mind tricks are toys to manipulate. Use your fire, child.'*

Ember groaned as hands reached around them and helped them to sit up. They rubbed their face. Their head pounded. Cress's mind magic may be a 'toy,' but it still left an after-effect of 'ouchie.'

"My brain hurts."

Dad's hand was cool on their forehead. "Well, you let an idiot play with your mind. What did you expect?"

Aunt Nuri's fiery eyes gazed at her with her phoenix head tilted. *'Be better next time. No witch should get the upper hand on a phoenix's mind.'*

Ember stared at her blankly. That didn't help. They reached their hands up and Dad pulled, yanking them to their feet. As they looked around, they saw they were still in the same room, but everything was still and quiet. Quick as they could, they stripped and began the shift, letting the freedom of their feathers take over. Once in bird form, they saw that their dad had shifted back as well. They were going to need to eat a feast for dinner.

The three swooped out of their prison. Ember was surprised to find how many floors down they'd been kept. They knew there was one basement level of cells, but multiple? They got through the first level and found another set of cells, and then a second. It wasn't until the third floor they found what felt more like a home … a house? A mansion.

What do these people need with so many levels of prison cells? Gods above, they're horrible!

The three circled above the house once they got free of the confinement of the three floors above the basement levels. Ember glorified in stretching their wings in the skies. They did a loop of elation. *I'm free!*

Behind them, they felt the power from Dad and Aunt Nuri as they extinguished the fires. Once the fires were put out, they followed the other two to a line of five cars. Felix's car was among them, as was Mom and Dad's. Ember dropped behind their parents' car and started their shift back to human.

The bird didn't want to give up control so soon; they'd been locked up in the cell and Ember had forced themself to stay human through all the trauma. Ember had to fight to change back. With a push of power, and a promise of a day in the sky, the shift to humanity began.

Once in their human skin, they raided the car and found clothes someone must have packed for them: underclothes, jeans and a t-shirt. They had to dig to find a pair of old gym shoes. Putting on clean clothes felt amazing.

Dressed, they found Dad and Aunt Nuri. They threw themself into Dad's arms for a big hug. They wanted to hide away, but knew it wasn't over yet. He squeezed Ember tight, whispering nonsense words of endearments to them. Then, the three started the walk to the house.

Aunt Nuri wrapped an arm around Ember and gave them a squeeze. "The others are in the mansion already, searching for any survivors."

"All the magic users left from the floor I'd been held in, I think." Ember said, rubbing their temple. Their memory felt suspect. "Anyone else left will be human."

Aunt Nuri's arm felt comforting. "I'm glad we got you out. And like you, we can save them. I know this group of thugs will hire more humans to act as pawns to take to slaughter, but at least today we'll save a few."

As they crossed the fallen gate, Dad checked his phone. His phone vibrated with text messages. Once they made it inside, shock took over Ember when they saw who stood waiting for them.

Why is Daisy here? Was she part of Infinite WISDOM and knew I'd been in the cells? But no, that's not possible. She's here with Felix. Could she have come to the realization that Infinite WISDOM is wrong? Do I have my friend back? Is she joining our fight?

In the end Ember decided they'd figure it all out later. They ran over and hugged their friend, their chosen sister.

Pulling away, they realized everyone else had left the two of them alone. Ember dragged Daisy to one of the fancy couches. They feared in a fancy-pansy place like this, the couches weren't sitting couches, but only for show. Uncomfortable facsimiles put in the room to be pretty. A pleasant shock went through them as they sank into the soft cushions. They were sitting couches after all.

"What are you doing here?" Ember asked. "I mean, I'm so happy you're here, but you may be the last person I expected."

Daisy explained her week. She'd spent time researching things on the internet and it landed her in the hospital.

"Gods above, Daisy. I'm so sorry I wasn't there to visit you. I would've come and read to you every day if I'd known, if I had been around. I can't imagine how awful it's been. You were there all alone while your parents had to work?"

Daisy leaned in, linking her arms with Ember's. "Me? You were locked in one of the fire princess's basement cells for all this time. Did they ... do anything to you?"

"Do you want the truth?"

"Are you going to tell me the truth? Like for reals?" There was an edge to Daisy's voice, but Ember knew the questions were asked with sincerity.

Ember burned with shame. They knew they'd had to keep secrets, but now their secrets were exposed.

They faced the kitchen where they'd heard Dad helping the fallen with Aunt Monte. "Dad, we're opening up now, right? No more secrets."

"Not with our friends and allies. I don't know how far this will go, but the people here and now know. Tell your friend, she deserves your truth."

Ember took both Daisy's hands in theirs and began telling their tale. As they spoke, Felix brought them each a bowl of ice cream to eat then left, giving them the illusion of privacy. Ember was so hungry, the bowl of chocolate and vanilla goodness with M&Ms and fudge made them want to swoon.

At the end, Daisy looked ready to cry. "Gods above, Ember! How many times have you died this month? How much did it hurt? Are you okay? Like mentally?"

Felix walked in from the kitchen during that litany of questions. Dad's fuming face loomed behind him. "Too many. Because of the magical moonstone, which I left in the basement, I don't think they realized what I was." They faced the door to the kitchen. "Dad, we need to get both my stone and that box. I don't want them retrieving it. Also, is there a way to stop them from making another one?"

Aunt Nuri joined them from a back hall. "He already texted the people searching down there. All the moonstone is gone. They must've collected it after they knocked you out. Someone is checking the jeans you'd been wearing, but if it isn't there, we'll get you more."

"You can have the chunk you brought back for me. Your group collected two pieces and I don't care to have one." Dad sounded gruff. "No more quests, no more visiting Phoenix Forest, no more chances to end up in the clutches of these jerks."

Mom came in and pulled Ember into a hug. She pushed back, staring intently into Ember's eyes. "Are you okay, love? Do you need to go home?"

"No, let me stay. I need to see this place cleansed, and talking to Daisy is helping."

She nodded and got back to directing others in finding survivors.

It took a few hours to collect all the humans. Daisy sat with Ember, who didn't have the energy to do much but observe. They had three mind mages who worked on clearing up the compulsion for them to sleep. Some of the mind workings were easier to overcome than others. Then they set to searching for any evidence of illegal activity they could find.

It wasn't until they searched a guard's room in the first-floor basement that they found a data drive. A virus had been uploaded in all of the computers and fire set to the papers. Aunt Nuri took it all for Monte, explaining that she was great at hacking; it was why she'd given up healing.

Satisfied, the group left. Felix and Daisy joined Ember's family for a steak and potato feast. Ember knew things were going to change soon, but the few minutes of normalcy soothed a tension that had built in the days of captivity.

Chapter 42 - A Retreat

Ambrose

Ambrose walked away from the cell where her father held Ember, a classmate, a teenager, a witch. When she'd gotten down there, Ember had been in the room with the box and that phoenix fire. That meant, if Ember hadn't used air magic to blow the fire into the window, Father and Mr. Shade planned on killing them.

This is not what I thought Infinite WISDOM was about. All these killings are horrible. I don't know when Father changed, but it's disgusting.

She shook her head. Mr. Shade, Father, Cress—this wasn't about bringing witches together. This was about tearing the world down. And doing it in the most brutal, sexist way possible.

Father had told Cress to magically knock everyone out on the bottom floor. He knew the other side was coming with fire while knowing nothing about their holding cells. It was still death he was dealing in.

He just wants the other side's hands to be as bloody as his. It's disgusting.

When she'd agreed to be one of the faces of this movement, it wasn't about killing random people and holding witches in cells. She wanted power—her family's power ... and her eventual power—but how far was she willing to go? She knew her family deserved power; they were great leaders. Well, maybe Father was a bit suspect, but Ambrose knew she could lead.

When did it grow to be so anti-human that Mr. Shade wanted to kill? She bristled. But what harm was there if the humans and magic users lived separate lives? It wasn't like they mingled normally ... not really.

But now, for some reason, her father and Mr. Shade had it out for a teenager. A person her age. It made no sense. Harming someone who was a magical *nobody.*

Ambrose didn't like Ember, but that was teens being teens. It wasn't about killing someone. She didn't hate Ember enough to kill them. Embarrass them, sure—but something more permanent?

A shiver traveled down her spine and bile filled the back of her throat.

The glint she'd seen in Cress's eyes told her he'd have killed Ember in a heartbeat.

In general, she disapproved of Tad Shade and Infinite **WISDOM**'s imprisonment of humans but holding a witch ... the bile dropped lower to churn in her gut.

If the attack hadn't come, would they have tried to kill Ember? Is that what the fire had been about? Why had there been a void bubble with fire in that room? What were they doing with her classmate, and how long had Ember been locked up? Gods above, why hadn't she thought to ask *that* before?

Ambrose pursed her lips, tired of not knowing anything. "Shouldn't we head to the elevator and get out? If the roof is on fire, we can still get out by the garage, right?"

Father glanced at her. "Ambrose, don't try to think, dear. Remember, you're the face of the movement, not the brains. Just do as I say."

Anger boiled up, as it often did when he spoke to her like that. Dismissing her, like a common servant. It hadn't always been like that. Before Mr. Shade showed up, he would speak to her ... if not like an equal, then at least with a modicum of respect.

She made fists and her arms trembled. Mother came up and placed a hand on her shoulder. "You know not to aggravate your father, dear. Listen to him. Your job is to be seen, not heard, and to do as you're told. When will you learn?"

Ambrose clamped her jaw shut and followed with the others. They came to a door in the far back end of the lowest basement. Once Cress finished with his duty, Father pulled out a key, sliding it into the lock. It led to a narrow, dimly lit hall. He shut and locked the door behind them, covering their tracks.

The passageway wasn't wide, so they were forced to walk single file. The women were safely tucked into the center, though Ambrose was probably one of the strongest magically in the bunch. She didn't care. If one of the men died, it was probably for the better. One less misogynist in the group couldn't hurt.

She followed behind Cress. The path dipped low as they continued to walk, minute after minute. The electric lights were dim but were enough to show where they were going. It suddenly occurred to Ambrose that she had no idea what their destination was. "Where are we going?" Her feet began to hurt, and she wished she'd worn a warmer jacket.

"I didn't say 'talk.'" Father snapped. "I said 'follow.'"

Behind her, Mother spoke softly. "This leads to a secondary garage three miles from the house. From there we can go to the summer home."

Ambrose rolled her eyes. *Was that so hard to say? When did Father become such a sexist jerk? Knowing the endpoint wasn't going to slow anyone down. I bet Cress, the idiot, knew all this. I'm probably the only one in the whole group who didn't know.*

They finally started heading uphill. The people in the front walked so darn slow. Ambrose wished they'd entered the passage in an order that allowed those who walked faster to lead the group. Then she could've gotten to the secondary garage and waited. Trudging along like a tortoise didn't make her feet hurt less.

She still thought they could've just gone to their normal garage and taken one of their cars. It wasn't like they were in a war. It was probably Ember's people coming to get them.

Again, why did Father and Mr. Shade take them? What was the point? Beyond every man in this movement being a sexist idiot. The whole organization was run by imbeciles. Most of the message was good though, wasn't it? Magic users supporting each other. Stop the humans who were trying to bring down the magic users. If it was true, she wasn't surprised that the humans were afraid of them. She was more surprised it'd taken two hundred years to get to this point.

I wonder what it would take to overthrow the men and reorganize into something more stable and intelligent. Infinite WISDOM has a good structure and foundation. Father and Mr. Shade are just taking it in the wrong direction. I bet I could lead this organization better.

Thinking of overthrowing Mr. Shade lightened her steps.

Chapter 43 - Laziness Is No Excuse For Bad Manners

Ember

Ember sat at the dining room table. They couldn't believe Daisy sat there between Felix and their dad. Aunt Monte helped Mom serve steak and mashed potatoes to everyone with a side of fresh salad.

Everyone seemed happy to have rescued Ember, yet apprehensive because Dad and Aunt Nuri outed themselves as phoenixes in the process. Mostly, the mood was festive.

Aunt Nuri and Dad dug in right away. Shifting and flying took a lot out of a phoenix.

"Did they feed you while you were there?" Mom gaped as Ember snagged a second helping of steak and potatoes.

"Not really. They gave me a bit of food, but one of the meals was poisoned, so I was wary after that."

Mom sighed, face tight. "I'm sorry you had to deal with that. Did you ever figure out what they were trying to accomplish?"

Daisy looked shocked. "You were poisoned, and that was the full reaction? My parents would be freaking."

A few people at the table chuckled. Amusement broke through some of Ember's melancholy from the past several days of captivity. "I know, but unlike you, I can't truly die. It hurt, sure, but Mom knew at the end of the day I was coming home."

Daisy's eyes were still huge, and she shook her head. "Still seems odd. Like ... really odd. 'Oh, honey, you were poisoned and killed. Rough day. Want more potatoes?'"

There were a few chuckles at her representation of Ember and their mom.

Ember turned back to Mom to answer her question. "They asked about why I wouldn't die, and what I was doing in the cave. I'm not sure they really cared either way. They didn't push when I didn't answer them. In the end, they were kinda dumb. They figured out I was a phoenix, then decided their conclusion was wrong because I never rose from ash, and the fact that I was a witch. So, having magic saved me, really. In the end, I'm not sure if they knew or what they knew. Mostly they were upset that I wouldn't stay dead." They huffed out a laugh. "Oh, and the Everfire they collected from the cave. Maybe they're trying to weaponize it?"

Felix's face scrunched in frustration, eyes narrowed. "When do we go after them for what they did?"

Aunt Monte leaned back. "Give us tonight to celebrate before you start planning our next campaign. We just got Ember back."

Aunt Nuri grinned fiercely. The glint in her eyes made Ember realize she never wanted to be on her aunt's bad side. "But then it's on. Weaponize our fire, more fools them. They will not get away with going after my family, forcing our hand with coming out, and expect nothing. We've battled stronger and smarter magic users than them. They will not divide our world ... not two hundred years ago, and not today.

Felix chuckled nervously at her words. "Okay, I guess I can wait."

After a moment of taking things in, Daisy finally relaxed and did her happy food dance as she ate. Her hands came up and out to the side and her shoulders shimmied. *Gods I missed her!* "I'm just excited that we're all together and there's no more secrets."

Aunt Nuri smiled at her. "Oh, hon, there's always secrets."

Daisy laughed. "Well, sure, but I know more than I did two days ago, and I'm just going to stick with being happy, otherwise I'll focus on the fact that my best friend is invincible. You know, that and other weird facts."

Ember shrugged. "Like you don't have weird things about you. Anyway, it'll take time, but we'll get through all of the secrets ... or at least most of them. Think of it as a surprise gift each time we talk. But, for now, can we discuss what the fallout will be for outing the phoenixes? I mean, I met one of our kind in the forest. He was a bit of a jerk, but he seemed young and terrified of our last name. What you two did ... I mean, thank you, but what will happen now?"

"The elders won't be happy," Aunt Nuri said with some authority. She got up and headed to the kitchen. She rummaged until she found a new bottle of red wine to serve the adults. "But at the end of the day, it wasn't their choice. My guess is, any reaction the elders and greater phoenix community have will take a few days to manifest, maybe even weeks. Don't worry. We have time."

Dad guffawed. "No, they won't be happy, but they haven't been happy with us in over two hundred years. The shunning was just the final straw. You knew they'd been hoping for a reason to kick us out of the compound."

"You know, when I spoke with Pat and Lesly, they said our home is still there waiting for us. It's been kept empty. There are servants who clean it once a month or so to make sure if we ever were to return, then we'd have a place to live."

"Why?" Dad snorted, shaking his head.

"Ash, our parents were royalty. Just because they felt they'd lived long enough and decided to leave this world when we were babies, doesn't mean we aren't considered royalty as well."

Wait ... what? Ember felt woozy. "Phoenixes have royalty?"

Aunt Nuri said, "Yes"

At the same time Dad said, "No."

Dad sighed. "Your grandparents were part of the founding creators of the current compound. It's been in its present location, gods above, for ... Nuri?"

"Maybe two, three, millennia? Forever. That's all you really need to know."

Dad sipped his wine and closed his eyes. "I don't know. You're right, the length of time doesn't really matter. A really long time. Nuri and I are ... Well, we're old. Older than we look. I don't know if I know that number off the top of my head either. But, Ember, you know that. You once said 'older than dirt,' and I think that sounds about right."

Aunt Nuri snorted.

Dad waggled his eyebrows at her. "I mean, you are technically younger than me."

"Gods above, you are a doddering old idiot. I'm the elder twin."

Dad's jaw dropped open. "You are?"

"Focus, brother. Yes, Ember, we are royalty. We were kicked out because the elders ... the *other* elders felt we'd influence too many phoenixes with our radical ways."

Ember rubbed their forehead. "The radical idea that other beings besides shifters were worth saving?"

"No, dear, other beings besides *phoenixes*. Our people are *very* reclusive. Your dad and I expanded our world outside of our own. Other shifters have historically intermingled; it's why we didn't think a phoenix and witch could have a kid. No other shifter has had a kid when they've mated outside their kind. In my lifetime, the largest number of phoenixes alive was never above two hundred. Is it any wonder the others fear our worldly ways?"

Once Aunt Nuri stopped talking, Felix shook his head, as if snapping out of a trance. "So, phoenixes have always avoided the greater world, even before your 'extinction.' Your people only came out because the two of you encouraged the wild and crazy few to help magic users in stopping a war. If the War of Peace had been lost, the elders understand how bad it would've been for them, right?"

Mom sipped her wine. "Yes and no. The young are always so passionate. From what I understand, they thought themselves above mere mortals. They figured they could lay low and survive any outcome. That magic users would die out eventually." The disgust in her voice was unmistakable.

Aunt Monte searched the faces at the table. "Is there a chance they'll ignore your stunt today?"

Aunt Nuri lifted a brow. "You don't know the elders. There is no way they're going to ignore what happened. If they find out about our doings, they'll demand an accounting of our actions. We'll be summoned, or at least I will. They know about Ember, and it took everything I had to put off their meeting when I went there before."

"Ember will not go there without me," Dad grumbled.

Daisy sat still. She pushed her plate a few inches away. "What do you think they'll do? Do you think you all are safe? Is Ember safe? They could stay with me at my house. My parents love them, you know."

Though Daisy's offer warmed Ember to their soul, they were tired of running. As soon as their family decided to stay and fight after the camping trip, and then Dad and Aunt Nuri came to save Ember by having them fly out of their prison as a phoenix ... "I don't want to run and hide. What are they going to do, break into the house and steal me away?" A sense of irritation and determination filled them. They weren't going to be run from their home, not for anyone.

All the adults stared at them. Aunt Nuri shut her eyes. "I don't think they will, but at the end of the day, it's been over two hundred years. I don't know how scared these people are. Anything is possible. I could see them trying to take you away to 'raise you right.' There's a school that trains phoenixes. It's a good school. You're the only fledgling phoenix I know of not raised in the community. As well as Sadie and Ash are teaching you, there are pieces of the lore you don't know."

Ember grumbled low in the gut. "If they try to take me, I'm burning my way out and flying home. They can't keep me against my will. I played that game once. I'm not doing it again. Mr. Shade only had a chance because I was hiding who I was. These elders will know I'm a phoenix. I'll have nothing to hide." A smile spread on Ember's face. "No one will imprison me again."

Dad cheered and Aunt Nuri's grin was a bit terrifying.

"No, dear," Mom said with a warm smile. "They can't. More than that, if they don't keep you in a magic-blocked room, I can pick you up with spatial magic. I don't think they'll be lining it with moonstone. Speaking of, that's going to be your new set of lessons. You need to learn how to move yourself, not just other objects."

Daisy's glass dropped to the table. Felix caught it before anything spilled. She sputtered. "What ... Did you just ... Spatial magic? Are you kidding me? First you tell me there are phoenixes and now this? You've got to be kidding me. There is no way! Like, no. Just no. That's a dead magic. Now you all are just messing with me."

Ember started to laugh. They couldn't stop themself. Felix smiled at them, chuckling along with them. Smiles grew on Mom's and Dad's faces, as well as Aunts Nuri's and Monte's faces.

Finally, Daisy exploded. "What is so funny?"

Ember snorted. "I'm a phoenix, and you get a bit scared, but you're more mad that I didn't tell you. You find out that my dad and aunt are old as dirt ... not even a blink. There are elder phoenixes who may kidnap me, they are scary and powerful ... you want to hide me at your place. There have been so many things discussed, and you're like, 'no big thing.'" Ember waved their hand to emphasize their words. "But spatial magic, a proficiency, well, no, that's a line you are unwilling to cross. That is *one thing too many.* You're like, nope, no, no, no. I'm sorry, I just ... it's funny."

Ember held out their hand and pulled a new soda from the fridge without getting up. It appeared in front of Daisy. "Thirsty?"

Daisy squealed. "Gods above! You could've warned me. But yes, if you want to know, I am thirsty, and this is what I wanted. As my best friend, you probably should've offered it sooner. And since you didn't even have to get off your butt, there is no excuse."

That got everyone at the table laughing.

Chapter 44 – The Shunning

Ember

After dinner, Felix, Daisy, and Ember decided to walk to get ice cream. Felix hadn't had any the first time around, so they had to get more ... it was only fair. No matter what the threat or fallout from the exposure of the phoenixes would be, they figured it wouldn't arrive in the next hour.

The idea of getting out and moving felt good. Ember had been in that cell for so long, and walking seemed like a gift. The evening was beautiful, the night was clear, and the temperature was just warm enough that a light coat was all that was needed.

Gods, moving without having to pace feels like a luxury!

Daisy sighed. "After so many days in the hospital, and then my parents hovering over me last night, this walk is so nice."

Ember smiled at Daisy. "My thoughts exactly." They sneered, thinking of what Cress and the others had done to their friend, and them not knowing Daisy had been hurt. "I can't believe they put you in the hospital. I mean, I can, but ... the fact they're putting anyone in the hospital is insane to me. And Cress and Ambrose supporting it... it's disgusting."

Daisy shook her head. "And Simon. That's the real disappointment. He's smarter than this. It isn't like he's friends with the popular group."

Felix gazed off into the stars. "I wonder why. Your point is a good one. He's never cared for the popular crowd."

"He's mad about losing a job last summer." Daisy explained about the library job that went to a human.

Felix groaned. "Gods above and below. That arrogant ... he is taking his frustration about that one event out on everyone. Why can't he step back and see the bigger picture?"

Daisy shrugged. "I don't know. I agree with you. I tried to talk to him about it, but he's convinced his situation is proof of a larger problem."

They walked for a bit more in silence before Daisy asked, "Are you at all worried?"

Ember scrunched up their face. "Am I worried about the other members of my extended family?"

"Yeah."

"Yes and no. It would be naive to say no, but Dad and Aunt Nuri are powerful. Mom and Aunt Monte are no shrinking violets themselves. I have strong adults watching out for me. I know that the elders are people to worry about, but I think they should worry more about *us*."

Felix whooped. "That's right! Your family is amazing."

They arrived at the confection shop, and each got a cone. Felix ordered rocky road, Daisy cookies and cream, and Ember got s'more to love. They focused more on eating on the way back than talking.

Ember thought about the phoenixes and their compound. They wished there wasn't such animosity between their family and the others. They wondered what the phoenix school was like. Were they really behind in their education? What did that even mean? Would it affect them in some way? How many other fledgling phoenixes were there? Did Aunt Nuri say three? Or four? So few ... did it really matter in the end? Would it make sense having a phoenix in the compound that could do witch or other proficiency magic? Would they even allow their mother in? Could they stop her if Dad wanted her there?

In the end, did it matter? Ember liked their school and friends. They didn't want to leave. They fought hard to stay at Feniks Secondary School. Why would Ember want to give it up now?

Gods above, everything about phoenixes and their compound is a question, and I bet the answers wouldn't be ones I'd like.

"If you ended up at their school, how many students would even be in your classes? And what would happen to your current schooling?" Daisy asked. Apparently her mind was still running parallel to theirs. This was why they'd always been such good friends.

Felix's brows came together. "Didn't Vi say something about you being one of five new phoenixes?"

"Four," Ember corrected, finally remembering. "So, if there are only three others, the classes must be very specialized. I don't see how it would be different from my parents' home schooling. If I'm immortal, doesn't getting a basic education from public school make more sense? I have my whole life to learn from them, right?"

Daisy laughed. "You do know you're asking the wrong crowd, don't you?"

"I do. I'm just venting. Okay, ice cream's done. I'm getting tired after not really sleeping or eating for days. I really want to hang out with the two of you, but I think I'm about to crash here and now." The wave of exhaustion hit them hard.

Felix slid an arm around them. "How about you get home before you fall asleep out here? I'm guessing your room would be nicer than the sidewalk."

"I mean, if you insist. Just about anything is better than where I've been." A tremor ran over Ember's body, and Felix tightened his arm. Ember leaned into him gratefully.

As they got to the house, Ember saw something tacked to the door. "What is that? Is it something that explodes? Should I approach the house without you two?"

Daisy rolled her eyes. "It's paper. Are you blind, or just that tired?"

"Probably tired," Ember admitted.

They got to the door, and Ember saw it was an envelope. It was hanging from a hook on the door from a large, enameled, phoenix-shaped pin. On the envelope, in large letters was: "Ash and Nuri Savita." In the upper left corner was a stylized E.

Opening the door, Ember yelled, "Dad, Aunt Nuri, you've got mail. Didn't you hear the noise of delivery?"

Dad was the first to arrive. Like Ember, he left the letter until Aunt Nuri could see how it was hung on the door. Aunt Nuri took one look and tore it down. Everyone piled into the living room.

Aunt Nuri glared at the envelope as she tore it open.

Ash and Nuri Savita—

Your shunning has been lifted. Please return to the phoenix compound with your families. The magic users will be welcomed by our community.

-The Elders

A weighty silence filled the room. A chill shot down Ember's spine. *Gods, what now? Are we really going to do this?* Their friends both gaped. Mom looked annoyed. Dad's face was contorted with disgust. Before Ember could get to Aunt Nuri, Aunt Monte started to laugh. "I told you so!"

Thank you for reading Veiled Phoenix!
Please leave a review online.

Check out my website to find all the links to my socials
and find information on my next series!

Coming Soon:

- Battle Phoenix

- Pebble's Story

  - Xenagogue

  - Yugen

  - Zephyr

About the Author

Huckleberry Rahr is a mathematics instructor at the University of Wisconsin-Whitewater. She spent many years teaching math around the Midwest and in Papua New Guinea with the Peace Corps. Her parents  instilled a love of reading from a young age.

She grew up with lesbian moms who had a huge collection of women authors with heroines as the protagonist. Her favorite genre was fantasy and science fiction, that is, until she discovered urban fantasy. What her mom's library lacked were books with characters that looked like her family: diversity in background, gender identity, and sexuality. She decided if she couldn't find that series, then she would write it.

9 781959 981602